Erica

FIRE IN THE WOODS

Jennifer M. Eaton

Month9Books

Enjoy your race through the woods!

Month9Books

For my husband and kids.
You believed in me before I'd typed a word.

FIRE IN THE WOODS

Jennifer M. Eaton

1

The walls shook.

My favorite sunset photograph crashed to the floor. Again.

Why the Air Force felt the need to fly so low over the houses was beyond me. Whole sky up there, guys. Geeze.

I picked up the frame and checked the glass. No cracks, thank goodness. I hung the photo back on the wall with the rest of my collection: landscapes, animals, daily living, the greatest of the great. Someday my photos would be featured in galleries across the country. But first I had to graduate high school and get my butt off Maguire Air Force Base.

One more year—that's all that separated me from the real world. The clock wasn't ticking fast enough. Not for me, at least.

Settling back down at my desk, I flipped through the pages of August's National Geographic. Dang, those pictures were good. NG photographers had it down. Emotion, lighting, energy…

I contemplated the best of my own shots hanging around

my room. Would they ever compare?

Another jet screamed overhead.

Stinking pilots! I lunged off the chair to save another photo from falling. The entire house vibrated. This was getting ridiculous.

Dad came in and leaned his bulky frame against my door. "Redecorating?"

"Not by choice." I blew a stray hair out of my eyes. "Are they ever going to respect the no-fly zone?"

"Unlikely."

"Then next time you have my permission to shoot them down."

"You want me to shoot down a multi-million-dollar jet because a picture fell off the wall?"

"Why not? Isn't that what the Army does? Protect the peace and all?" I tried to hold back my grin. Didn't work.

He grimaced while rubbing the peach fuzz he called a haircut.

So much for sarcasm. "It was a joke, Dad."

A smile almost crossed his lips.

Come on, Dad. You can do it. Inch those lips up just a smidge.

His nose flared.

Nope. No smile today. Must be Monday—or any other day of the week ending in y.

The walls shuddered as the engines of another aircraft throttled overhead, followed by an echoing rattle.

Dad's gaze shot to the ceiling. His jaw tightened. So did mine. Those planes were flying way too low.

My stomach turned. "What—"

"Shhh." His hand shot out, silencing me. "That sounds like…" His eyes widened. "Jessica, get down!"

A deafening boom rolled through the neighborhood. The rest of my pictures tumbled off the walls.

Dad pulled me to the floor. His body became a human shield as a wave of heat blasted through the open window. A soda can shimmied off my desk and crashed to the floor. Cola fizzled across the carpet.

My heart pummeled my ribcage as Dad's eyes turned to ice. The man protecting me was no longer my father, but someone darker: trained and dangerous.

I placed my hand on his chest. "Dad, what…"

He rolled off me and stood. "Stay down."

Like I was going anywhere.

As he moved toward the window, he picked up a picture of Mom from the floor and set it back on my dresser. His gaze never left the curtains. How did he stay so calm? Was this what it was like when he was overseas? Was this just another day at the office for him?

The light on my desk dimmed, pulsed, and flickered out. The numbers on the digital alarm clock faded to black. That couldn't be good.

Were we being attacked? Why had we lost power?

The National Geographic slid off my desk, landing opened to a beautiful photograph of a lake. The caption read: *Repairing the Ozone Layer*. I would have held the photo to the light, inspected the angle to see how the photographer achieved the shine across the lake—if the world hadn't been coming to an end outside my window.

I shoved the magazine away from the soda spill. My heartbeat thumped in cadence with my father's heavy breathing. "Dad?"

Without turning toward me, he shot out his hand again. My lips bolted shut as he drew aside the drapes. From my vantage point, all I could see were fluffy white clouds over a blue sky. Nothing scary. Just regular old daytime. Nothing to worry about, right?

"Sweet Mother of Jesus," Dad muttered, backing from the window. His gaze shot toward me. "Stay here, and stay on the floor. Keep the bed between you and the window." His hands formed tight fists before he dashed from the room.

Another plane soared over the roof, way too close to the ground. My ceiling fan swayed from the tremor, squeaking in its hanger.

I trembled. Just sitting there—waiting—it was too much. I clutched the gold pendant Mom gave me for my birthday. If she was still with us, she'd be beside me, holding my hand while Dad did his thing—whatever that was.

But she was gone, and if all I could do was cower in my room while Dad ran off to save the world again, I might as well forget about photojournalism right now.

Wasn't. Gonna. Happen.

Taking a deep breath, I crawled across the floor and inched up toward the windowsill. Sweat spotted my brow as my mind came to terms with what I saw.

Flames spouted over the trees deep within the adjacent forest, lighting up the afternoon sky. The fire raged, engulfing the larger trees in the center of the woods. I reached for my dresser to grab my camera and realized I'd left it downstairs. *Figures*.

I gasped as the flames erupted into another explosion.

The photojournalist hiding inside me sucker-punched the frightened teenager who wanted to dash under the bed. This was news. Not snapping pictures was out of the question. I flew down the stairs. The ring of the emergency land-line filled the living room as I landed on the hardwood floor.

Dad grabbed the phone off the wall. "Major Tomás Martinez speaking."

The phone cord trailed behind him as he paced. His fingers tapped the receiver rhythmically—a typical scenario on the days he received bad news from the Army. I stood rapt watching him, hoping he'd slip up and mention a military secret. Hey, there's a first time for everything. I'd have to get lucky sooner or later.

"Yes, we lost power here, too…Yes, sir…I understand, sir…Right away, sir." He hung the receiver back on its stand and glanced in my direction. "I told you to stay upstairs."

"What'd they say? What's going on?"

"I'll tell you after I find out." He snatched his wallet from the counter and slipped the worn leather into the back pocket of his jeans.

"You're leaving? Now? Did you hear that last explosion?"

"I know. That's why I'm being called in." He picked up his keys.

"For what? You're not a fireman."

His gaze centered on me. I shivered. Dad in military mode

was just. Plain. Scary.

"It's a plane. A plane went down."

The memory of the low-flying jets and the rattling of what must have been gunfire seared my nerves.

"Went down or was shot down?" The journalist in me started salivating.

"That's what I'm going to find out."

The door creaked as he pushed down the handle. The blare of passing sirens reverberated through the room.

"Why would they shoot down a plane?" I glanced at my camera bag perched on the end table. My shutter finger itched, anticipating juicy photos to add to my portfolio.

"Everything will be fine. For now, just stay in the house."

"Stay in the house? But this is like, huge. I want to take some pictures."

His jaw set. That gross vein in his neck twitched. "You can play games later. Right now, I need to know you're safe."

"No photojournalist ever made it big by staying safe."

"Maybe not, but many seventeen-year-olds made it to eighteen that way. Stay here. That's an order."

The whooting of a helicopter's blades cut through the late afternoon sunshine. Butterflies fluttered in my gut as Dad disappeared through the screen door without so much as a backward glance.

Seriously? He expected me to just sit there—with the biggest photo opportunity of my life going on outside?

I ran to the window and brushed the curtain aside. The Air Force pilot who lived across the street ran to his jeep, a duffle bag swinging from his arm. Lieutenant Miller from next door left his house and exchanged nods with Dad as they both slipped into their cars.

The sound of another explosion smacked my ears. The ceiling rattled, and I steadied myself against the wall. How many times could one plane explode? I took a deep breath and forced myself to relax. I lived on a military base for goodness sake. The Army and the freaking Air Force were stationed next door. You couldn't get much safer than that.

Flopping onto the couch, I clicked the power button on the remote control three times. The blank television screen mocked me. *No electricity, idiot.*

Another siren howled past the house. My gaze flittered back to my camera case. When in my lifetime would I get another chance to shoot pictures of something like this?

"This is crazy." I slid my cell phone off the coffee table and dialed my best friend. No service. Ugh!

I grabbed the corded phone. Her voicemail answered: "Hey, this is Maggs. You know what to do."

"Maggie, it's Jess. Where are you? The whole world is coming to an end outside. Call me."

Another helicopter zoomed over the roof. How many was that now? Three? Four?

My gaze trailed to the name above Maggie's on the contact list.

Bobby.

The part of me that feared the chaos outside yearned to call him. Bobby would come. Leave his post if he had to. Protect me. But did I really want Bobby back in my life?

Not after he and his MP buddies beat up poor Matt Samuels.

All the kid did was take me to a movie. It wasn't even a date, but Bobby didn't care. If he couldn't have me, then no one could.

I gritted my teeth as I slipped my phone back into my pocket. Suddenly, I wasn't as scared as I thought.

Tucking back the living room curtains, I snooped on the neighbors gathering outside their houses. Mrs. Sanderson and the lady across the street both herded their kids inside, their faces turned toward the sky. The fear in their eyes struck me. What an amazing photograph that would have been.

A few guys began walking toward the thruway. One of them held a cheap, pocket camera in his hand. He had to be kidding. What kind of shot did he expect to get with that?

I let the curtain fall. Staying in the house was just too much to ask. This was the story of a lifetime. I couldn't let it slip by without getting something on film.

Grabbing a black elastic band off the end-table, I twisted my hair into a pony tail. One brown lock fell beside my cheek, as it always did. I clipped that sucker back with a barrette and slung my camera case over my shoulder.

I hesitated at the front door. A picture of my parents hung askew beside the window. I straightened the frame. Mom's smile warmed me, but Dad's eyes bored through me, daring me to face his wrath if I touched the doorknob. I stood taller, strengthening my resolve. He'd understand after I got into National Geographic.

The odor of smoke and something pungent barraged my nose as I opened the door. A fire truck wailed in the distance, warning me to keep away. But I couldn't. I pulled my collar up over my nose to blot out the smell and headed toward the main road.

A parade of emergency vehicles whipped by at the end of the street. Lights flashed and sirens blasted through the neighborhood.

The cacophony froze me for a moment. Nothing like this had ever happened before. We lived in New Jersey for goodness sake, not Saudi Arabia. I glanced back at the house. Keeping it in view made me feel safe, but I knew I needed to get closer to get a good shot.

This was it. The big league. I could do this.

Turning left toward the airstrip, I watched the last fire truck become smaller before its whirling lights passed through the gates onto the tarmac. The fire blazed well within the tree line, maybe even farther than I originally thought. The smoke reached into the sky, blotting out the sun. I raised my lens and waited for the clouds to shift and give me the perfect lighting— until a smack on my arm ruined my setup.

Maggie.

A smirk spread across her face. "Hey, Lois Lane. I figured you'd be out here."

I sighed, watching a flock of fleeing birds that would have maximized the emotion of the shot—if I'd taken it.

"Lois Lane was a reporter. Jimmy Olsen was the photographer."

"Whatever." Her golden curls bounced about her face. "This is like, crazy. My dad took off like World War Three or something."

"Yeah, mine, too."

I shielded my eyes. The smoke rose in gray billows. Almost pretty. I raised my lens.

"You want to know the scoop?" Maggie's perky form fidgeted like a toddler who couldn't hold in a secret. She loved eavesdropping on her father, the general. Unfortunately, that kind of gossip could get you carted off by the MPs. Never stopped her though, and I adored her for it.

"You know I do. Spill it." I brought the clouds into focus and snapped the shutter three times.

Her grin widened as she feigned a whisper. "It's not one of ours."

"What do you mean?" The stench in the air thickened. I covered my nose.

"The plane. They don't know whose it is. Isn't that exciting?"

"Heck yeah." I raised my camera and clicked off ten successive shots. If a terrorist got shot down over American soil, Jess Martinez was going to have pictures to sell. This was the kind of break every photographer dreamed of.

I adjusted my camera-case beside my waist. "I'm going in closer."

The air around us grew hazy. Maggie coughed. "Are you nuts? This is close enough for me."

"Stop being such a wuss." I tugged her wrist. It never took much more to convince her.

Maggie prattled on while I shot off round after round of gripping photographs. My heart fluttered as each preview image appeared on my screen. For once I was actually doing it. I was being the journalist I was meant to be, not the caged-up little girl Dad wanted. And boy, did it feel good.

The closer we came to the chained-link fence surrounding the runways, the more people gathered around us. A man, ignoring the whimpering Labrador on the end of his leash, gawked at the clouds. *Click.* Two women caught excited children and dragged them away. *Click.* The MP from down the street shouted, "Yes sir, right away sir," into his cell phone and jogged from the scene. *Click*—all amazing images to add to my portfolio.

Pushing to the front, I slipped my fingers through the metal fencing. The paved tarmac sprawled before me, backing up to the trees. Soldiers on the far side of the airstrip formed barricades against the tree line. I centered my lens between the silver links and chronicled their maneuvers.

A breeze whipped up. The heat slapped my face like sitting too close to a campfire. I covered my lens to protect the glass as the people around us flinched and backed away. One woman ran, crying into a hankie.

"Should we be able to feel the heat from this far away?" Maggie asked, shielding her face with her arm.

I shrugged, unease settling on me as the smoky cloud arched toward us. The breeze stretched the formation, driving it north over our heads and toward the houses.

My stomach did a little fliperoo. The spunky, fearless photojournalist slipped away, leaving a scrawny, slightly-unsure-of-herself teenager behind. "I gotta go."

"Why?"

"My dad told me to stay inside. He'll be calling on the house phone any minute to check on me."

"The major's getting more neurotic every day. You're almost eighteen for goodness sake."

"I know, but I still get the *While You Live Under My Roof* lecture every day."

The ground rattled. Another billow of fire wafted into the sky. I steadied myself, transfixed by the sheer magnitude of the ever-growing bank of smoke.

Wow. How bad did I want to stand there and use up my memory card—but I wanted to *not get grounded* more. I began walking backward, snapping off shots with every step.

Maggie strode beside me. "Do you ever stop taking pictures?"

Click.

"Not if I can help it."

***

I shimmied open the front door. On the far side of the living room, the corded phone rattled on the receiver, mid-ring. My keys clanged to the wood floor as I sprang toward the table to grab the handset. "Hello?"

"Where've you been?"

"Nowhere. I was—in the bathroom." I clenched my teeth, holding my breath. Would he buy it?

"Are you okay?"

"I'm fine. Why?"

I could imagine his Major Martinez no-nonsense expression

on the other side of the phone. "Listen, it's really important that you stay inside tonight. I'm sorry I can't be there, but I need you to lock the doors, and stay away from the windows."

I crinkled my forehead. Sweat settled across my brow. "Why? What's wrong? There's nothing, like, nuclear or anything, right?"

There was a pause on the line. "No—nothing nuclear."

I drew the curtain back from the rear kitchen window. The smoke cloud over the woods had darkened. The smell of burning pine tickled my nose as a humming tone on the other end of the call agitated my ear.

Dad spoke muffled words to someone else. "Jesus H. Christ," he whispered, returning to the phone.

"Dad, is everything okay?"

"Please just promise me you'll stay inside tonight."

Yikes. His Major Tomás Martinez voice had drifted away. That was his 'daddy's scared' voice. I hadn't heard that tone since the night Mom died. I shuddered. "Dad, if things are that bad, shouldn't I be with you?" Silence lingered, and a scratching noise reverberated in the background. "Dad, is someone else on the line with us?"

"Jess. I am asking you to stay inside and lock the doors. Can you do that for me…Buttercup?"

Buttercup?

My breath hitched. Crud. That meant something. Buttercup was a word he and Mom used when something was wrong. Something was definitely up. "I got you, Dad. I'll stay inside. I promise."

"Thank you." He paused. "I'll be home as soon as I can."

"Yeah, okay." My hand trembled as the phone clicked back into the cradle.

I checked the front and back door and ran to the stairs. The fire cast a magnificent glow behind the trees outside my bedroom window. I slid down the screen and clicked off a few rounds of shots, hoping to catch the eerie blues and pinks behind the shaded leaves. Whoa. *New favorite sunset shot for sure.*

Settling down on my bed, I started scrolling through today's pictures. Something was weird about the fire, but I couldn't quite place my finger on it. Flipping through June's National Geographic, I glanced through the photographs of the explosion in Nanjing, China. The colors in my shots were so much more vivid, more dynamic, more, well, *colorful*. Not that I knew anything about explosions, but something itched that little button inside that told me I had something special.

The lights suddenly flicked on. I gasped and laughed at myself. Perfect timing. I settled at my computer, hooked up my camera, and started the upload. I couldn't wait to enlarge those babies.

2

Trumpets!

My eyes popped open as round after round of incessant choruses of Reveille echoed over the base PA system, shocking the world and demanding everyone get up and take notice that the ungodly time of O-six-hundred-hours had arrived.

A groan escaped my lips as I pushed up off my desk. Every muscle in my neck and back screamed at the same time. I must have fallen asleep waiting for my pictures to upload. Rubbing the back of my neck, I stood as the last trumpet bellowed its obnoxious call.

God, I hated that stinking song.

The screen-saver flicked off when I jiggled my mouse. The website from last night was still waiting for me to confirm my order. I smiled and clicked the button. It'd be a few hours before the store opened and I could pick up the pictures that would change my life. Once I added the best of yesterday's shots to my portfolio, no one would dream of refusing my college application.

The sun sparkled through my windowpanes. In the distance,

three dark birds circled over the forest in a beautiful, blue sky. A thin tendril of smoke trailed from the trees, a small reminder of yesterday's chaos. The coolness of the glass enlivened my skin as I pressed my forehead against the window. Despite the unbelievable shots I'd taken, I was glad it was finally over.

I stumbled through the hallway and peeked in Dad's room. His bed hadn't been slept in. So much for his day off. Ignoring the grumbling of my impatient stomach, I treated my sore muscles to a shower and got dressed.

The digital clock on my dresser blinked four-seventeen. I made a mental note to fix the time later.

While liberating a few knots from my hair, I made a beeline to the refrigerator. Fruit, eggs, milk...Boring. I shoved aside a few food savers and smiled.

"Bingo."

I slid out a plate of German chocolate layer cake. Smacking my lips in anticipation, I plopped back in front of my computer and scanned the photos I'd sent to the drugstore print shop. I could hear Dad now: "Why don't you just send the pictures to the PX. It's cheaper."

Yeah, they're cheaper all right—and pixely.

Not to mention the fact that they might confiscate a few of the shots I'd taken of the soldiers. My brow furrowed as I scanned the photos of the platoon gathered near the edge of the forest. In every shot, the soldiers were facing the woods. If they were there to keep the people safe, wouldn't they be facing out?

Swallowing down the last bite of cake, I walked downstairs and peeked out the front window. No sign of Dad yet, but I wasn't about to sit there and wait for him. I dialed up his cell, but his voicemail answered.

"Hey Dad, it's Jess. Everything's fine. No problems last night. I'm going to walk down to the drugstore to pick up some pictures, okay? Don't worry, I'm going in completely the opposite direction from where the fire was, so I won't be anywhere near the cleanup. See you later."

I hung up and grabbed a notepad and pen. Standard Major Martinez protocol dictated a note as well as a message. I flipped to an empty page and let him know where I was going, sealing it with a smiley-face.

Outside, a summer breeze caressed my face. I inhaled the crisp morning air and crinkled my nose at the slight hint of smoke lingering from the fire. Yuck.

Quiet greeted me throughout the compound, as if yesterday's calamity never happened. Funny, how quickly everything adjusts back to normal. I guess the fire really wasn't as big a deal as I thought.

The heaviness still hung in the air, though. Not that I thought a plane crash would take it away. Everything about Maguire, and the other three military bases I'd lived on, stifled me like a prison without walls, and the pressure seemed to tighten every day.

Day trips with Mom used to help, but now that she was gone, and with Dad sinking further and further into his shell… Well, things just weren't the same without Mom.

Relief swept over me as I passed the guard shack and walked into the real world. I laughed at myself. I was only a few feet away from military ground, and most of those houses were probably still Army or Air Force families all squashed together since they merged Fort Dix with Maguire. It was civilian land, though, and it smelled like freedom. Well, smoky freedom at the moment, but still freedom.

I headed toward the woods and allowed my thoughts to drift up and away, clearing my mind and letting it wander. Senior year began in a few weeks, and I'd have to start looking for colleges.

Looking…funny. There was only one choice. Columbia. Their arts department was the tops. My application was already filled out, and these photographs were going to cinch it for me.

Dad dreamed of me going to West Point. We'd already sent in the paperwork, but I didn't care that every Martinez since my great-grandfather went there. I had to live my life, not his.

A larger than life advertisement on the side of a passing NJ Transit bus made me smile. *Fire in the Woods, starring Jared Linden and Chris Stevens. In theaters September tenth.* Jared leaned forward in the photo, ready to pounce off the side of the bus. Chris Stevens stood beside him, shirtless with hands in pockets and beautiful blond tresses falling seductively toward one eye. I loved Chris's new haircut, and Jared—Yum. Five foot ten inches of pure tall-dark-and-handsome. They were both just to die for.

A sudden movement drew my attention from the bus. I skidded to a stop. To my right, maybe a hundred feet from the forest, stood the most beautiful buck I'd ever seen. I held my breath trying not to move as he stared me down. A majestic twelve-point rack of antlers scrolled from his head, and his white and brown tail flickered incessantly. After a long, breathless wait, his mouth swirled in a chewing motion.

Nature in its most beautiful form.

An eerie shadow cast across the grass as the sun shone through his rack. The silhouette formed little fingers that seemed to reach for me. Wow. If I took that picture at just the right angle…

Shoot. My camera sat safely at home, not attached to my hip where it should have been. Diversity in the portfolio was a must. I needed a picture of that guy. I inched forward and the buck raised his head, shifting the shadow from sight.

"It's okay," I whispered. "I won't hurt you."

I reached into my pocket and fumbled for my phone. The aperture on the camera feature opened, and I lifted the screen toward him. Without warning, the deer sprang into the air. It flipped its tail toward me and bolted into the woods.

"Awe, man."

Clutching my camera-phone, I ran to the trees and squinted into the brambles. The buck's dark, shiny eyes blinked within the brush. He chewed twice before he trotted deeper into the foliage.

"Come on, dude, I just want a picture."

I ramrodded my way into the forest, the branches whipping back as I set them free. The morning warmth gave way to cool, damp air beneath the trees as I hopped over a group of fallen logs and ducked under a giant poison ivy vine climbing up a tree. I paused, listening to the woods. Silence greeted me, followed by the chirps of two birds chasing each other from tree to tree in the upper canopy. I slowed and fought to catch my breath. He was gone.

My chest throbbed as I leaned my hands on my knees.

Sheesh, he was fast. I chuckled to myself. What was I thinking?

A puff of smoke rose over some brush on my right. I pulled the bushes aside and found the remains of a small, smoldering campfire. Some people were so irresponsible. I tossed dirt on the embers until they winked out. Good deed for the day: done.

Turning to head back out of the woods, I froze. A noise blasted through the forest, screeching like a smoke alarm gone haywire. A stabbing pain tore into my brain. I slammed my hands over my ears, but I couldn't fight the drills boring inside me. Head pounding, I howled, but my own voice fell victim to the vibrations within my mind.

I dropped to my knees. "Please stop! Make it stop!"

The squalling encompassed everything. Tears pooled in my eyes, blurring my vision before trailing down my cheeks. I wailed in misery.

Until it stopped.

I shook, reeling from the unexpected silence. A faint hum lingered, a frightening reminder of the sound's intensity. Hands still covering my ears, I sucked in a short breath and dared another. Holding as still as possible, I scanned the trees.

What the heck was going on?

Sobbing, I blinked back fresh tears and wiped my cheeks clean. A leaf fell to the ground at my feet, but the rest of the forest remained motionless. The chirping birds had vanished. Nothing stirred to disrupt the eerie quiet—not even a gentle rustle of the wind.

I cringed, frightened by a thrash behind a large fallen tree. Ignoring the instinct to flee like the buck, I inched forward and peeked over the log.

A guy, maybe seventeen or eighteen, lay curled in a ball on the ground. His hands pressed against his ears as he whimpered through twisted lips. A tight-fitting white tee-shirt clung to his back, slightly untucked from his faded blue jeans. His soulful whimper clawed my heart as he rocked steadily on the woodland floor.

Biting my lip, I mustered up the courage to speak. "Are you okay?"

He grunted. "Please stop! Make it stop!"

"The noise? But it's gone now."

He twitched and moaned. The brush beneath him crunched with every movement.

"It's okay," I said. "Just breathe. It's over. Everything will be all right."

Panic centered in my chest, as if something reached inside me and tugged. A haze seeped into my thoughts, and I shook my head to clear it. What was wrong with me?

The boy hadn't reacted to my questions, almost as if he couldn't hear me. A helpless, panicked swirl within my ribs gave me pause. I had to do something, but what?

My hands balled into fists. "What's wrong?"

I shoved aside a stray branch and jumped over the log. The boy stopped rocking as I approached, but his body quaked with long, labored breaths.

"It's okay. It's over."

He didn't respond. I looked through the tree trunks and over the bramble and ferns…only leaves and vines and trees blending into more trees for as far as I could see. There was no one else to help him. I ran my fingers through the hair at my temples, massaging the sensitive skin where my brain still pulsed with a dull ache.

Pull yourself together, Jess.

The guy pushed up on one arm. His long, dark bangs fell over his face. Cautiously, I placed my hand on his back.

"Hey, are you all right?"

His entire body flinched. He popped out of his crouch with a cry of alarm. He kicked his feet against the leaves and dirt, backing himself away. A murmur escaped his lips as he smashed against a tree trunk. His turquoise-blue eyes widened. His gaze darted in every direction.

Were his eyes actually turquoise? I tilted my head to the side. Yeah, they really were. Must be contacts or something.

I raised my palms, keeping my distance. "It's okay. I won't hurt you."

He focused on me, mouth open, taking in huge gulps of air. His right hand reached up and held his left shoulder as he bit his bottom lip. Beautiful white teeth grazed his slightly tanned skin before he closed his eyes and swallowed hard.

I stepped closer. "Are you hurt?"

The guy scrambled away, sliding beside the tree.

I raised my hands. "Okay, okay. I was only trying to help." I eased down on a patch of moss. "What do you think that was anyway?"

His eyes centered on me—freaking me out with their odd color. I wanted to look away, but I couldn't. My eyes burned and grew heavy—until he blinked.

A waft of air entered my lungs, and I let it out slowly. Why was I holding my breath? I rubbed my eyes. What was wrong with me? I felt, I don't know, different—like a cloud covered me. No, like a blanket. A nice, safe blanket.

A wince contorted the boy's face as he stretched his neck. He crinkled his nose, his breathing settling to a more normal pace.

His gaze seemed to search through me, and the foggy feeling deepened. I relaxed, taking in his strong, round cheeks and delicate jawline. I must have won the lottery or something... stuck in the middle of the woods with a guy who—come to think of it—looked a lot like Jared Linden.

"So," I began, trying not to focus on those muscular arms nearly busting out of his tight tee-shirt. "What's your name?"

"Your name?" His hair fell in loose waves along the bangs, flipped back over short-cropped sides...exactly like Chris Stevens's hair, but much darker—almost black.

"Yeah, you know—your name." I pointed to my chest. "I'm Jess."

I waited for an introduction that didn't come. He just looked at me, blinking hard like something was stuck in his eyes.

"And you are?"

He squinted. "David?" His eyebrows arched, almost as if he were making sure his name was okay.

"Are you asking me, or telling me?"

A maddening grin shot across his face. Jared Linden eat your heart out. Damn, this guy looked like he should be on a magazine cover, not out traipsing around in the woods—or whatever he was doing out here.

"David," he said. "My name is David."

"Okay, now that we got that out of the way, are you all right? Is your shoulder hurt?"

He shifted to the left. A grimace twisted his lips. "My shoulder? Umm, yeah. It hurts in the back."

"I took first-aid last year. Do you want me to take a look at it?"

"Take a look at it?" He blinked twice.

"Yeah. You'll need to take your shirt off, okay?"

"Shirt off?" He placed his hand down, crushing the jagged leaves of a fern.

"Okay, did you hit your head or something, because you're, like, repeating everything I say."

He blinked his eyes hard again. His breathing came in shallow wheezes, as if every lungful hurt. I half expected to find a gunshot wound, but I'd probably have seen the blood by now. At least I hoped so. It'd be embarrassing if I passed out and he ended up taking care of me instead.

"Here. Let me help you." I reached for the bottom of his tee-shirt and helped him lift it over his head.

"Ouch." David grabbed his shoulder before I could get the shirt over the other arm. The white fabric hung in the crook of his elbow, dragging the ground and picking up a few pine needles.

"Sorry, I didn't mean to hurt you." I shifted to kneel behind him. His gaze tracked me like I had a knife or something. "Okay, let's take a look."

I chewed the inside of my cheek and took the longest look of my life. He was flawless. Absolutely flawless. Slightly bronzed, unblemished skin covered strong shoulders. He almost seemed air-brushed. I reached out to touch him, and his muscles rippled and tensed.

A gasp escaped my lips. Dang. I mean seriously: Da-ha-hang. If I didn't distract myself, I was gonna drool all over him. "So, what do you think that loud noise was?"

"Loud noise?"

"There you go again, repeating me." My jaw fell open. "Holy cow. You weren't in the plane crash were you?"

"Plane crash?"

"Still repeating."

He shook his head. "No. No plane."

A light wind blew overhead, bringing life back to the forest. The birds resumed chirping as I slipped beside him. "Did you see it, the crash?"

He nodded. "Yes."

"You didn't get hit by shrapnel or anything, did you?"

His lips formed a word, but stopped. "I, I don't know."

"Crap, talk about picking the wrong time to be in the woods." I moved behind him again, and ran my hand along his back. I couldn't find any trace of injury, but his skin seemed hotter than Hel...well, really hot.

"What's the last thing you remember?"

His shoulders twitched. "You asking if I was okay."

"Don't you remember holding your head and screaming in agony?"

He rubbed his forehead. "Oh, umm, yeah. It was...strange."

"Strange is kind of an understatement, don't you think?" I removed my hand. "I can't see any swelling. Where does it hurt?"

"In the shoulder middle."

I ran my hand across his back lightly once, and applied gentle pressure in the center of the blade.

He cried out.

"Oh, sorry." It hit me that I'd barely passed first-aid class. I had no idea what I was doing.

He grumbled, flinching. "Can you first aid it?"

I laughed. "First aid it?"

"Can you help me?"

I sat back, just missing a daddy long-legs scurrying across the ground. "David, I think you need to go to a hospital."

He raised his hand. "No. No hospital."

"But you're hurt. You probably need an x-ray."

"No. I definitely don't need one of those." He stood and cried out, clutching his arm.

"Listen, are you in trouble or something? Are you running from the police?"

"No…not the police."

I propped myself against a small tree. "So you *are* running. From who? You're not, like, a criminal or anything, right?"

"No. I just don't want to be found." His gaze drifted downward.

Way in the back of my mind, a little trickle of doubt and fear struggled against an overwhelming need to help him. I should have done the smart thing and run, but I couldn't just leave the poor guy there.

"Listen. You don't have to tell me what's up, but you're hurt. You at least need some ice."

He looked up. "Ice?"

"You know—to keep it from swelling."

A deep furrow crossed his brow. "Can *you* get me ice?"

"I guess. Do you want to walk back to my place with me?" I shuddered. Did I just invite a guy I didn't even know back to my house?

"No. Bring it here."

Relief washed over me, but not because I was afraid of David. I was more afraid of Dad finding me alone with a boy. Bring ice? No problem. I glanced around the trees, no longer sure which way I'd come from.

"The only problem is I'm not sure I'll be able to find you again. I'm not even sure if I can find my way out."

He motioned behind me. "You are six-hundred and twenty-seven point five meters from where you entered the woods."

I stared at him as my geek-meter went haywire. "You're kidding, right?"

He paled slightly and shrugged, glancing away. "Yes, of course. You did come from that direction, though."

He was probably some kind of a math nerd or something. Damn cute math nerd, though. "Okay. I'll be right back." I started walking.

"Jess?"

My hair grazed my cheek as I turned back toward him. "Yeah?"

David eased himself against the log. "Thank you."

"No problem." *As long as my dad isn't home, that is.*

I imagined all the possible Major Martinez interrogation questions. None of them ended up good. I turned to the woods and quickened my pace. I had to get in and out of the house before Dad got home.

3

I sprinted down my street and stopped at the edge of the sidewalk. Busted. Dad's car sat in his favorite parking space, still creaking as the engine cooled. How in God's name was I supposed to sneak a bag of ice out of the house with Dad home? The back door!

The handle of the rear screen door clicked as I tiptoed into the kitchen.

Dad's voice came from the living room. "I did tell her to stay home. Mom, I just don't know what to do with her anymore. She doesn't follow orders at all."

Why was he talking to Grandma about me? Didn't matter. I had to get that ice. I inched toward the freezer.

"I know she's not one of my soldiers. Believe me. If she was, she'd think about the big picture and not focus on herself all the time. And she wouldn't do such stupid things. I swear she does this to piss me off."

I gritted my teeth and slid the ice tray out of the freezer. What Dad considered *stupid things* were all the things that were important to me that he didn't understand. If he'd look up and beyond that stupid uniform he wore all the time, he'd realize there was more to life than—

"And this dumb photography thing—dammit Mom, I wish you never bought her that camera."

I froze. My heart wiggled its way into my throat.

"Give her space? Let her make her mistakes? What kind of advice is that?"

Photography wasn't a mistake. It was my life, my passion, my—

"Mom, I need help with her. I thought I could manage it alone, but I can't. All I'm asking is for you to come for a week or so, just until school starts. There's too much going on and I just can't trust her anymore."

Can't trust me?

Grandma?

My stomach did a somersault and missed the landing. The ice container slipped out of my hands and crashed on the floor.

"Mom, she's back. I gotta go."

I dropped to my knees, taking deep breaths as I scooped the slippery cubes off the linoleum. My hands shook. Why couldn't he understand how much that camera meant to me? Why couldn't he understand that his dreams weren't the same as mine? I shoved the container back into the freezer and sat down at the kitchen table. I doodled the deer's antlers on the edge of a pad, trying to calm myself down as I prepared for the impending fight.

Dad barreled around the corner. "Jess, where have you been?"

"I told you, I went to the store."

"You were supposed to stay home."

"You said last night. I went out this morning."

His face reddened. "When I tell you to stay home, I need you to stay home."

"I left a note and everything, didn't I? And I called, like a good little soldier, but as usual, you didn't pick up the phone. You never pick up the phone."

"Don't you try to turn this around on me."

"Don't worry. I didn't do any more stupid things." I pushed past him and stormed up the stairs.

"Jessica!"

I slammed my bedroom door. The covers poofed up around me as I flopped onto my bed. Only think about myself? Dumb photography? What did he know? I rolled over and hugged my pillow. It was the same argument, different day. Nothing would change. Ever.

By now, Dad was probably half way to counting to a hundred to calm down. He'd need to get to two-hundred before he'd come up here and give his stylized lame apology. God, I hated that part.

I rubbed my face, remembering why I'd come home in the first place. I needed to find a way to smuggle some ice past Dad. But how? There was no chance of getting out of the house again until he stopped focusing on me.

A prisoner until the game played out, I decided to kill time with Maggie. I slipped my phone out of my pocket, and dialed her up. "Hey girl."

"Hey, you. What's up?"

"My dad as usual, but guess what just happened in the

woods? I was chasing after a deer—"

"Again?"

"Yeah. Anyway, there was this noise, and it felt like my head would explode, and then there was this guy, and he heard it too."

"A guy?" She giggled. "Okay, now I'm interested. I thought you were going to tell me another stupid *Jess chases an animal* story. So, fess up. Was he cute?"

A sigh slipped from my lips. "Didn't you hear about the noise? I mean, it was really loud. Did you hear anything?"

"Nope, no noise. Now spill it about the guy."

I rolled over onto my stomach. "His name is David."

"Isn't David the name you made up for your dream prince?"

I giggled. "Omigosh, how'd you remember that? We were, like, thirteen."

"I remember those juicy stories you made up about him— all tall, dark and Greek-God delicious."

The more I thought about it, David actually did look a lot like—

"So was he running through the woods taking pictures of animals, too?"

"No. Can you keep a secret?" I rolled onto my back. "He's hiding out there from someone."

"Hiding? Girl, you're not hooking up with a serial killer or anything, right?"

"He's not a serial killer. He's like, seventeen, eighteen tops."

"Didn't you see that movie *Scream*? Those two were—"

"Can we come back to reality please?"

"Okay. Okay. Okay. So, what's he running from?"

"Dunno." I rubbed my fingertips, remembering the heat radiating from his skin. "He said it wasn't the cops. I'm hoping he talks to me when I go back."

Maggie snickered. "You're going to meet him again in the woods? Miss Goody-Two-Shoes, are you finally going to do something naughty? And without me?"

I sat up, knocking the pillow off my bed. "No. I just want to help him. He's hurt."

"I bet you want to help him." She giggled.

"Stop. You are so bad."

"But seriously, Jess. You don't know anything about this guy."

I chewed the top of my lip, thinking about Dad's conversation with Grandma. Was I being stupid? I needed to make a good decision here. "You know what? You're right. Can you come out there with me?"

"You know I'd love to meet your prince charming but I need to go school shopping while my mom's credit card is still squeaking, and tonight is family movie night. No getting out of that in the Baker household."

"Oh yeah, I forgot." Oh well. So much for reinforcements.

"You know what? Just don't go. Tip off the MP's that someone's out there, and they'll find him."

"You want me to turn him in?"

"No, not turn him in, but if he's in trouble...You know... They have shelters for kids like that. Confidential and all. They won't call his parents."

I fingered the chain on my neck. "No. It doesn't feel right.

He needs my help."

Someone knocked on my door three times.

"Maggs, I gotta go. My dad's revving up for another pep talk."

"Okay, but be careful if you go out there, okay?"

"Yeah, whatever." I clicked off the phone and opened my door.

Dad's hand was poised at eye level, about to knock again. His chest expanded for the obligatory breath before an apology speech. "Jess, I don't want to fight with you. I just wish you'd listen once in a while."

I folded my arms. "I only went to the store." *With a little side-trip into the woods.*

"It's not just that and you know it." He ran his palm across the top of his cropped hair. "You know it's been hard without your mom here, but I'm trying."

"I know." Dang he was good with the guilt trips. An uncomfortable silence lingered, stifling me like an invisible curtain.

"Listen. I've never been able to keep you cooped up, and I realize you're into all that photography stuff, but until things die down and I can confirm everything is secure, I need you to stay in the house."

Crap.

You see Dad, I can't stay in the house. There's this drop-dead gorgeous guy in the woods, and I promised to bring him ice. Nah. That wouldn't go over well. Certain things a girl should just keep to herself.

"Dad, what's going on? And what was all that *buttercup*

stuff about last night?"

He rubbed his face with his palms. "You weren't really old enough when your mom and I came up with the word buttercup. I was hoping you'd understand what I was trying to say."

"Mom told me once to listen if you ever said buttercup during an emergency. That's all I remember."

"Well, we were in an emergency. You did good."

"There was someone on the phone, wasn't there? They were making sure you didn't tell me anything."

Dad leaned against my doorframe. "You know I'm not allowed to talk about work."

"Work smirk. I don't care about security clearance."

"There was a possibility of danger. I just needed to know you were safe." He kissed my forehead. "I gotta get back."

"You're leaving again?"

"Yes. I'm sorry, but the whole base is on alert status."

"For how long?"

"It depends on how long it takes us to find…"

I waited for a word that didn't come. "Find what?"

His head tilted to the side. "Nice try."

"Can't blame a girl for trying."

So, the army was looking for something. Interesting.

"I'll be back in the morning for a bit. We'll have breakfast, okay?"

"Uh-huh."

Dad headed down the stairs, and I counted to a hundred before following.

So, the army was all jacked up in another one of Dad's top-secret operations. I still had no idea what Dad did in the army, but from what I could gather from Maggie's eavesdropping habit, Dad's division dealt with dangers of the "who" kind, not the "what" kind. They called my dad to track people down. If Dad was involved, whoever they were looking for had to be pretty big potatoes.

David was hiding from someone, and he was hurt. Could he be running from the military? A vision of David's bright eyes and perfectly cut jaw flashed through my mind. I shook my head. Why would Dad be hunting a kid? He certainly had better things to do. Terrorists and the like were out there. Real criminals. There was no way Dad could be looking for David. My gaze settled on my camera case. I grabbed it…just in case.

Shooting over to the kitchen, I opened up the cupboard, pulled out a gallon-sized Ziploc, and filled it with ice. The bag fit neatly into the bottom of my backpack. I threw together a few peanut butter and jelly sandwiches and tossed them in with a couple bottles of water and my camera. The ice chilled my back as I threw the pack over my shoulder.

I hesitated, my hand on the front door. Dad wanted me to stay home. *Until everything was secure.* That meant that there was a safety risk, and if Dad was involved, it had to be a pretty big one. He expected me to be a good little soldier and stay inside. But how could I?

David was out there, alone. Hurt. I couldn't just leave him there, especially if there was some kind of dangerous fugitive on the loose. I'd made him a promise, and I had to keep it.

4

I yanked my jeans free of a thorny bush. I swear I had to be crazy. Just that morning something screeched in the woods so loud it almost burst my eardrums. But here I was, wandering around in those same woods, probably lost, bent on finding and helping a boy I didn't even know. My chest ached with pressure from my short, choppy breaths. Why did the forest seem so much more sinister than it normally did?

"*Auoi calinart est.*" A gruff, masculine voice echoed through the trees.

The language was odd, musical. Kind of like singing, or maybe Norwegian—or maybe a Norwegian guy singing. I couldn't decide.

An elderly man wearing a long, dirty winter jacket slapped a tree branch as he sped-walked around a bush. He nearly plowed into me.

"Sorry," I said, backing off the path.

The man gazed up at me. His nose crinkled as if a foul odor suddenly hit him. He blinked and continued on his way, but his icy cold countenance hung with me for a minute. And his eyes…No one had eyes so blue. Except maybe David.

I shivered. Not sure why, but the old dude creeped me out. His head bobbed as he moved through the bushes. He had to be delirious, wearing that warm coat in the middle of August.

"Pardon me." A woman with gorgeous long blond curls ran up the same path. Her jacket brushed against me as she passed. When she caught up to the old guy, she grabbed him by the arm. They muttered, heads close, before he shoved her away and continued down the trail. The woman turned her face toward the sky, fisted her hands, and continued on after him.

The dude had to be her father or something. Why else would she take that kind of crap from him? I sniffed out a laugh. I hoped that wouldn't be me and my dad in twenty years.

I pushed through the brush and plodded on. The trees were probably laughing at me, because I was pretty sure I'd seen the one with the big, black knot in the bark at least three times, now. Stinking, stupid, big, black, knotty tree.

A rustling of leaves deep within the trees startled me. I froze, and stared down another gorgeous, enormous buck. Or was it the same one as that morning?

"Hey, beautiful," I whispered.

Swirling antlers blended with the landscape. He barely seemed to notice me.

"Good boy." I clawed for my camera, slipping it out of my pack. "Just stay right there." I pressed the picture button and zoomed in. *Click*. Gotcha. But a closer shot would be even better.

I inched forward. Majestic black eyes emitted a sense of serenity, calming me from within their gaze. *Crack*. The twigs broke beneath my feet. Dernit. The deer's ears twitched.

"It's okay, buddy. It's me, remember?"

Two little baby steps brought me closer. I held my breath, trying to keep quiet, but my phone vibrated, the ringtone reverberating through the trees. The buck bolted.

"You're not going to chase him again," I told myself. A grin broke across my lips. "Oh, yes you are."

Jumping over fallen trees and stomping in muddy patches, I followed him deeper into the woods. My phone finally stopped ringing, but the buck was long gone...again. I laughed and leaned over, resting my hands on my knees. I was starting to make a habit out of this.

"Jess?"

I screamed and whirled toward the voice.

David raised his hands. "Sorry. I thought you saw me."

"Saw you? I was looking at the stinking deer." I held my hand to my heart, willing it to stay within my chest. "You scared the crap out of me."

His lips contorted into the cutest pout as he settled onto the ground. "Sorry."

"Well, wear a bell or something next time. Geeze!"

Okay, heart. You can slow down now.

I caught my breath. "Are you feeling any better?"

"Maybe." He rotated his shoulder. "Either that, or I'm numb."

Dirt and pine needles scattered in a puff as I dropped my backpack beside him. "Okay, let's get to it, then." I grabbed the Ziploc bag.

"What's that?"

"Ice. What did you think?" The cubes scraped together inside the plastic.

"Umm…" His eyes widened.

"If your shoulder is swollen, and you won't go to the hospital. You need a cold compress."

He swallowed hard. "Okay."

David bent forward. I brushed traces of bark and dirt clinging to his back as I knelt beside him. The muscles in his neck and arms tensed.

"Loosen up. It's just ice." I carefully placed the bag on his injury.

David trembled. He steadied himself against a sapling, gripping the slim trunk in a shaky fist. "It burns! Ouch, it burns!"

I pulled the bag away from his skin. "How can it burn? It's cold." I set the Ziploc on my leg and let the ice chill my skin. "Look. No burn. You can't be such a big baby. This is supposed to help. Can we try again?"

David nodded, but flinched as I lifted the bag.

"Okay, tell you what…" I picked up his tee-shirt from the ground. "Let's get this back on you."

His head popped through the opening, and a gentle tug brought his right hand through the armhole. I elevated his left arm as slowly as I could, but he still stifled a groan as the rest of the shirt slid on.

"This is like torture," he whispered.

"Sorry." I gently replaced the bag. "Your shirt should protect a little against the ice but still leave it cold enough to stop the swelling." I smiled, proud of myself for remembering something from first aid.

David grimaced. "It's still pretty cold."

"It's supposed to be. That's the point."

David's eyes closed. He took in a deep breath through his nose, and his lips parted slightly to release it. I watched the tight, white cotton expand and retract across his back with each breath. Holy shmoley. *Okay, Florence Nightingale, get a grip.*

David's body quaked, and he grunted through clenched teeth. He grabbed the sapling, snapping it in two.

"Hey, what'd that tree ever do to you?"

His hands formed into trembling fists. He shook like a rocket trying to take off until he bolted upright. The ice fell to the ground.

"I c-can't," he stammered. "It's just too cold."

"All right." I picked up the bag. "But I don't think it was on there long enough to help you."

"Then I'll have to deal with the pain. I'll get over it." He grimaced, settling back down on the ground. "Eventually."

He rubbed his shoulders. His gaze seemed distant.

"Are you okay?" I asked.

"I can't seem to get warm."

"Warm? It's like eighty degrees. It's gorgeous out here."

"I know, but I keep getting a chill." He scuffed the dirt, making an imprint with the front of his sneaker. A spider shimmied from the divot and crawled up a tree to his right.

The sun funneled through the canopy, flickering splotches of light into his hair. What was it about this boy? I just wanted to sit there and stare at him. Well okay, he was gorgeous, but it was something more than that. I felt compelled, like a gentle tug inside, drawing me to him. I bit back a grin. It's called hormones, Jess. Let's just keep it together and don't make a fool out of yourself.

The wind blew lightly through the treetops, rustling the branches over our heads as I slid down beside my bag. "Are you hungry?"

"Yes, famished." His eyes lit up, the color actually brightening. It must have been the sun.

"Great. I made a few PB&J's. I hope that's okay."

"I guess."

I handed him a sandwich. He flipped it over, squinting at the jelly running down the crust.

Okay, so, I wasn't Betty Crocker. Get over it.

I removed mine from the plastic wrap, and David followed suit. He watched me take a bite before tearing into his own.

What did he think, it was poisoned or something?

"This is good." He swallowed and nodded. "Really good."

A snicker escaped my lips. "I guess anything would taste good if you hadn't eaten since yesterday."

"Mm-huh. Thank you." He finished the last bite and ran his tongue slowly along his pointer finger, licking off a glob of jelly.

I shifted my weight, watching his tongue glide across his skin.

Wow.

I bit my lip and cleared my throat.

Get. A. Grip. Jess.

Looking away—definitely a good option. "Listen, you

can't stay out here. There is some kind of dangerous fugitive or something on the loose."

"Or something?"

The spider beside him dangled from a branch before swinging back up, a stream of silk glistening behind it.

"That's about all I know. I just thought you should know. You know?"

Ugh. How much dumber could I sound? Why did I act so goofy around this guy? Pfft. It had nothing to do with the perfect tan, the washboard abs, those unbelievable arms...

"So, what does this fugitive look like? It's not a young girl with long brown hair and blue eyes, is it? Because that would kind of suck."

I laughed. "If I were a fugitive I wouldn't be making PB&J for some sappy guy in the woods."

"Well, I guess today's my lucky day, then."

He licked another finger. I forced my eyes back up to the spider web. The sunlight caught the square outline of the miniature piece of art before it disappeared, fading in and out like a mirage.

My stomach churned anxiously. "So, do you want to tell me why you're out here?" *Please, please, please don't tell me you're a dangerous fugitive.*

He looked down. "I told you..."

"I know. You don't want to be found. I get that, but the Army is out there looking for someone suspicious. If they find you..."

David's eyes sprang open. He leapt to one knee, just missing the spider web. "Where are they looking?"

"I don't know. Around, I guess."

A refreshing breeze blew through the woods, invigorating me, but a shiver rattled David's shoulders. "It's getting colder."

Dark clouds wafted over the treetops, shrouding the forest in a dim gray before the sun broke through once more.

"It might rain, but it's still, like, eighty degrees."

He wrapped his arms around himself and sat hunched over. A pang deep within my gut warned something wasn't right, that I should run, but the sensation quickly ebbed away. As if erased.

I knelt beside him. "Are you sure you're okay?"

"I'm just cold."

"Maybe you have a fever? You should really see a doctor."

"No. No way." He raised his hands in a defensive position.

"All right—if you tell me what's going on, maybe I can get help, but we're not really getting anywhere here with me doing all the talking."

"Okay, let's talk." He looked to the right and moved closer to the web. He seemed to focus on each strand the spider spun.

The sunlight sparkled in his dark hair and gleamed within the web. I couldn't help myself. I grabbed my camera and adjusted the focus so both David and the web popped crisply from the outlining scenery.

Whoa. The preview looked like a magazine ad. The lines in his face, his nearly pore-less skin—just perfect.

David smiled as I raised the lens again. I set off the shutter on high speed repetition, hoping to get some of the sparkle from the spider's web.

"You like to take pictures, huh?"

"Yeah. It's an obsession of mine. You don't mind, do you?"

He shook his head, and I snapped some more. The last one had a beam of sunlight in the background. Damn if I couldn't sell those as pictures of Jared Linden and gotten away with it.

I closed the lens. "I'm still waiting for your story. I love photography, but I'm not that easily distracted." Well, not right now, at least.

"I'm not sure where to begin. Do you get along with your dad?"

I leaned back, surprised. "I guess. I mean, most of the time. He's a little judgmental, though."

"Mine too. In a big way."

"Is he the reason why you're out here?" A fly buzzed my ear. I swatted it away.

David shrugged. "Indirectly. If he'd just listen, just try to understand…"

"I know what you mean. My dad's got this crazy idea I can't make good decisions."

"Yeah, mine too. He said I was worthless, and I've never done a selfless thing in my life. What does that mean, anyway?"

"My dad thinks I don't listen."

David propped his elbow on his knee and rested his chin on his fist. "Well, you're listening now."

I smiled. A little girly tingle jittered through my chest. He was cute, and said the right things. Score another notch in that lottery ticket.

My cheeks burned up in a flush under his sparkling gaze. Those eyes—so darn blue. I broke our stare, clearing my throat. "So, you had a fight with your dad, huh?"

"Something like that. I tried to prove I was worth

something."

"Did it work?"

He took a deep breath and let it out in a puff. "If it did, I wouldn't be here."

The fly buzzed around David's head and darted toward his right, snagging itself in the spider web. The more it thrashed, the more the webbing ripped and covered its wings…until the struggle abruptly ended. The web seemed to wink in and out of existence as the spider inched toward its prey.

Despair settled into my gut. The thought of being totally overpowered—and to die like that—it just didn't seem fair. The clouds drifted, and the web faded once more. So beautiful, but nothing more than an elaborate trap.

David's gaze moved from the spider back to me. He seemed to search through me, and his brow furrowed. Did I surprise him somehow, or was that confusion in his eyes?

His expression faded into a smile. "Jess, you…"

Another cooling breeze encircled us. David clamped his arms around his shoulders. His hands shook as they rubbed his skin.

The hair on my arms stood on end as the sky darkened ominously overhead. "David, are you all right?"

He wheezed, his body trembling as he bent over into a ball.

"Okay, that's it," I said. "I'm getting you out of here." I lifted him to his feet. He barely struggled, but drew away once we were standing.

"I can't leave the woods," he said.

"Oh, yes you can."

I nestled my camera into my backpack and flung the bag

over my shoulder. David's body seemed rigid as I pulled him to his feet.

"Jess, please don't..." His words were lost between chattering teeth.

"Don't nothing. You need help."

I yanked on his arm. Luckily for me, he was too busy trembling to fight me. We slunk through the trees, stopping each time David's chill shook him too hard to walk.

This is insane, Jess. You don't know anything about this guy. Lord knows what's wrong with him, and...

A moist tap hit my head, then another. I glanced up. The clouds thickened. Another raindrop grazed my nose as a few birds flew for cover.

Great. A rainstorm was all I needed.

David studied a drip running down his arm, and turned his eyes up to the trees. "What..."

"Come on," I said, giving him a tug. "The trail is this way." At least I hoped it was.

Ferns scraped against my jeans as I pushed branches away from my face. I stopped once to untangle David's shirt from a sticker bush before the woods opened up to the dirt path beside the road. It wasn't where I'd come in, but it was close enough to get home.

David tensed as we stepped away from the trees. Small circles appeared on the ground, darkening the sand from tan to brown as scattered droplets fell from the sky.

David retreated toward the woods. "I can't...I can't."

"You don't have much of a choice now, do you?" I led him forward.

His muscles relaxed, but his eyes told me it was in defeat rather than agreement. David hunched his shoulders, ducked his head, and stumbled as I nudged him forward. I slowed my pace, hoping it would help him keep up.

This is crazy, Jess. Just bring him to the...I stopped, alarmed by the movement at the gates to the base housing. Two men in uniform tossed their packs beside the door to the guard house. One fumbled with keys.

In the entire four years we'd lived on that base, I'd never seen guards stationed at the entrance. A wave of adrenalin swept through my body. Sweat formed at my temples.

David gripped my arm. Turquoise eyes, wide with fear, met mine.

A twinge in my gut forced my whole body to tremble. I was right all along. It was him. He was the guy they were looking for. We were in deep shi…well, we were in a lot of trouble. Or was it just me? Was I in trouble? Was David dangerous?

I forced a smile. Every part of me screamed to run, to flee to the guards and tell them, but when I looked into David's eyes, the mistrust melted away, disappeared.

Wait. Why did it disappear? I was scared to death a minute ago, wasn't I?

His eyes softened me. I was safe with him. I always had been.

"I'm not going to turn you in. I promise."

His shoulders relaxed. "Can we please go back to the woods?"

"There's no way to warm you up out there. Now come on, and act natural."

I kept watch on the guard house as we walked toward the gate. One of the guys talked on a cell phone while the other unpacked his bag. *Just keep walking.* A large raindrop pelted my shirt, then another.

David brushed away a rain droplet dribbling down his cheek and looked toward the sky. He gaped, his eyes questioning. Why did rain freak him out? Everybody's seen rain, right?

His nose and lips distorted before he ducked his head down again. Not really as inconspicuous as I'd hoped for, but at least he was keeping up.

Relief washed over me as we passed through the gate. I couldn't believe it. We'd actually...

"Excuse me."

Oh. Crap.

Every muscle in my body tensed. I could feel David's bicep contract as I turned toward the MP. "Yes?"

"Can I see some ID please?"

"Oh, umm, yeah."

I reached into my pocket and grabbed my wallet. He made note of my driver's license on a clipboard.

The MP motioned to David. "And yours?"

"He doesn't have his license yet," I stammered. "He's only sixteen."

My tense muscles got even tenser. There was no way David would pass for sixteen. He looked eighteen, nineteen. My brow furrowed. Just how old was he?

A crack of thunder boomed overhead. David nearly jumped into my arms. The wind whipped up. I glanced to the MP. *Please let us go, dude.*

David turned from my shoulder and stared at the MP. The officer moaned and blinked his eyes. He looked up at the sky and handed my license back.

"Okay. You're cleared. Thank you." He walked back to the booth, massaging his forehead.

No way.

I shoved my license back in my pocket. "I don't believe it."

David didn't comment beyond a tremor as I maneuvered him across the street.

We'd been incredibly lucky. The guy hadn't even made a note of David. Maybe MP training wasn't as hard-core as I'd heard.

We moved past a bush near the edge of the sidewalk, and a sparrow hopped out. The bird fluttered its spotty brown wings as it snatched a squiggling worm on the concrete.

David reared back, nearly knocking me over. "What the…"

I tightened my grip on his arms. "Dude, it's only a bird. Chill out!"

"I'm sorry. It frightened me."

His eyes remained on the little brown-spotted minion-of-doom as it hopped onto the road. What kind of idiot got spooked by a bird? I didn't push it. David obviously had serious issues. Hopefully they weren't the homicidal kind.

I cringed.

No. He was just a guy who needed help. No homicidal anything.

David's gaze shifted from left to right. "Where are we going, anyway?"

"Don't be so scared. It's not like the whole world is looking for you. What are the chances of your father just happening to be on Maguire, and driving down this road at this very minute?" I tried to gauge his reaction, but his expression didn't change. He was worried about more than his father, I could tell. Was it really the MPs? The regular police? Worse? Maybe eventually he'd open up to me.

As we turned onto my street, an open-top jeep sped toward us. David cried out and jumped away from the road. One of the soldiers inside waved as they drove by.

"I really think I need to go back to the woods," David said.

The jeep turned the corner, not even hesitating at the stop sign. "It's nothing. They're only going to work. You need to lighten up."

You should bring him back to the gate. Turn him in. This is bigger than you, and you know it. If the Army is looking for him something is seriously up.

I scoffed at my own idiocy. Paranoia was so un-cool. He'd be fine. He was just out of sorts with a fever or something. Besides, if he was a fugitive, and I helped him, I may just be setting myself up for the story of a lifetime.

Or a lifetime behind bars.

I decided to go with the first scenario. Much better karma.

Head tucked down low, David allowed me to guide him while I kept a careful watch on the neighbors' windows and front porches. The last thing I needed was a nosy housewife calling my dad.

David dug in his heels as we turned up my walkway. He wrenched against my grip. "What's that?"

"My house."

"Your house?"

"Yeah, this is where I live. David, are you delirious or something? Where did you think I was taking you?"

I placed my hand on his arm. Perspiration beaded on his brow and his tee-shirt seemed far damper than it should have been in the light rain.

Sweat?

David scrunched his eyes closed and stumbled foot over foot. A torrent of unintelligible words streamed from his lips as his body went limp.

My knee slammed on the pavement as I reached down to catch him—but he was nowhere near as heavy as I expected. Weird.

His eyes opened and rolled back into this head. He coughed once before his gaze re-focused on me.

"You're done. I'm calling an ambulance."

He grabbed my arm. "No! I just need to get warmed up."

I shook my head and helped him back to a standing position. "I think it's more than that, and something really strange is—"

"I promise you, I'm just cold. Please just…" His words lost themselves inside a moan, and another shaking chill brought us both to our knees. David's shoulders stiffened between my hands, becoming board-rigid before shaking fitfully.

"Shoot," I whispered, rubbing his arms in a fruitless effort to warm him.

The sky opened up. Rain pummeled us. The sound roared through the compound.

David's pupils fixed on a point behind me. His jaw

vibrated in time with the tremor. Dark wet tresses matted to his forehead. Water trailed from his bangs and down his cheeks.

I gripped his face and pointed it toward mine. "David. David, listen to me. I need to get you into the house."

His eyes didn't focus. His teeth chattered.

"Okay. Let's hope you heard me." He grimaced as I hauled him to his feet. His shiver tightened his joints. The stiffness in his body fought against me as we made our way to the door.

5

Beneath the overhang, I fussed with my keys and pushed the door open. With some finagling I dragged his trembling form inside and into the family room, where he collapsed on the couch.

"Stay here." Like he was getting up anytime soon. "I'll get some blankets."

I sprinted up the stairs, leaving muddy footprints on the carpet. Yeah, that wasn't going to get me in trouble or anything. I threw open the linen closet.

"Okay Dad, it's like this," I whispered to myself. "I know I wasn't supposed to talk to strangers, but he was really cute so I figured it was okay…then he got sick. I couldn't just leave him out there."

Yeah, that'll work. You are in deep dog-poop, Jess.

I threw two towels over my shoulders and grabbed a stack of spare blankets before padding down the stairs. Drying David's clothing proved fruitless, but at least his hair wasn't dripping anymore. Dad had left his gray sweatshirt hanging on the back of a chair. I peeled David's wet tee-shirt from his back, trying to be careful of his injured shoulder, and pulled the warm fleece over his head.

Still stricken with the chill, David rolled himself into a ball. I unfolded the blankets with a flourish and swaddled him in pink and yellow fuzz.

"Okay. If that doesn't warm you up, nothing will."

I admired my domestic-ness until the covers began to quake again. He had to have a fever. I cranked the thermostat up from seventy degrees to seventy-five.

"David, I'm going to get a thermometer."

Chattering teeth answered me.

Just call an ambulance, Jess.

No. No ambulance. He'd been clear on that. No hospitals. Until I found out what was going on, I needed to keep that promise.

I walked right by the telephone to the bathroom and grabbed the thermometer from underneath the toothpaste in the medicine cabinet.

Closing the door, I cringed at my reflection. Yesterday's eyeliner oozed down to my cheek. My bangs hung wet, lifeless, and clinging to my forehead. Lovely. I ran a fingertip under each eye, alleviating most of the raccoon syndrome. Who was I kidding? I'd never win a beauty pageant anyway.

I uncapped the thermometer as I returned to David. He groaned. His chill rattled the coils in the couch.

"David, I'm going to stick a thermometer under your tongue." I had no idea if he could hear me over his shivering.

After pressing the button to clear the digital readout, I pried his mouth open to slide the prong between his lips. His hand clutched the edge of the blanket. His fist shook against his chest.

"Come on, David. Snap out of it."

His eyes squeezed shut. His mouth formed a pained, straight line.

"It'll be okay." A puff of air blew out of my lips. Saying the words didn't help me to believe them. What if I was wrong? What if he really needed a doctor? What if he died?

I touched the chain on my neck, twirling the links around my fingers. The phone sat on the end table. One call to 911 would bring an ambulance, which was what he really needed. I reached for the phone and sighed. He seemed petrified of the hospital. But was it right to let him die just because he was afraid?

The clock on the wall ticked, filling the room with its cadence. David's teeth rattled against the plastic tube in his mouth. What was taking that thermometer so darn long to beep?

I grasped my pendant, willing myself to do the right thing—if I could just figure out what the right thing was.

My mother's words seeped into my mind. "I had this necklace blessed. You'll never have to worry about anything while you wear it." Her image soothed me like a hug. I closed my eyes and fed on her strength.

"All right, Mom," I whispered, "here goes nothing."

Another tremor rocked David's body as I unhooked the chain and refastened the clasp behind his neck. I touched my fingers to the golden oval.

"Please God," I whispered. "Please help him." The shiver

subsided, but his breathing seemed labored.

Darnit. What was I supposed to do?

I frantically searched the room for something to help. Pillows, magazines, remote controls, everything a good Jersey home should have other than something to stop a person from freezing to death.

Three logs lay unburned beside the fireplace, leftover from the spring thaw. Perfect. I placed one of the logs on the steel grate and shoved some newspaper beneath it. Luckily, the dry wood caught quickly. I checked David's blankets and glanced at the thermometer's digital readout. *112. 113. 114.* "What the…"

David convulsed and bit down, snapping the thermometer in two.

"Holy crap!" I picked up the half that fell on the blanket and tossed it on the table. My finger shot between his lips, and I pried his mouth open, praying he didn't bite me by accident. I dug the rest of the thermometer from under his tongue and threw it over my shoulder.

His head fell to the side, his body as limp as a rag doll. I did my best to hoist him to a sitting position as his eyes rolled back, exposing ghostly white orbs.

"Omigosh, this is not happening. David! David!" No answer. I slapped his face.

His eyes sprang open, centered on me, and froze. His lips clamped together. His body shook as if it were preparing to explode. His muscles hardened like bricks beneath my fingertips. The skin around his eyes crinkled. The set of his eyes screamed for help.

"Come on, David. Snap out of it. Come on!"

His eyes remained fixed on me until the convulsion subsided. A blink told me he was still in there. I eased him back until he rested on the couch without my support. His gaze locked with mine. Color returned to his face.

I reached out and touched his arm. My fingers trembled. "Please tell me it's over."

David closed his eyes and rubbed his chest, taking in several long, full breaths. He blinked and squinted as if the light hurt his eyes, before scanning the room.

His movement seemed hesitant and sleepy, as if he'd just woken up. The licking flames in the fireplace caught his attention. His lips turned up in a grin.

"Warm. Thanks," he whispered.

I ran the back of my hand across my forehead, dabbing away the sweat. "Thanks, nothing. You have, like, a hundred and fifteen-degree fever. We need to get you to a hospital."

His eyes darkened. "No. I told you—"

"David, this is serious."

He reached out and touched his fingers to my chest, just below the collarbone. "I am serious." His irises seemed to brighten beneath his dark lashes.

A soothing sensation rolled over me, relaxing my muscles one at a time. My apprehension slipped away, while something deep in the recesses of my mind begged me to run. I blinked and allowed the calm to overcome. "All right, but I'm not a doctor, you know. I have no idea what I'm doing."

"I don't need a doctor."

Yeah, so he'd told me. I kneaded my hands together, doing

my best to remember what they taught in my first aid class. "So, okay, fever. A tub of ice, right? Ice water will break a fever?"

He raised his palms and leaned away. "No! No more ice. Please…"

"But David you're really sick."

"No, I'm not." He rubbed his temples. "I, I…have a disorder."

"A what?" The fire crackled behind me as the room continued to heat.

"It's…thermo-nucleic disorder. Have you heard of it?"

"No." I crossed my arms.

He straightened. The pink blanket fell to his waist. "I have an extremely high body temperature. I don't do too well in the cold."

"You're trying to tell me you're always that hot?"

He placed his hands on his lap. "Pretty much. I'm feeling better, though. Thanks for the fire."

I kept my arms folded. Seriously? He must have thought I was a…

His smile warmed me more than the fire, and I relaxed.

A disorder, of course. It made total sense—unless he was pulling my leg.

His smile faded as he tugged the chain of my mother's pendant out of the sweatshirt. He fingered the golden oval. "What's this?"

I scooted aside the blankets and sat beside him. "It was my mom's. She gave it to me when I was twelve. She told me that whenever I wear it, I could hold it tightly and know that she was with me…that everything would be all right."

David ran his thumb over the etching and turned the charm over. The starburst cross on the front glistened in the firelight. "That's beautiful. Why did you give it to me?"

I shrugged. "At the moment you kind of needed it more than I did."

"The fire warmed me, not the necklace." He reached for the clasp behind his neck.

"No. Keep it for now…until I'm sure you're okay."

The fire cast a light glow on the right side of his face. "If you can help me stay warm, I'll be giving this back to you pretty quickly."

I narrowed my eyes. "Wow, I can't believe this. You really can't take the cold? At all? What do you do in the winter?"

He laughed. "I try to dress more warmly."

I fiddled with my thumbs, recapping and sorting through everything that'd happened. Despite being completely relaxed, I knew something was very wrong. I fought back the feeling of ease as it tried to overtake me again. Why was I being so complacent when something was obviously up? What was wrong with me? Focus. I needed to focus.

"David, why are they looking for you?"

"You mean my father?"

I stood. "No. I mean the Army. Is it because you have some kind of funky disease? Am I in any danger? Did you break the law? What—"

"I'm going to have to take notes if you keep asking questions without letting me answer."

I folded my arms. "Then start answering."

He pursed his lips. "I'm not contagious, and I would never hurt you."

"So you *do* have some sort of freaky disease. Is that why they're looking for you?"

He chewed his upper lip, his face pensive. "I promise I'll tell you everything, but right now I don't think it would do either of us any good. Can you please just trust me for now?"

"I don't know you. I'm not even sure why I brought you here."

David stood and curled his fingers around my hands. "Trust me. We're alone. If I wanted to hurt you, I'd have done it already."

"But David…"

He stepped away from me and grabbed his temple.

"Please don't tell me you're getting another chill."

"No." He sat on the couch, jostling the pink blanket. "Just dizzy."

He closed his eyes and stretched his neck as I sat beside him. "David, I don't know what to do."

"I think I'm just tired." He cuddled into the corner of the couch.

Shifting the blankets out from under me, I stood and threw one over him. David blinked and smiled, sending a rush of tickling energy through me, heating my cheeks. What was it about that smile? Why did I turn into a heaping sack of melted jelly when he barely even looked at me?

My hands shook. Distraction. I needed a distraction.

"Tell you what. You get some rest. I'll see if I can scurry up something to eat for dinner." Yep. Food. That would work.

Nothing helps a girl keep her calm and focus like a good old-fashioned dose of carbs and calories. I walked toward the kitchen. "I can always make peanut butter and jelly again if I need to."

David drew the blanket up under his chin. "I'd rather have more PB&J if you have it. That was great."

I turned, leaning on the doorframe. "That's what I said."

His lashes flickered closed, and his face softened. A placid rhythm developed in his breathing.

Maybe he was more tired than I thought. I walked back and sat beside him on the couch. Trailing my fingers across his forehead, I brushed back his long, dark bangs.

Who was he? Why was he here, and what the heck was going on? I rubbed my chin. He asked me to be patient, but all these questions were killing me. Was I sitting on the story of my life, or was I setting myself up for disappointment, and perpetual, eternal grounding?

The firelight cast a stunning shadow behind him. Eerie, ethereal. I pulled out my camera and rattled off shots from several angles, but the photos in the preview screen did little to convey what my eyes saw in real life. Maybe they'd look better when I downloaded them later.

Making my way into the kitchen, I opened the cabinet and reached for the peanut butter and a loaf of bread. I slathered as much jelly as I could without it sloshing out the sides of the sandwich. Admiring my finished masterpieces, I licked the jelly that still clung to the knife. Waste not, want not, Mom always said.

I smashed a quarter wedge into my mouth and placed the

rest on a napkin, leaving it on the coffee table beside David. His lips rose in a half-smile as he slept.

Boiling hot skin met my fingertips as I touched my hand to his forehead. I winced, fright overtaking me for a moment, before I settled myself.

Duh. Of course he was going to feel warm. Temperature disorder, remember?

The sun broke through the clouds outside. Cheerful sparkles glimmered on the water droplets still clinging to the window screens. At least the rain was over.

I eased into the armchair and watched David sleep. So many questions muddled inside my mind. What was he running from? What's really wrong with him?

Although the storm outside had abated, the storm inside still slumbered on my couch. I should have been terrified of him, but I wasn't…and it drove me crazy.

And what about Dad? He could burst through the door at any moment. What would I say? How would I deal with the unavoidable life-long punishment? I covered my face. *Crap.* I was in way over my head.

The rhythm of David's breathing transfixed me, lulling me to sleepiness. I blinked twice, and grabbed my phone. I Googled 'rare temperature diseases' and scrolled through listings of pointless topics. Raynaud's syndrome. Nope didn't make your temperature high. Lyme's disease…nah, didn't seem likely. Cold urticaria…allergic to cold temperatures, causes hives in the cold. I glanced in his direction. No, there was never a mark on him, and they didn't say anything about constant high temperatures.

I clicked off my phone and rubbed my eyes. The sun had gone down, and the last embers in the fire had died out. I spied a carton of synthetic logs under the kindling newspapers. I added one to the grate to keep the fire burning.

David rolled over in his sleep, his bangs falling toward his right eye. I brushed them aside and sat on the floor staring at him. Was he telling the truth? Could he really have some sort of freaky temperature problem?

The clock on the wall clicked to nine-thirty. I tousled my hair and found it damp from the heat. Sweat beaded on my chest and dripped down into my bra. Gross.

David's cheek was warm, but not sweaty. His breathing remained deep and regular.

He may have felt fine, but I felt like I was going to yack. I headed up the stairs to my bedroom and hoisted the window open, letting in the cooler outside air. A light breeze blew the curtains beside my shoulders, refreshing me from the heat in the house. I rested against the sill and turned my face to the sky. A thousand lights in the heavens glinted and sparkled, settling my uneasiness. I breathed deeply, enjoying the sweet scents of Mrs. Miller's garden until a star overhead winked out. Then another.

I grasped the windowsill and pushed against the screen—holding my breath as the stars wiped away before my eyes. A deep, dark blanket stretched out over the house, consuming the sky quickly and more completely than any cloud cover.

I reached for my necklace. Startled by its absence, I froze until I remembered it lay safely around David's neck. My gaze drew back to the sky. A black mass hovered over the houses, continuing to blank out the stars. One by one the little pinpricks of light returned as the form passed overhead and moved toward the airstrips.

No lights. No landing gear. Just black—And really, really slow. A blimp? In the middle of the night? And no noise at all?

I shivered and backed away from the window. Keeping an eye on the mass, I fumbled for my phone and dialed Maggie. I recounted my entire day, right up to the apparition that'd just flown over my house.

"Did you see it?" I asked.

"So they flew a plane over your house. It's not the first time."

"Have you been listening to a thing I've said?"

"Come on, girl. I don't care about the plane," Maggie said. "I want to hear about the hottie. He's actually there in your house? Right now? And your dad's not home?" Her giggle always sounded maniacal. "Are you going to *do it*?"

"No! Maggie, come on."

"But seriously. What are you going to tell your dad?"

I shook my head. "I was thinking of the truth. I can't send David back into the cold, and I can't really hide him either. Right now he's passed out on the sofa."

"Holy cow. The major's going to have a brain aneurysm."

"Believe me, I know." I tucked back the curtain and peeked up at the stars. Everything seemed perfectly normal—now. "Maggs, that plane, or whatever—it was weird. I mean, really weird. I couldn't even hear it, but it must have been huge."

"Hon, maybe you were dreaming."

"I wasn't."

She held a long pause on the line. "Are you going to deal with the real problem, here? What do you think is wrong with Prince Charming?"

I checked the window again and slumped onto the bed. "I have no stinking clue. He says he has this funny disorder."

"Okay, so what is it?"

I rolled onto my back. "He said it was something like thermo-dynamic disorder. Or maybe it was thermo-nuclear disorder. I don't know…something that makes him really hot, and he freezes when it gets cold out. I tried to Google it, but I couldn't find anything."

"You already knew he was really hot."

I ignored her. "It was so bizarre. I couldn't get him warmed up, no matter what I tried."

"You know, if it happens again, you can always smother his body with yours."

"What?"

"Seriously. I see it in the movies all the time, and they told us that in first aid class too, remember? Sharing body heat and all." She snickered. "And I hear friction…"

"Maggie!" I sat up and tossed my pillow back to the head of my bed. Not that the idea of snuggling up with David was all that gross, but I didn't need her to know that.

"Okay, okay, but I'm going to research it to make sure he doesn't have the plague or something."

"Whatever. I'll talk to you tomorrow."

I smushed my forehead against the window screen again and counted stars. Not that I knew how many were supposed to be up there, but tallying them made me feel better. Scattered light clouds left from the earlier storm dotted the sky, but otherwise the stars shone as brightly as any other night. I closed the window, pulled the blind down, and leaned against the edge of my dresser. I knew there was no way I was going to be able to sleep.

I grabbed my comforter and pillow and padded down the stairs. Throwing the bedding on the chair beside David, I placed my fingers on his forehead. Still hot. *Duh – Temperature disorder, Jess.*

First things first: I needed to make sure Dad didn't have a conniption when he walked through the front door so he didn't shoot David or something. I grabbed the note pad from the counter and scribbled: *Don't be mad. I'll explain in the morning* on the yellow-lined sheet. I taped the note on the couch behind David.

Lame, but it was all I could come up with. Tomorrow was not going to be fun.

I eased back into the chair beside David and yanked the lever to raise my feet. Using the blanket to prop up my side, I cuddled into my soft down pillow and watched David sleep. So many questions…but tomorrow I'd get some answers.

Hopefully David would comply. If not, Dad might beat the answers out of him.

6

The trumpeting throng of Reveille smashed its way into my dreams. *Stinking P.A. system!* I crushed my pillow around my ears, but the blaring trumpets pierced the feathers and shot straight into my brain. There was no escaping the military wake-up call: an evil tune perpetuated by evil men joyously pressing a button and cackling as they woke the world.

The trumpets faded. I growled, willing myself back into sleepy-land as I did every morning. A scrumptious smell teased my senses before I fell back into dreamy land.

Mmmmm, bacon.

I salivated, dreaming of the crispy strips crunching in my mouth.

Wait. Bacon? Bacon's cooking? Dad's home!

I sprang out of the easy-chair, stumbling in half delirium and falling onto the sofa.

Omigosh, David. I tapped the empty blankets. Where was he?

Someone scraped a pan in the kitchen and turned on the faucet. I rolled David's blankets into a ball and tucked them on the side of the couch. I snatched the pieces of the thermometer off the table and slid them into my pocket.

"David?" I whispered.

Silence lingered—except for the bacon sizzling in the kitchen.

The napkin I had placed David's sandwich on the night before still sat on the end-table, holding a few stray crumbs. I shoved it into my other pocket.

"David?"

Horrid images of him bound and gagged to a chair in the kitchen crossed my mind.

The note was no longer on the sofa. Had Dad read it? What *would* Dad do if he caught a boy in the house? Would he have woken me up to see what the deal was, or would he have shot first and asked questions later?

I counted to ten, calming myself, and walked through the archway.

Dad looked up from the stove and raised an eyebrow. He wore the same jeans and tee-shirt he'd left in the day before. "Hello, *pequeña*," he said.

I glanced about the kitchen. No sign of David. At least he wasn't tied up.

"Morning, Dad." I kissed his cheek.

"So, you're feeling better? I'm surprised to see you up. I figured you were sick."

"Me? Why?" I flopped into a chair.

He scraped some eggs onto a plate. "Well, first it was hot as Hell in here when I got home, and it's not like you to start a fire, and I don't think I've ever seen you sleep in a chair, and all those blankets…" He looked up. "And I saw your note. If you were that sick, you should have called."

He hadn't found David.

Think fast, Jess…and make it good. "Well—I had this chill. I, I turned up the heat, but it wasn't getting hot enough, so I started a fire, and I guess I fell asleep. Sorry."

He used those 'daddy thinks you're lying' eyes on me. Probably because I was babbling like a guilty idiot. Time to change the subject.

"So, anyway, did you catch the bad guy?"

"Who said there was a bad guy?"

I propped my elbows on the table. "Come on, Dad. I'm not stupid."

"We're still investigating the crash."

"Does that mean you're leaving again?"

"Not immediately. I need to report back in around noon, but I'll be home tonight."

I poured myself a glass of orange juice. "Dad, does the investigation have anything to do with a huge, quiet plane?"

"What? No!" His quick reply told me he wasn't completely telling the truth. It also didn't help that he nearly dropped the pan. Time to keep pushing while his guard was down.

"I saw something strange last night. Why would a plane fly over the houses without lights on?"

He bit the side of his cheek…typical Major Martinez stall tactic when he was about to lie.

"I don't really know." He turned back to his cooking. "Jess, I asked Grandma to come help out for a bit, but I'm thinking it might be a good idea if you stayed with her instead, you know, until this all blows over."

Oh, no you don't. "No way. I hate Grandma's. You know that."

Grandma's. The pit of doom. Well, maybe not doom, but boredom anyway. She lived in a retirement village for goodness sake. What would I do all day? He slid eggs on a plate and handed it to me. He topped it off with extra bacon. *Sorry, Dad. I can't be bribed.* Well, not this time at least.

"Sweetheart, I just don't know when I'll be called or have to do another overnighter. I want you safe."

I grit my teeth. "You don't think I'll stay in the house." Of course, he'd be right. I wasn't about to admit to that, though.

His lips formed a straight line. "You know what? You're right. I don't trust you. You had a chill last night because you went outside. You got caught in the rain, and you were soaked."

My mouth dropped open like a Venus fly trap. I snapped it closed.

"You're going to Grandma's."

"I'm not a baby. I don't need a sitter."

I folded my arms and put on my defiant face. He knew I was serious because I hadn't touched the bacon. Yep, I had willpower. Not much more, though, so I hoped he'd back down quickly.

He placed the pan in the sink. "How about you stay with Maggie?"

I shuddered. "Dad, you know I can't stay there. You know...Bobby." Yeah, spend the week in a house with my ex-boyfriend. Not. A. Good. Idea. I should have considered the "ex" factor before dating my best-friend's brother.

He mashed his hands into a towel and chucked it on the counter beside him. "I need to know you are supervised. Period. Grandma either watches you here, or at her house. Which is it?"

Tally up another argument to lost. "She can come here."

"Good. Negotiation over."

Crud. Why couldn't I ever win at that game?

I picked up my fork. My stomach twisted. I was pretty sure it wasn't excited about the pending bacon.

Dad was easy to dodge. He never stayed home. Grandma rarely left the house when she visited. She'd move from room to room, buffing and waxing until the house sparkled. I'd be trapped.

Maybe I'd get lucky and this whole thing would blow over before she was able to get on that plane?

"Do you really think there's someone dangerous out there?"

He pointed to my plate. "Eat up. I don't want you getting sick again."

Yikes. Complete avoidage of my question. Not good. But it couldn't really be David, could it? Shoot, I wished Dad would spill some classified beans. Right now two plus two equaled ten. Nothing seemed right.

Something was obviously up with David. He'd admitted as much. But he seemed harmless enough. He couldn't possibly be a threat to any sort of national security. Could he?

I poked a piece of bacon in my mouth. Salty goodness coated my tongue with each crunch, but my mind kept drifting back to David. I glanced out the window, expecting to see him slink by. I swallowed, forgetting to enjoy my favorite vice.

Where was he?

***

I pretended to watch TV while Dad farted around for hours. Plans had been made, and Grandma's plane would land around seven a.m. the day after tomorrow. At least I had a full day and a half to find David before the Grandma lock-down.

As for today, I had to spend the day at Maggie's. At least that's where Dad thought I'd be. A quick call to Maggie and it was all planned out...unless Dad thought to call Mrs. Baker and confirm. If he did, I was skunked.

I packed a bag with all the essentials. Namely, a blanket in case David was cold, and my camera. Yesterday had shown me how a photo op could happen at any moment, and I needed to be ready with more than a camera phone.

Dad dropped me off at Maggie's, and I waved as I walked toward the porch.

Hyper-focused as usual, he didn't even check to make sure I went inside. Perfect. No need to worry about Mrs. Baker. I glanced down the street.

Deserted. Where were the kids? Joggers? Exercise junkies? Weird, but at least there wasn't anyone around who might slow me down while I looked for David.

Now, where would I hide if I was an obnoxiously cute guy with a temperature disorder? The only place I could think to look for him was back in the woods, so I followed my steps from the previous day.

Half way down the street, Mrs. Nicholson scooted her six-year-old, what's-his-face, into the house. She furrowed her brow as I passed.

"Jessica, does Major Martinez know you're out?" she asked, holding the screen door ajar.

"Yeah. It's all good. I'm going to the playground." Sounded plausible. The playground was in that general direction. Sort of, anyway.

"Today?" She tilted her head to the side.

Army housewives…they listened to their husbands, they panicked, and then worried about everybody else's business. This wasn't the first time the Army scrambled over nothing at all. I learned that by the time I was ten. Why adults took so long to catch up, I didn't know. I smiled, waved, and continued on. I just hoped she didn't call my dad.

Movement at the gates ended my cadence. An MP stood at the guard shack, looking over papers on a clipboard.

Crap. Why were they still monitoring the gate?

I kept walking. He looked up and held his hand out.

"Just a minute, miss," he said. "Would you mind opening the bag?"

Sweat crept over my brow. "Why?"

"We've been asked to check all baggage."

No use fighting it. "What are you supposed to be looking for?"

"Classified."

Classified, my rear-end. His security clearance probably

wasn't much higher than mine.

I opened my camera case and showed him the contents. I wouldn't even let Dad fiddle with my camera. I wasn't about to let this guy's pudgy fingers grease up the lens. I snuggled it safely back in its compartment as the MP unzipped my bag and removed the blanket. He raised a questioning eyebrow.

It's none of your business, jerk. I looked away, hoping to avoid questions.

I had to stop fidgeting though. I probably looked as guilty as sin.

The MP handed the duffle back to me. I started squishing the blanket back in.

"So, is that it?"

He made a note on this clipboard, glancing at me. "You're Jessica Martinez, right?"

I straightened. "Yeah, why?"

"We met at Bobby Baker's graduation party."

Ouch. The night Bobby and I broke up. Not a good time.

I threw my bag over my shoulder. "Sorry, I don't really remember. Can I go now?"

He nodded. "Sorry for the inconvenience, Miss."

I marched past the gates, my hands frozen into fists until I stepped onto the sidewalks near the civilian housing. I didn't stop until I stood before the open grassy area where I'd first seen the deer.

"Okay, David," I whispered. "Where are you?"

I treaded over yesterday's muddy footprints, and pushed aside the broken bramble I'd dragged him through last night. Instant cool embraced me the second I passed under the forest's welcoming limbs. I searched for him for hours. Well, I was lost for a few of those hours, but I was looking while trying to find my way out.

The air grew cooler, and I fingered the blanket in my bag. David was going to be cold. I couldn't leave him out there alone. Then again, maybe he decided to go home, or maybe he got caught by whoever he was hiding from. I could very well have been looking for someone who wasn't even out there anymore.

Evening's coolness seeped into the forest. I glanced over my shoulder, unease stabbing me. He could be anywhere. Staying out there was stupid, and the sun was going down. If I didn't get home before Dad…Well, let's just say Dad getting home before me was not an option. I'd end up in reform school or something.

Still—turning down the trail that led out of the woods was the hardest thing I'd ever done.

7

Score! No Dad to be seen. I skipped into the kitchen, plucked some chop meat out of the fridge and threw it onto a frying pan. While it sizzled, I grabbed a box of taco shells from the cabinet. I could manage a little Mexican food, and it would look like I'd been cooking for a least an hour.

I chopped up some lettuce and tomatoes and stirred the seasoning package into the meat. I'd made a typical 'Jess is cooking' mess before Dad came in.

A day's stubble marred Dad's square jaw. He rubbed his swollen eyes and looked up at me. "How'd you get home?"

Oops.

"Oh, umm, Mrs. Baker dropped me off." Score one point for Jess. I was turning in to a half-decent liar. Felt like crap about it, though.

He slumped down on a kitchen chair and held his forehead.

"Dad, are you okay?"

"I've had better days. Thanks for cooking, *pequeña*."

I scooped together a taco for each of us and sat down. "So, what's going on?"

He chewed and swallowed. "I talked to Grandma. She's still going to be here Thursday morning, but she's going to pick you up and the two of you will be on the next plane to Florida."

"But..."

He raised his hand. Why did that always stop me dead in my tracks? "They're not dropping this investigation. They're making evacuation plans for all the neighboring towns."

"What? Why?"

"For the worst case scenario."

I set my tortilla shell on my plate. "And what are the chances of having a worst case scenario?"

"Slim, but not impossible."

He stared at the bitten end of his taco. His mind seemed far away.

David was a freaking kid for goodness sake. What were they making such a big deal about? Unless it wasn't David at all. Maybe they were afraid of the same person David was hiding from. I wiped my hands on a napkin. There were just too many possibilities. Too many maybes to try to wiggle around. I wanted answers, and the guy sitting beside me had them.

"Okay, cryptic-talk time. If there was something wrong, which there probably isn't, would it have to do with the plane crash?"

His lips hinted at a grin. "Yes."

I jumped, surprised by the swiftness of his response. Good. He was willing to play. "And they are afraid of what...fuel leakage? Radiation? What?"

"None of the above."

"So they really are looking for someone?"

The sudden flex of his neck muscles told me 'yes'.

"You're kidding. How dangerous could one kid be?"

He raised an eyebrow. "Kid?"

Oops. "Well, you know. Maggie and the rumor mill. Are they really going to evacuate everyone?"

His face remained blank. "Not everyone. Just the civilians."

"That's crazy."

The set of his jaw told me he didn't agree. "I just don't want you anywhere near here."

"Dad, you just said the chances of them evacuating us are slim."

He shook his head. "I wish I could tell you more, but I need you as far away from here as you can get. Do you understand?"

Wow. He used the 'Daddy loves you' voice. That's pulling out the big guns. Something in his eyes told me not to argue, like this was bigger than both of us. "Okay. I'll pack a bag. But you need to get some sleep or you're gonna die of sleep deportation or something."

"Sleep deportation?" He grinned.

Hell hast frozen over…the man actually grinned!

"You know what I mean."

"I will, sweetie. I promise."

***

I rolled over in my bed, my face sinking into a soft pocket in my pillow.

Grandma's. Ugh. Maybe I could talk her into taking me to the Everglades or something so I could take pictures. That's one day covered. I supposed Universal Studios was out of the question. She wasn't even close enough to a beach to enjoy the weather. What a lousy way to end the summer.

A cool tremor ran through my veins as the hair on my arms stood up. My stomach lurched, and I started to sweat. Every sense I had sprung into hyper drive. My ears heard the smallest of noises—the clock ticking downstairs, the light hum of the refrigerator in the kitchen, the crickets outside my window, and someone—breathing. Yes. I definitely heard someone breathing, and—a presence. My skin crawled as I imagined beady eyes watching, leering.

Mustering all of my courage, I rolled over, ready to laugh at myself. Instead, I screamed as a silhouette of a man moved toward me and covered my mouth. I struggled, thrashing wildly, slamming my fists against his chest.

"Jess, it's me."

My heart bounced against my ribcage like a dribbling basketball until my vision cleared and big, sparkling turquoise eyes caught what little light illuminated the room.

"David?"

Relief swept over me. The pressure against my lips receded.

I shoved him away. "David, you scared the crap out of me again. What are you doing here?"

Heavy footsteps thumped on the wood floors.

"My dad! Get under the bed."

David dropped to the floor and slid his long, lean form beneath my bedframe. I hoped there wasn't anything embarrassing under there. My door banged open, and the sudden light burned my eyes.

"Jess!" Dad called. "What's wrong?"

I squinted, my eyes struggling to focus in the bright light. "Huh?"

He opened the closet and checked behind the door. "Why is the window open?" He walked over and closed the panes, clicking the locks. "I want the windows and doors closed and secured at all times, do you understand?"

"Yeah, Dad. I'm sorry. I was, well…hot." *Did I leave the window open?* "Why are you freaking out?"

"You screamed. What happened?" Demanding, hyper-focused eyes scanned the room. This maniac was not my father.

"I dunno. I guess it was a dream. I'm sorry."

Dad's eyes relaxed and he eased himself down on the edge of my bed. "I guess I'm a little jumpy. I'm sorry, too." He fiddled with his thumbs. "I just got off the phone with General Baker. I've been called to full active duty."

My heart stopped. "What? When?"

"In the morning. I've talked to Mrs. Miller, and you can stay with her until Grandma picks you up."

"Wait. What? Dad, no!" I was seventeen, for goodness sake. I was not about to get baby-sat by my next-door neighbor. "I'll stay inside. I promise."

His eyes told me I'd been caught too many times.

"Or, I can go to Maggie's." Screw Bobby. I'd rather deal with the ex than a babysitter.

"This isn't a game, Jess." He looked toward the window. "I didn't think there was a chance in Hell the pilot survived that crash, but…"

Say what? Was I just let in on a little intel? I closed my gaping jaw and waited, leaving the door open for him to keep spilling his guts.

"We thought he headed south, deeper into the woods, but a camp was just found less than two miles from here."

David's camp?

Dad took a deep breath. "Tomorrow there will be a calculated news leak. We're going to tell the public that he's out there, and he has an infectious disease. We're counting on the general public to turn him in."

Holy shi…Crap. A bead of sweat trailed down my inner-arm. "*Does he* have an infectious disease?"

My father stared at me. How could a man's eyes be so completely devoid of emotion? What had the Army done to him?

"Dad, this is crazy. That camp could have been nothing… just kids playing around."

"It wasn't. They found…"

Finish that sentence. Please, please, please finish that sentence.

He sighed, and for the first time I could remember, his eyes seemed to soften. "Jess, I need you to do this for me. I'm not coming back any time soon. I can't focus on my target if I'm worried about you."

How could I say no? And I really needed to get him out of there, since he was pretty much sitting on top of the guy he might be looking for. I nodded, lowering my eyes.

"Thank you, sweetheart." He kissed my forehead. "I don't

know what I'd do if anything happened to you."

If anything happened to me? A shiver weaseled up my spine. He left, closing the door behind him.

The darkness hovered around me, heightening the pressure in my chest. What was going on? My mind numbed, blotting out the thought of a plane ride beside grandma and her dumb crossword puzzles.

I sat there, lost, until the bed jostled beneath me. "Oh! David. Come on out." I jumped up, flipped on the light, and twisted the lock on the door.

David shimmied out from under my bed. I brushed a dust-bunny out of his hair.

He looked toward the door. His beautifully sculpted chest pressed against Dad's sweatshirt with every breath. "Your father is in the Army?"

"Yeah."

David rubbed his arms and continued to stare at the door.

"Don't worry. He won't come back unless I scream again."

My comforter barely budged as he settled on my mattress. My heart jumped into my throat and choked me. If Dad ever caught a boy sitting on my bed—I shook away my stupidity. I had a story to focus on.

"David, why are they hunting you?"

He lowered his gaze. "I guess because I'm different."

Or sick with a disease they don't understand.

The implications sunk deep within. Whatever the *different* was, the Army was involved. Dad knew what was going on, and it scared the crap out of him.

David was a military target. I was standing there talking to public enemy number one, and for all I knew, this guy was the key to Pandora's box.

I reeled in my flight reflex. I wasn't getting ill, so he wasn't contagious, and David totally scored brownie points for not trying to kill me. Deep down, I knew I wasn't in any danger. I trusted David, and I needed to hear what he had to say.

"Different, huh? How different?"

He lifted his gaze to me. Turquoise. I bet those eyes weren't contacts. It had to be some kind of lab experiment gone wrong or something stupid like that. I prepared for the worst, but what kind of threat could this sweet, timid guy possibly pose?

"I'm very different. I think you know that."

His lashes fluttered, as if drawing me in, yet keeping me from seeing what was really inside. That's what I wanted more than anything else, though—to see inside. To really know what was going on. Why wouldn't he let me in?

I guess he had no reason to trust me. We'd only just met. Then again, he was sitting in my bedroom. On my bed. With the guy who was searching for him just down the hall. Come to think of it, was he stupid or something? Did he want to get caught?

"David, why did you come back here?"

His head jerked up. "What do you mean?"

"You snuck into my room in the middle of the night. You freaked me out and almost gave my dad a coronary."

"Sorry." He hunched his shoulders. "It started to get cold. I got scared. I didn't think. I didn't mean for you to get into trouble."

Could he get any sweeter? Fugitive my left butt cheek.

This guy wasn't a threat to a fly, let alone a nation.

"I'm not in trouble yet, but if my dad catches you in here, we're both in deep shi…well, we'd be in big trouble."

He glanced toward the door again. "You have no idea."

But I'd like to have an idea. How did reporters normally handle this? Badger the witness? Beat the info out of him? What did I have to do to find out what was going on?

David stood and stretched his arms behind his neck. His biceps nearly split the stitching in Dad's sweatshirt. He glanced in the direction of the door again. The light in the hallway went out.

Safe at last—for the time being, at least.

"So," he whispered. "I guess you could say I met your father. Where's your mom?"

"Umm…she, umm…" Boy, did that catch me off guard. I opened my mouth to speak, but couldn't form the words. Why was I afraid to say it out loud? It'd been over a year now. It was bad enough Dad wasn't dealing with it. One of us had to face the truth. "She's dead. My mom is dead."

David flinched. "Oh. I'm sorry." His gaze fell to the floorboards. "My mother is dead, too. It happened while I was pretty young."

I jolted in surprise. "Really? How young?"

His gaze returned to me. "I was only a kid. I'm not really sure."

The sadness in his eyes nearly matched the ache in my heart. "Do you remember her?"

"Yes, I remember her. I think of her every day just to make sure I don't forget."

Okay, so I guess it's safe to say he's not a clone, or a fabricated human, or a robot or…Shoot. Who cares who he is? He was finally opening up to me, and opening up easier than I ever had about something so personal.

Had I thought of Mom every day? Maybe at first. But less and less. My stomach churned.

"It was my fault," David continued. "She died because of me."

I sat beside him, crossing my legs. "What do you mean?"

"She was coming to retrieve me from the play center. I asked her to stay later." He wrapped his arms around himself. "If we had left on time, she'd be alive right now."

I placed my hand on his arm. "Wow. I don't know what happened, but I'm sure it wasn't your fault."

"No? Tell my father that."

The fire in his eyes chilled me to the toes. My stomach knotted, poking me from inside. I knew all too well how he felt.

"My Mom and I were in the car when it happened. I don't even remember the crash. I woke up in a hospital." Painful memories flooded me. The antiseptic smell, the beep of the machine by my bed, the vacant expression on Dad's face. "I've never been a hundred percent sure my father didn't blame me, although he's never come out and said it. He's been different ever since."

"How so?"

"He doesn't really laugh anymore. We used to play a lot together, and now he's all business."

I closed my eyes. My mind wandered back to my mother's

funeral—Dad sitting on the bench, staring at Mom's open coffin. "He never cried. He just sat there at attention the whole time, staring at nothing. And ever since, he won't even talk about her. It's like he doesn't even feel any emotion. How can't you cry?" I rubbed my dampening eyes. "I cry about her all the time."

He adjusted his weight. "I guess we have a little more in common than either of us would like, huh?" He rubbed my back. "I'm sorry for bringing it up."

David's forehead crinkled, and his eyes searched me, as if piecing me together one odd-shaped section at a time. He blinked, and a gentle smile appeared on his face as he slid his arm around my shoulder.

My heart fluttered three full beats as my body absorbed his strength. Holy crap he felt good. I tensed as he leaned toward me and brushed his cheek against mine. It was nothing, just a brush of our skin, but the touch was wildly sensual, as if my cheek experienced contact for the very first time.

"Thanks, Jess. I'm really glad I found you."

I avoided the awkwardness by shifting away. "I believe I was the one who found you."

He dropped his gaze. "I'm sorry, I didn't mean to…"

Dumb thing to say, Jess. "No, that's not what I meant. I mean, like…"

He laughed. I'd laugh at me too.

"I'm sorry, David. If you want to put your arm around me, you can."

"My arm?"

"Yeah."

His neck tensed, and I thought a wave of disappointment crossed his features. What did he expect? *Duh, Jess. He's sitting on your bed*—but no, it didn't seem like that at all. He seemed—sad.

He held out his arm.

I didn't feel a shred of fear or inkling that he'd take advantage. And boy did I want those arms wrapped around me. I cuddled into his embrace, instantly warmed by the heat permeating his sweatshirt. Well, duh. He was like a hundred and fifteen degrees. I smiled to myself.

A hundred and fifteen degrees of perfect.

I should have cared about why the Army was looking for him. I should have cared about who he was. I should have cared about why he got cold so easily—but I didn't. Nothing about him made sense, but it didn't matter. Dang the story, and dang my father. All that mattered was this.

I couldn't remember the last time I felt so at ease with a guy. Probably because it was never. I sank into a deep void of nothing, drinking in the right-ness. So calm, so safe, so perfect.

My doorknob jiggled. My heart leapt into my throat.

Dad's voice boomed through the door. "Jess?"

I jumped up from the bed and realized David was gone.

The door slammed open.

"Who's in here?"

"No one."

Dad ran to the window and looked out, side to side, and up. *Up?*

"I thought I heard voices." He looked in my closet.

"I don't know. Maybe I was muttering or something."

His eyes narrowed. "Muttering?"

"I don't know, Dad. Why are you freaking out?"

"Why was your door locked?"

"Because I'm scared." At least I didn't have to lie about that. "You tell me that someone's on the loose, and then you wonder why I locked the door?"

His eyes softened, just like they had earlier. Maybe, just maybe, the father I grew up with was still in there, hiding behind a façade of an emotionless soldier.

He pulled my head to his chest and kissed my hair. "I'm sorry, *pequeña*. I just want to make sure you're safe."

He backed away, straying dangerously close to the bed.

Please don't look under. Please, please, please don't look under.

He turned back to me. Crazy Army Dude was definitely gone. This was my father, the man who taught me how to ride a bike, the man who hiked around Lums Pond with me, the man who'd taught me how to read. I never realized how much I'd missed him.

"You don't want to go to the Miller's, do you?" He folded his arms.

I shook my head. "I feel like it's babysitting."

Seventeen years of piggyback rides, tickle fights, and walks on the beach settled across his face. I liked it. "I'll call Mrs. Miller in the morning and ask her to drive you to Maggie's instead."

"Really?"

"Yeah. I'll have Grandma pick you up there."

I nodded. Probably looked like a bobble-headed idiot.

"Yeah, okay. I'll let Mrs. Miller know when I'm ready to go. Thanks, Dad. I mean, really. Thanks."

"All right. Sleep good."

He kissed me on the forehead and left the room.

I locked the door behind him. A lot of good it did last time, but it made me feel better. Not much, but it was something. I strode to the window and pushed it open. I looked back, forth, and oddly enough, up. Nothing out of the ordinary. But Dad was totally freaked. Maybe it was more than just David. Something else must have been out there. And whatever it was frightened a man who'd served a tour in Iraq.

Maybe I was wrong. Maybe I *should* be scared.

David appeared beside me, and I tensed to keep from jumping. Damn he was quiet.

My gaze trailed out the window again. No ladder. Just military-grade white vinyl siding. Not even a bush to climb on. "How'd you get up here anyway?"

David's eyes widened. "I…climbed?"

There it was again. Answering my question like he hoped the answered was okay. Well heads up. I wasn't buying it. Climbed? That's some damn good climbing. Friggin' Spider-Man. "All right, listen. Enough is enough."

He nodded. "Yes, it is. I guess we need to talk."

Finally.

But was I ready? Would I be able to handle what he was about to tell me?

I had to. No matter how bad it was, I promised myself I wouldn't freak out.

David tensed, and his face mottled into a grimace. He

clutched his arms to his torso and creased his brow as a tremor overtook him.

"Not again." I slid the window shut, picked my sweater off my chair and threw it over his back. The pink angora bought out the subtle highlights in his otherwise jet-black hair. Didn't stop the shiver, though.

Body heat. Friction.

Get out of my head, Maggie!

David crouched into a shaking ball at my feet.

Great. Now what? "Umm—give me a minute."

I threw open my closet door and hauled out my old beat-up plastic heater. Unraveling the short electrical cord, I reached under the dresser and plugged it into an extension. I placed the unit on the center of the floor and set that sucker to maximum.

"Here," I motioned to the heater.

He scooted across the floor, stopping mere inches from the unit, and rubbed his fingers together. "This is great. Th-th-thanks."

I sat beside him, rubbing his shoulders. Why did I have to open that window? He was fine. He was going to tell me everything. How could I get him talking again?

"Listen," I began. "If you tell me why you're really so cold all the time, maybe I can help."

He looked at me, and then back to the heater. "I'm afraid."

"Of what? Me? If I was going to turn you in I'd have told my dad to look under the bed. I can't live like this. I need to know what's going on."

The sound of the fan inside the heater filled the otherwise silent room.

David hugged his knees, looking more like a terrified child than a wanted fugitive. "I'm not from here."

His words coated me with a sense of doom. Was he a spy? A defector? Double agent? Impossible. He wasn't much older than me, for goodness sake.

He quaked. "Jess, I'm sorry. I'm really cold."

Shoot. "Give me a minute."

I jiggled my sleeping bag out of a box in my closet and rolled it out in front of the heater. David ran his fingers across the dull, gray fabric.

"It's seen better days, but it's warm."

"Thanks." He drew the quilted fabric around his arms, leaving most of his body uncovered.

"You're kidding, right?" I plucked the bag from his shoulders and flattened it out on the floor. "Haven't you ever seen a sleeping bag before?"

"No, I guess not."

Who's never seen a sleeping bag? I unzipped the side. "It's a bag. You get into it, and you zip it shut around you."

"Really? Wow, that's a great idea."

My eyes narrowed. "It's the best thing since grated cheese. Are you trying to be sarcastic or something?"

David nodded, but I didn't buy it. What country could he be from that didn't have sleeping bags?

He fingered the zipper. "I'll be kind of confined, won't I?"

"Yeah, I guess, but you can always unzip it."

"What if your father comes back?"

Good point. No matter what we did, Dad would be an issue. And I obviously couldn't put him back out into the cold.

"I need a good place for you to hide."

David's gaze trailed to the closet. "Can I sleep in there?"

"In my closet? Seriously?"

He pulled the sleeping bag from the heater and flattened it out in the small space between my hanging clothes and the floor. He wouldn't even be able to stretch out in there. Didn't stop him from trying, though.

Twisting at odd angles, he managed to ease himself between the two halves of thick fleece. He fumbled with the zipper until I took the end from him, zipping the bag up to his chin.

"Thanks. This is really warm." Calm coated his features, as if everything suddenly was right in his world.

But it wasn't right in *my* world. He hadn't finished telling me what the heck was going on.

"David?"

A cute little snore filled the room.

Crap. I rubbed my temples. "All right. You sleep, then. But tomorrow, we need to talk."

David grunted in reply.

Perfect. Just perfect.

I leaned on the edge of my bed. The pulsing red button on the heater illuminated David's face, tucked like a little doll in the bottom of my closet. The effect was almost eerie.

I grabbed my camera, adjusted for the low-light, and snapped a few pictures of him.

Sheesh. The resemblance to Jared Linden…it just wasn't natural. I mean, they say that everyone has a doppelganger in the world, but this was just crazy.

Creepy crazy, but at the same time, incredibly beautiful. Gentle, soft lines formed David's face, giving him an air of complete serenity. Too bad I didn't feel so secure with the sleeping arrangement.

Boy in the room.

Dad on a rampage.

Fugitive on the loose.

Jess in deep shi…shoot I was in trouble.

I eased the louvered doors shut, leaving a crack so he could breathe, but still concealing him if Dad decided to pop in to say goodbye in the morning.

Setting my camera back on my dresser, I cuddled under my comforter and tilted my pillow toward the closet. What a crazy couple of days. Everything was nuts, but at least I knew David was safe. Unless Dad found him, that was.

I glanced toward the door. Would Dad come and check up on me? What if he opened the closet again? Trembling, I closed my eyes, but I knew sleep would be at a premium that night.

8

Sunlight stung my eyes, waking me. I rolled over and squinted at my alarm clock. Ten twenty-two. No six A.M. Reveille? Someone must have broken the speakers again. *Whoever you are, I love you.*

Last night's events flooded back into my mind. I bolted upright.

David.

I sprang from my bed. My bare feet sank into the warm carpet. Why did my floor feel hot? I ran my fingers through the moist hair matted to my forehead. My night-shirt clung to me, the fabric so wet it had changed from a dark pink to a deep fuchsia. Balmy air filled my lungs.

But where was the heater?

The white extension cord wove from beneath my desk and snaked along the floor under my closet's louvered doors. The mild hum from the unit's fan reverberated from within.

"David?" I held my hand up to the door, my fingertips sampling the heat rushing from between the slats. It felt like the Sahara in there. I slid the door to the left. A gush of hot air assaulted my face, forcing a single step retreat.

David still lay wrapped in my sleeping bag with the heater propped beside him, cuddled like a moth in a cocoon. A light snore rose from his lips.

Well, that certainly kept him warm enough.

I smoothed back my damp tresses. The stifling heat in the room may have made David comfortable, but my stomach threatened major pukeage. I unlocked the bedroom door, and closed it softly behind me, allowing the cooler temperature of the hallway to relieve my lungs.

I tiptoed down the stairs and drew aside the curtains in the front window. Dad's car was already gone. In the kitchen, I found an envelope on the counter marked "Jess". As if anyone else lived in the house. I passed my finger under the seal, exposing six crisp, clean fifty dollar bills and a credit card. All right Dad! I withdrew a note from between the bills.

My father's messy penmanship scrawled across the paper: *Remember, Grandma will be here tomorrow morning. This is so you can have some fun and pick up some school clothes while you are in Florida. Stay at Maggie's until she gets here. Dad.*

I tapped the envelope against my palm. One more day to figure out what was up with David. Maybe if I could keep him warm enough, he'd finally tell me the truth.

I took a quick swig of OJ before climbing the stairs to the shower. The massage setting on the spigot eased some of the pain in my sore muscles. Some. Not all. I had no idea what I was going to do about David when Mrs. Miller came to pick me up.

"Jess?"

I screamed and clutched the shower curtain, pulling the pink plastic up to my neck as I peeked out into the bathroom. "David, what are you doing? Can't you see I'm in the shower?"

His eyes opened wide and his jaw dropped. He stood in the center of the steamy room, gaping. "I—I'm sorry. I just wanted to know where you were."

"Well, duh. Couldn't you hear the water running?"

"Yeah." He continued to stare at me.

Was he really that dense? "David, give me a minute to finish up, okay?"

His brow furrowed. "Do you want me to wait in your room?"

Was he for real? "Yes. Anywhere but here."

He wiggled his hands into his pockets and strode back into the hallway. Cute, but a total douche.

I stepped out and dried off. What was it with this guy anyway? And Dad thinks *I* have no common sense. He'd never be able to handle David.

I laughed at myself, grabbed the clothes I'd left on top of the hamper the night before, and slipped them on.

I crinkled my nose at my reflection in the mirror as I ran a comb through my bangs. If I were pretty like Maggie, maybe David would…I shook the thought from my mind. David was about six feet of drop dead gorgeous. Yes, quirky, but you could get away with the odd thing with pecs like that.

The mirror reflected simple Plain Jane Jess. *A guy like that is never going to go for you.* I dabbed a stroke of eyeliner against my bottom lashes, and fluffed my hair. It sure didn't hurt to try, though.

My cell rang. *MAGGIE* flashed on the screen. "Maggs, you are not going to believe this. He's here again. He spent the night."

She squealed. "Omigosh, did you *do it*?"

"No. He slept in my closet."

A mild pause hung on the line. "In the closet?"

"I know. It's kind of weird, but I really like him. He's sweet. You know—nice."

"Nice? Everything about this guy is odd, Jess."

"He was cold. It was warmer in there."

Her exhale fizzled through the phone line. "Is he feeling better at least?"

"Yeah, he seems fine today."

"So, what are you going to do with him? You can't keep him hidden from the major forever."

I pinched the bridge of my nose. "My dad would freak if he knew I had a boy in the house."

Maggie snickered. "Do you know how many guys I've hidden in my closet?"

"But I'm not actually doing anything."

"Yet," Maggie finished. "It sounds like you want to."

I shrugged. "I admit he's good-looking, but I...I don't know. I'm so confused."

The tapping sound of her keyboard clicked in the background. "You know, girl, I couldn't find a record of any disorder that makes your temperature really high. What did he say he had?"

"Thermo nuclear something or other."

"I looked for that. No such thing."

"I don't know what he said. Does it matter?"

"If he's in your house breathing the same air as you, it matters. I'm gonna keep looking."

Oh-oh. Maggs just dropped into sleuth mode. No biggie. The worst she could do was find a way to help me keep him warm—without the friction.

"Hey, listen. Mrs. Miller is supposed to pick me up soon. Can you just drive me instead?"

"Me, oh, umm, yeah. Hold on." She seemed to hold the phone from her face. "Mom, is it okay if I go get Jess instead of Mrs. Miller?"

Her Mom's voice sounded like the teacher from Charlie Brown in the background. Completely unintelligible.

Maggie returned. "Man, my parents are acting like we're being invaded or something. Don't worry. I'll schmooze her over and have her clear it up with Lieutenant Miller's wife. Call me when you get rid of the hottie and are ready for me to pick you up. Okay?"

"You got it. Thanks, Maggs."

I clicked off the phone. *Get rid of the hottie.* Why did I think that was going to be easier said than done?

The sound of wooden doors opening and closing banged from within the kitchen as I climbed down the stairs. I rounded the corner and smiled.

David closed the cabinet he was searching through. "I'm hungry. Can we have PB&J?"

I wrinkled my nose. "For breakfast?"

"But I liked the PB&J."

Mom always said the way to a guy's heart was through

his stomach, and I managed to find a guy who actually liked something I could make. Peanut butter and jelly sandwiches—who knew?

"The only problem is I think we're out of bread." I walked past the counter and opened the fridge. "I can make ham and cheese sandwiches without the bread. How about roll-ups, just like we're kids."

"Roll ups?" He leaned on the counter.

I slapped a piece of ham on a plate, covered it with cheese, and rolled it up into a small tube. Not really a breakfast extravaganza, but it was almost noon, anyway.

David's jaw tensed. He walked around me and chose a banana and an apple out of the fruit basket by the window. "How about some of this?" His gaze darted back to the ham. A slight grimace touched his lip.

"Do you have a problem with ham?"

A purplish tint blemished his skin. I swore he was about to yak.

"David, are you a vegetarian?"

He tilted his head slightly to the side. "Yes?" He leaned forward. His voice sounded as if he were asking if it were okay.

Could he get any cuter? "Why didn't you tell me? That's okay." I couldn't fathom how anyone couldn't like ham, but being a gracious host, I smushed the offensive slice of pig into my mouth.

I grabbed a few bags of veggies from the refrigerator and threw them on the counter. "I can make some stir fry. Sound good?"

"Okay. But no roll ups."

"No meat, no dairy. Got it."

I pretended to peruse the vegetables. So, he didn't eat meat, he's not used to the cold, and he's never seen a sleeping bag. But he also looked like he'd never seen a bird. Where were there no birds?

Grabbing a knife, I began chopping the broccoli. "Last night you were about to tell me where you were from." I brushed away the little green crumbles, pretending I wasn't as interested in his response as I really was.

"Yeah, that." He picked a knife from the block and grabbed a fistful of carrots from a bag. "I've been thinking about how to explain." He pressed down on the knife. Slices as thin as paper curled up in a growing pile on his plate.

"Impressive. Were you a chef in a past life or something?" I turned on the stove.

He placed the knife down. "I wish it was that simple."

My cell phone rang. David flinched.

"It's okay, it's just Maggie." I swiped across the bar on my phone's screen. "Hey, Maggs. This is a really bad time. David and I are—"

"He's still there?"

I glanced over to David. "Yeah, we're making lunch."

"Jess, get out of the house."

"What?"

"Just make an excuse and run."

I smiled at David and walked into the living room. "What are you talking about?"

"I think he's the reason for the security alert. He's the guy they're looking for."

A little ball formed in my chest and twisted. "Yeah, I kinda know, but it has to be a mistake or something."

"There's no mistake. I added two and two together and got David. You have to get out of there."

I glanced through the archway. David set the knife down and popped a carrot slice into his mouth. "Will you get a hold of yourself? He's not dangerous."

"How do you know?"

"Because he's fine. We're cutting up vegetables for stir-fry."

Maggie growled into the receiver. "With a knife? I'm calling Bobby."

"No! Are you crazy?"

"Jess, I'm scared. I've never seen my dad like this. Something huge is going on and you just happen to find some guy in the woods?"

The part of me that wanted to be safe struggled with the side of me that wanted to get back to David's explanation. Now was not the time to freak out.

"Tell you what. Come over. Meet him. If you still think he's a terrorist or something, I will dial Bobby's cell for you. Deal?"

Silence hung on the line. I paced the living room, waiting for her answer.

"All right," she said. "But I'll have my finger on the speed-dial."

"Fine. You won't need to use it."

"I'll be there in about fifteen minutes." She hung up the phone.

Whatever. It felt like the whole town had gone nuts. I turned back to the kitchen. "Ugh, Maggie can be so…"

David jumped as I entered the room. He stumbled back, bumping into the counter and steadying his right hand on the stove.

The stove. The *hot* stove.

My heartbeat drummed my ears. I gasped.

A putrid stench rifled through the air. Smoke rose from between his fingers as his skin melted and bubbled on the hot burner.

"David, your hand!"

He cried out, ripping his arm away and cradling his fingers inside his elbow.

The stove continued to sizzle where he had left most of his skin behind. Holy shi…Gross! O*kay. Okay. Keep it together! You can do this.* I switched the power off on the stove and reached for him.

"Let me see it."

"No. You definitely don't want to see this." He winced, and held his clenched fist to his chest.

"I've had first aid training, remember?" I glanced toward the stove. A lumpy, blackened hand print sent trails of rancid white smoke into the air.

But was that even possible? His hand was only on there for a second or two. Skin shouldn't burn that quickly. Unless you're David, and everything about you is bizarre.

One thing for sure—he was hurt, and I was all he had. "David, this is really serious. You're going to need a doctor."

A bead of sweat trailed from his hairline to his cheek.

"You're probably right."

"I'm calling an ambulance."

I picked up the phone, but David, still clutching his hand, kicked it out of my reach.

His eyes teared up. He shoved his fist under his arm. "I told you, no hospital."

"Okay, you can be an idiot, or you can let me help you."

He sprinted to the sink. "Just let me take care of this. I'll be okay."

Apparently, the choice of the day is idiot. I turned on the water for him. He placed his wounded hand into the stream and rested his cheek on the opposite arm. Breathing labored, he hid the ghastly sight from me. Not that I really wanted to see it, but he needed serious help. This was no time to be chivalrous.

I opened the corner cabinet and pulled out gauze and tape. "You need to at least let me bandage it."

He dabbed his palm against his shirt and looked at it. "It's not that bad."

I shook the box of gauze at him. "Did you see how much of your hand you left on that stove? You'll probably need a skin graft or something." I opened the box.

Frowning, he backed away. "I'm okay. It doesn't even hurt anymore. Here, give me the bandage." He held out his good hand.

Raising an eyebrow, I held out my own palm. "Give me your hand so I can look at it. I need to see how bad it really is."

He drew his injured hand tighter to his chest. "Jess, please, just let it go. It really doesn't hurt anymore."

A sense of tranquility crept over me.

No. Not this time. I didn't know who he was, or how he made me calm all the time, but I wasn't going to allow my instincts to slip into oblivion ever again. I wanted answers, and I wanted them now.

I grasped his wrist. He winced.

Didn't hurt?

My left butt cheek it didn't hurt.

I flipped his hand over, but he held his fingers in a tight fist. His pinky, blackened like char, stretched out slightly from the waxy bubbled skin beneath.

Oh Shi…dang. His hand wasn't on there that long, was it? Maybe I really didn't want to see the rest, but I had to.

"Open up."

His brow twisted, his eyes implored. "Jess, please…"

Let it go, Jess, he said he's fine.

Pushing my own thoughts aside, I gritted my teeth, threw the box of gauze on the counter, and pried his fingers opened. Well, I tried to at least. Darn he was strong.

A puff slipped from his lips. "I didn't want you to find out this way."

He opened his hand.

Sometimes your brain can't compute what your eyes see. Sometimes you need to stare, hoping maybe you'll wake up and find out everything was a dream. Unfortunately for me, I didn't wake up.

David's lower lip quivered. Agony and fear quaked in his eyes. I held his gaze. Thoughts of him freezing in mild temperatures, magically appearing in my room, staring at birds and spiders as if he'd never seen them before…All very strange. Maybe unexplainable. Or was it?

My gaze trailed back down his arm, along his strong wrist, and over the rolls of waxy-white melted skin, to the light purple mottled flesh it had once concealed.

Purple. Mottled. Flesh.

I took the deepest breath of my life and held it. Swallowing down hard, I bit my tongue, but I didn't wake up. The taste of copper spread through my mouth.

David's palm trembled in mine. "I really wish you'd say something."

I let his hand go and backed away. "I, I don't even know what to say." Hugging myself tightly, I paced the room, fumbling with pieces of a puzzle that were fitting incomprehensively in my head.

Another deep breath didn't help the freak-out simmering in my chest, building, burning, and begging me to high-tail it out of there. I forced in another slow, controlled breath as I walked into the living room. I sensed him following me, but I stared in the opposite direction, focusing on nothing.

Reaching the most calm I could hope for, I turned. "This is why the Army wants you. You have purple skin under your regular skin."

David looked down. "You're smart enough to know it's a little more than that."

9

My hands shook, my heart played hopscotch in my chest. "Okay." I paced the floor, rubbing my trembling fingers together. "So, what are you...some kind of science experiment gone awry?"

He laughed half-heartedly. "No."

"Genetic mutant?" I tugged my hair. "David, why the Hell is your hand purple? Why are they looking for you?"

"One thing at a time." He sat on the couch. "Can I have that bandage? This actually does hurt pretty bad."

My body dove into auto-pilot. I stormed into the kitchen, grabbed the box of gauze, and sat next to him. Biting my lower lip, I turned his hand over. The peachy-pink top layer had melted and peeled back, revealing deep lilac tones beneath. I ran my index finger over the darkest spot, and he winced.

"Why didn't you move your hand when it started to burn?"

"I did. I guess the outer skin layers couldn't handle that kind of heat."

Cringing, I ignored the implications of *outer skin*. First things first. I started a loose gauze-wrap. "How long will this take to heal?"

"I don't know. I've never been burned before."

A few pieces of white tape sealed off the dressing.

"Thanks," David said.

I bought some extra time by picking up the medical supplies piece by piece and arranging them neatly in the box. Out of plausible means of procrastination, I sat in the recliner and stared at the carpet. I counted how many strands of the pile I could see. At eight hundred and forty-one, I closed my eyes and turned to him.

"I'm waiting," I said, crossing my arms.

"I'm not really sure what to say."

"Okay, let me help with a topic. Why are you purple?"

David straightened. His lips parted, taking in a slow breath. "I was born that way."

"This is going to take all day if you're going to answer like that."

"Okay, I'm sorry." He brushed his fingers over the bandage. His lips tried to form several words before he raised his eyes. "I'm Erescopian."

"Meaning?"

He set his jaw, blinked, and began: "I was born on a transport ship. This is only the second world I've ever set foot on."

Huh? "Wait. What? Are you telling me you're from another planet?"

"Not really. I guess you can say my parents were from another planet. I was born in space."

A giggle burst from my lips. "Come on. Seriously."

David looked down and fiddled with the edge of his bandage.

I took a deep breath, searching for comprehension. "I don't believe in little green men."

"Technically I'm not little. I'm bigger than you are, and I'm not green."

My eyes narrowed. "You can't be from another planet. That's called science-fiction. Accent on the fiction. It's not real."

"Okay, what do you want me to do? Do you want me to lie to you?"

"Yes." My voice quaked.

"I, I…" He sighed. "I don't know enough about your culture to make up anything convincing."

I covered my face with my hands and rubbed my eyes. The calm settled over me again. This time I let it, relished it, but the truth still seeped in. "This is real? You're really from another planet?"

He nodded.

Eight hundred and forty-two, eight hundred and forty-three. I concentrated as hard as I could on the carpet. Anything was better than dealing with this insanity. I wish I didn't believe him, but I did. It explained a lot.

I looked up into his swirling blue eyes. Not blue. Turquoise. Not human. They'd never been human. How could I have been so blind?

Aliens. It was crazy. I mean, movies and books and stuff talk about aliens. It's entertainment, right? Not real life. My hands formed fists. I needed to keep it together.

This was a story. The story of a freaking lifetime, and I

was the only one who knew. I needed to find out what was going on. Be calm. Be cool. If he was going to eat me or snatch my body, he'd have done it already. I glanced at my camera. Should I take a picture of his hand? Get proof? Soon, but I needed to know what was going on first.

"How long have you been here?"

"My ship crashed the night before we met. I was scared, and I didn't know what to do. I ran, and then I met you."

"So you've only been here four days? How do you speak English so well?"

"I extracted your language from you a minute or two before we met."

"Extracted?"

He rubbed his chin. "You screamed when I did it. I'm sorry. I didn't know it would hurt you."

"That loud, screeching noise in the woods?"

"Yeah."

I held my forehead. "Holy crap."

A pounding on the front door started us. David darted to the door and peeked through the sidelights. "It's a girl."

"Maggie." I sprang for the door, unlocked, and opened it.

She ramrodded her way in, smashing the door toward David, concealing him.

"Are you all right?" she asked, looking around. "We've got to get you out of here. They are starting house-to-house searches. They know David's on the base somewhere. Sweetie, I have a really bad feeling that your friend..."

David kicked the door closed. The color drained from Maggie's face.

I squeezed her hand. "You were right, Maggie. David is the guy our dads are looking for."

"Hello, Maggie," David said.

Her eyes bugged out. She froze, agape. After a moment, she turned cautiously, as if standing on cracked glass. I moved beside David, slipping my hand around his elbow as her gaze slowly dropped over him.

The fear drained from her eyes. "Da-ha-hang," she said. "You sure don't look like you have a flesh-eating disease."

I crinkled my brow. "A what?"

"I don't know. That's what they said on the news." She blinked her eyes away from David and turned to me. "If they don't find him tonight, they're going to evacuate everyone."

Dread crept into my chest. What were we going to do?

"I don't have any diseases," David said.

"Obviously," Maggie absent-mindedly spun her golden tresses with her right pointer finger. She'd inched her way into guys' hearts with that little move since the sixth grade. It never bothered me before, but for some reason this time I struggled to keep from pummeling her to the ground.

She dropped her hair. "So—Jess is still alive, so I'm guessing you're not a serial killer or anything, so what's your deal, anyway?"

I thought of lying, but it didn't make any sense. I needed help, and Maggie was all I had. "He was in the plane that exploded the other day," I explained. "Well, it wasn't a plane exactly."

Maggie raised her brow, glancing toward David.

"Short-range communications conveyor vessel," he said.

"Huh-wha?" she asked.

"He's from another planet."

Maggie glared at each of us for a moment before bursting into laughter. "Yeah, right."

I should have figured it wouldn't be that easy, but if they were searching houses, we were in deep trouble. We needed to get this part over with, and quick. "David I know it will probably hurt, but show her your hand."

He unrolled the gauze, wincing, and held out his palm, tilting his violescent alien skin into the light.

I pointed at his wound. "His human-skin melted. That's his real skin underneath."

Maggie scratched her forehead. "I'm still not buying it. I've seen what they can do in the movies. That's not even all that good a make-up job."

I huffed. "Maggie, we don't have time for this."

"Does this help?" David grabbed the charred pinky sticking out from the gauze and twisted. The digit popped right off.

I nearly puked. Holding my stomach didn't help. "What the heck did you just do?"

"It's a prosthetic. My people don't have five fingers." He lifted his hand. The skin around where his pinky should be hung loose like a straw wrapper. The empty flesh wiggled as he flexed his remaining digits. Bile pooled at the bottom of my throat as he massaged the extra flesh on his hand. He pinched it, and the hole disappeared. You'd never know he'd just lost a finger. The skin simply closed over, leaving no trace of the missing pinky.

"Wait. That's like, impossible." The building nausea ebbed

away as our gazes met. I guess it wasn't impossible, because it just happened, but my stomach churned anyway. "That was really creepy."

Maggie folded her arms. "Yeah, and fake-looking. What's up with the freak show? Nothing you do is going to make me believe tall, dark, and gorgeous here is E.T.'s cousin."

I rolled my eyes. What would convince her? "David, tell her what she's thinking."

"What?"

"Read her mind. That will convince her."

He shook his head. "I'm not doing that again. You fell to the ground screaming when I extracted your language. I don't want to hurt anyone."

Maggie snorted. "Did you guys rehearse this? 'Cause you're not all that convincing."

"Just do it for a second," I told David. "Will it still hurt if you don't yank as much information out of her head?"

David looked down, sucking in his lower lip.

Maggie laughed. "Come on, E.T., I gotta see this. Read my mind. Tell me what I'm thinking."

David raised his eyes.

Maggie smirked as his gaze fixed on her. The clock on the wall clicked three times, and all expression melted from her face. She blinked and rubbed her temples. "Ouch."

David's eyes widened. "Why would you want to do that?" He looked away. "I'm not even sure what *that* is."

I smacked Maggie on the arm.

"What?" she giggled. "He's hot." Her forehead crinkled. "Hey! You just read my mind. That was sooo cool. Do it again."

David backed away. "I'm a little afraid to."

"Do you believe us now?" I asked.

"Wow," she said, rubbing her chin. "If you really are some kind of alien, that would explain a lot. Dad's been pretty cryptic on the phone, and he's totally freaked out. He has us all packed and ready to go to our shore house at a minute's notice." Her eyes glazed over David. "Boy would my dad love to get his hands on you."

"Maggie, you wouldn't."

"Nah, of course not. I'm not the goody-two-shoes military brat everyone expects me to be." Her eyes narrowed as she stared at David. "Do you still have that People Magazine from last month?"

What? "Um, Yeah. I think so."

I rifled through the magazines on the coffee table and found July's edition under Dad's Bass Fisherman Quarterly.

"Here you go."

She plucked the magazine out of my hand. "Huh, I was right." She held the cover up to David's face. "Do you know you look almost exactly like Jared Linden?"

Jared graced the magazine cover, lying in the grass and looking right back at me. I thought it earlier, but placing the photograph right beside David made it undeniable.

"Omigosh, you're right."

"Except his eyes are different," Maggie said, squinting at the photo.

David shrugged. "These are my actual eyes. The rest of me formed into what Jess was thinking of when we first met."

I gulped. "What?"

David ran the fingers of his uninjured hand down my arm. "When I pulled your language out of your head, I also took on a form that I thought would relax you. It's standard protocol."

Maggie perked up. "Cool. You're a shape-shifter? Like in the movies? That is so awesome. Change into something else."

"It doesn't really work like that. It's not something I can just do at a moment's notice." He re-wrapped his hand with the gauze. "This façade is a means of protection for a pilot in case they fall into unfriendly territory. You can only use it once. It's like wearing a suit, but I can't take it off."

"What happens if you take it off?" Maggie asked.

"I can't put it back on, and it's the only one I have. I had one chance to choose the correct form."

Maggie snickered. "You sure did pick a nice one." She walked around him, summing him up as if he were for sale. "So, Jess was thinking of Jared Linden, huh?"

"Yeah, and a few other people. I didn't have much time, so I cued in on the key things she was thinking about and let it go."

Maggie messed his bangs. "Chris Stevens's hair and shoulders. Adam Mayer's dimples." She turned toward me. "So, whose rear-end does he have?"

Oh no, she didn't. I blushed and headed for the kitchen. "I think I need something to drink. Anyone for an orange juice?"

Maggie's obnoxious ring-tone echoed through the house. She tapped on her screen and answered, "Hey, what's up?"

I was half-way through my second glass of OJ before David slid beside me at the kitchen table.

"Are you mad?" he asked.

"Am I mad?" Another swig of citrus rolled down my throat. "Mad that you read my mind? Mad because you stole the best parts of all my favorite guys? Mad that you are the man of my dreams, and I like you, and I thought you liked me, but you end up being some kind of an alien? No, I'm not mad at all." I slammed my glass on the table, splattering juice across the counter.

"I don't know what to say."

I gripped the edge of the counter. "How about sorry? Sorry for dragging me into this. Sorry for lying. Sorry for stealing stuff out of my head."

"All right. I'm sorry, but I only did what I was trained to do. I had no idea who you were and I needed to protect myself."

"From me?"

"Yes, that's why I…"

My jaw tightened as his words trailed off. "Why you what?"

His lips formed the beginning of three words before he closed his mouth completely.

I grabbed his arm. "What? What is it? What else did you do to me?"

David hugged his elbows. "I may have slipped in a little suggestion to not be afraid of me, and to trust me—no matter what."

Anger boiled in my gut and burst from my fist as I slammed it against his shoulder. He barely flinched, and it only made me angrier. "You've been controlling my mind? All this time? How dare you…what were you…"

He raised his hands. "No, no, no. I just slipped in a

suggestion to be comfortable with me. I never controlled you, Jess. You were always you. I never made you do anything other than feel safe when you were near me."

The spilled orange juice made an odd shape on the counter. Any other time, I would have taken a picture.

My mind scrolled through the past few days and all the stupid things I'd done—how my instincts prodded, nagged, and warned me, but I kept acting like I'd known him forever... like I could trust him with my life. I couldn't help but wonder... could I really trust him? I blinked as a whoosh of calm rolled through me. Of course I could trust him. David would never hurt me.

I pounded my fists against my forehead. "Ugh. I don't even know if these are my own emotions anymore."

"Jess, I never meant to hurt you. When we met, all I was interested in was hiding until I could go home. I never expected to..."

"Guys, we gotta get out of here," Maggie interrupted, slipping her phone in her pocket. "Janice says they are on Primrose now. We need to hide E.T. or they'll find him."

A flood of energy hit me, mingled with a need to protect David. Real, or some kind of freaky spell, I didn't know. Not that it mattered at this point. "Where can we go?"

"I have an idea, but you'll think it's crazy. And we're going to have to walk, because Bobby took my car again."

I jumped, hearing dogs barking in the distance. "Crazy is okay right now."

Maggie placed her hands on her hips. "Good. 'Cause I need you both to trust me."

10

I adjusted the hood of my dad's gray sweatshirt around David's ears as we stood in front of Maggie's house. "Are you sure about this?" I asked.

"Yes," Maggie said. "They already searched here, and what alien in their right mind would hide in the house of the general in charge of finding him?"

David's eyes darted from me to the house. He trembled, but I didn't think he was cold.

"There's got to be somewhere else," he said.

I wish there was. "Come on." I tugged his elbow.

He dug his heels in. "This is insane."

"Yes it is. That's why it'll probably work." I gripped his arm, dragging him toward the house.

"Probably?"

Warmth cradled my face as Maggie opened the door. The intoxicating aroma of slow-roasted beef wrapped me up and screamed *eat me*.

"Mom," Maggie called, "I'm home. Jess is here."

The door to the kitchen swung open. Mrs. Baker leaned

out, smiling. "Hey there, Jessica." She dried her hands in a towel and smoothed her apron. Her gaze fell on David. "Who's this?"

David straightened beside me.

"This is my cousin, David," I said. "He picked a bad time to visit, huh?"

Mrs. Baker nodded. "Last week certainly would have been better. I'm surprised Tom didn't mention him, but I suppose things have been a little crazy for everyone these past few days. I'll plan on an extra for dinner, then."

Mmmmm. The smell of Mrs. Baker's cooking tickled my nose, making my stomach holler *yes, please.* "That'd be great."

She headed off toward the kitchen. "Make yourselves at home."

The creak of the front door spun us around. Bile pooled in my throat. My heart pumped madly as General Baker hung his hat on the stand beside the door. Bobby entered behind him, ripping the Velcro from his MP armband and hanging it beside his father's hat.

I don't know which scared me more. General Baker, or the sight of Bobby and those pudgy lips I used to think were so kissable. I clenched my teeth and instinctively latched onto David's arm. Bobby's gaze fell on my hand. His nose flared. *Oh, snap.*

Visions of poor Matt Samuels facing down Bobby and his MP buddies flashed through my mind. I could tell by the look in Bobby's eyes, not much had changed over the summer.

The general cocked his head to the side as he surveyed the room. His wide body remained as straight as a board, as if moving would wrinkle his perfectly pressed uniform. He zeroed right in on David and approached us.

David's arm hardened like a rock.

"Who's this?" the general asked.

Maggs jumped between them. "This is Jess's cousin David. Isn't he cute?" She gave her dad a hug before leaning toward her brother. "Where are my car keys, klepto?"

Bobby dropped the keys into her hand, his gaze trained on David.

"Ask next time." Maggie slipped the keys into her pocket.

The general cleared his throat as his attention lingered on David's wrapped hand.

With a raised brow he opened his mouth to speak, but squeezed his eyes shut instead. A grunt scampered up his throat before he blinked three times.

His gaze returned to David. "How'd you lose your finger, son?"

I tightened my grip on David's arm as he spoke. "I—I caught my finger in a car door when I was a kid. There was nothing they could do."

General Baker's eyebrows inched up. "Interesting. The same thing happened to my brother when he was six."

Huh? Lucky guess? Wait. Did David read his mind?

The general gestured to the bandage. "What happened there?"

David raised his hand. "Jess cooked, and I'm not very good in a kitchen. I accidentally leaned on the stove."

A smile crossed the general's lips, and his eyes swept past David's bandages and focus on his fingers.

Omigosh! Did he just check to make sure David had another pinky?

"Be more careful, there." General Baker tapped David on the arm, and made his way into the kitchen.

Bobby watched the door swing closed behind his father. I tried to remember him like he used to be…curly blond hair and a football jersey. Not threatening at all. Just good old Bobby. It didn't work. Why did he have to end up being the jealous type? Sweat dripped from my arm pits. *Keep it steady, Jess.*

Bobby's gaze traveled over David. "Jess never mentioned having a cousin."

David straightened, but kept his cool. Good for him. I was sweating enough for both of us.

"I—don't live near here."

Bobby's nose twisted. "Where do you live?" His gaze lowered to my nervous grip on David's arm.

I released him, and my hands fell to my sides. It freaked me out how much a uniform and a crew cut could change Bobby. This wasn't the same guy I made out with behind the commissary. This guy was just. Plain. Scary.

Mrs. Baker poked her head out. "Margaret, could you help set the table?"

Maggie's eyes widened. "Umm, yeah, I guess."

She looked back at me and mouthed "I'm sorry" before slipping into the kitchen.

Bobby grabbed my arm and scooted me toward the front door. "Let me show you my new arm-band."

I scampered along with him. Not like he gave me a choice. David picked up a book from the coffee table and flipped through the pages.

"So who the Hell is this guy, Jess?" Bobby asked, releasing my arm.

It didn't hurt, but I rubbed it anyway. "He's my cousin."

"Don't give me that. Who is he, really?"

"It's none of your business."

His eyes softened before his gaze lowered. He almost looked upset. Almost. "You are my business, Jess. I care about you."

My stomach flipped. Two years ago, I would have danced a jig to hear him say that. I'd had a huge crush on Bobby. Every girl in school did. Class President, Most Valuable Player, Best Looking…there was no short run of accolades in his senior yearbook. He was the guy everyone either wanted, or wanted to be—and he was mine. Well, for a few months, anyway. The day he announced that he'd decided on a career with the Military Police, my little girl crush came to a resounding halt. Even the thought of being trapped on a military base for the rest of my life sent a heap load of bile in the wrong direction. So I broke it off.

You hear that Bobby? I broke it off.

"It's not your job to care about me anymore, Bobby."

I tensed as David appeared at my side. He seemed taller.

Bobby's chest puffed out. There was way more testosterone flaring between them than I was prepared to deal with.

David's neck seemed to tense. I guess he felt it, too.

My heart fluttered as Bobby took a step toward him. "Why do you look so nervous?"

"I'm not nervous," David said.

It was probably the truth. David had a look on his face like he would rip Bobby in two if he wanted to. I shuddered, wondering if he could.

Bobby leaned closer, not more than an inch from David's nose. "Who are you, really?"

Maggie banged out of the kitchen and threw a stack of dishes on the table. The three of us stood frozen, staring at each other as Maggs speed-set the table like a pro.

Her eyes remained fixed on us the entire time. I don't know how she got the silverware in the correct places.

She threw down the last napkin and joined us. "What are you guys up to?"

"Nothing." Bobby's word came out in a growl. His eyes didn't leave David. "Just getting to know Jess's—*cousin*."

Maggie smacked her brother's arm, lightening the mood in standard Maggie fashion. "Okay Mr. Brand New MP. Don't get yourself all in a ruffle." She placed her hand on the banister. "Come on guys. Let's go upstairs."

She gestured for us to follow. Bobby's eyes remained on David as we ascended the stairs, passing portraits of relatives in military regalia. The largest photograph, at the top of the stairway, showed General and Mrs. Baker with the President and First Lady.

I grabbed the handrail and looked down. Bobby's hands fell to his sides, and the anger fled from his face, replaced by— what—regret? I mustered up a smile, until Maggie backed up and grabbed my arm.

"Come on, Juliet. Show's over." She shoved me toward her room.

David slipped through the doorway just before me. I grabbed my shoulders, shivering as the adrenaline slipped from my body.

"I thought everyone was called to full active duty?" I asked Maggie. "Why is your dad here? For that matter, why isn't Bobby with the rest of the military police searching houses?"

She tousled her frizzy curls. "Yeah, sorry about that, but dinner is important in the Baker household. Dad never misses it. I think he pulls strings to get Bobby long breaks so they can come home together. I guess I should have thought that one over." She placed her hands on her hips. "You did good though. My dad's not at all suspicious."

"I nearly freaked when he started asking all those questions," I said.

"No worries." She fixed her hair in the mirror. "It's standard protocol to interrogate a suspicious boy in the house. Everything is fine."

Maggie turned on the radio while David swished aside the curtains and peered out the window.

I touched his wrist. "Maggie's probably right you know. They won't look for you here."

He folded his arms. "I'm scared, Jess. I was trained to be strong and focused and ready for anything…but I'm not."

I ran my fingers down his left cheek. The cheetah ready to pounce that I saw downstairs had disappeared, replaced by a frightened little cub. I wished I could erase some of the strain from his delicate features.

Maggie jumped onto her bed and sat crossed legged on her quilt. "So, E.T., what were you doing in that spaceship before it crashed? You weren't abducting people, were you?"

"Abducting? No." He glanced at me.

I felt dumb for not asking the question earlier. Everything had happened so fast. "What *were* you doing, David?"

He sat on the opposite corner of the bed. I slid between him and Maggie.

"I was sending a ready signal to our people on the planet."

"Ready for what?"

"Pick up. My job was to notify them that the transport was coming. Another ship would come after with the location."

David's jaw tensed, and he swallowed. Was he nervous about something? Well, other than the jealous MP and the Army general downstairs.

"So, there are more of you guys on Earth?" Maggie asked. "Are they all as cute as you, because…"

"Maggie!" I turned to David. "So, what happened?"

"A few black ships came out of nowhere. They were on me before I could react. I'd never experienced combat before. I didn't expect weapons fire."

"They shot you down," I said.

Maggie scoffed. "Typical. Welcome to our planet, now get out. Idiots."

I raised my brow. If they were idiots, her father was the king idiot, and mine was no better. "Was this, like, a rescue mission then?" I asked.

"They don't really need rescue. They aren't in any danger—or at least they weren't." He rubbed his face. "I guess I screwed up. Now your defenses know there are Erescopians on your planet. I just hope the Army doesn't find our scientists while they're looking for me."

"So what happens now?" Maggie asked.

David walked across the room, massaging his bandaged hand. "I guess I'm like them, now. I wait until the coordinates come, and I'll have to go to the specified location for retrieval." His hands fell to his side. "Unfortunately, I'll have to figure out a way to dodge your Army while I try to get there."

Maggie leaned forward. "So, you're the warm-fuzzy-pick-up-your-friends kind of alien—not the abduct-people-and-experiment-on-them kind of alien? I guess that's cool."

Leave it to Maggie to put things into perspective.

"When will you get the signal to leave?" I asked.

David rubbed the back of his neck. "I thought I would have gotten it by now. I'm not really sure when it will come."

"So what exactly is this signal? We can watch out for it, too."

"It's audible, at a frequency above your hearing capability. Don't worry. I won't be able to miss it."

Maggie rolled onto her stomach. "So we hide you until this signal comes. How hard can it be?"

David ran his fingers through his hair. "Has anyone else noticed that the guy looking for me is right downstairs?"

"It'll be all right," I said, taking his hand. I wished I believed it myself, though.

Maggie sat up. "Yeah, keep your skin on. Literally that is. Hey, what do you really look like under there, anyway?"

I cringed. The question had popped into my mind, too, but I didn't know how to bring it up. Leave it to Maggie to cut straight to the good stuff.

David shrugged. "I look a lot like you, but I have four fingers and four toes, and lavender-tinted skin. My markings are, umm…" He rubbed his stomach. "I can't find a word in your language."

I put my arm around his shoulder. "It's okay. It doesn't matter."

His smile sent a swirl of pure delight shooting through my nervous system and blasting out my toes. Yeah, that good. I didn't care that what I saw was some kind of costume. I'd never tire of looking at him.

The smell of gravy seeped through the door. Maggie breathed deeply. "Mmmmm, can you smell that? Who's hungry for dinner?"

***

Bobby forked an enormous helping of roast beef onto his dish and passed the platter to me. After placing two chunks on my own plate, I passed the tray across the table and gave David the salad and vegetables.

His nose turned when I slathered my meat with gravy and sliced it up. Sorry, dude. I was not passing up Mrs. Baker's cooking because my new alien friend was a vege-saurus.

A cell phone twittered. General Baker stood and plucked it from his pocket.

"Already?" Mrs. Baker said. "You haven't even eaten yet."

"Let me see what's going on." He left the table, holding the phone to his ear.

David fiddled with his fork, looking at the tongs. His gaze passed across the table. He seemed to concentrate on each person holding silverware before he bit his lip and scooped up a piece of cauliflower. I wondered what he ate with at home.

The general pulled out his chair and settled back in his place. He stabbed a piece of meat and stared at it before popping it in his mouth. His reddened cheeks bounced as he chewed. Once he swallowed, his attention settled on David, then moved to me before he placed his fork down. "You know, Jessica, I called Major Martinez earlier to ask him about David."

Busted.

My heart wiggled down into my toes. A hunk of meat lodged in my throat. I imagined the entire Army circling the house, aiming grenade launchers into the windows. Would the napkin on my lap make a good surrender flag?

"Unfortunately he was on radio silence."

Thank God! "Oh, umm, it's really hard to get him at work. I always have to leave a message."

His gaze lingered on David way to long.

"So, the two of you are staying here tonight, is that it? I'd really like to talk to Tom and make sure he's okay with that."

"No!" All movement at the table stopped.

Smooth, Jess. Scream 'the alien is sitting right here' why don't you.

"I mean…it was his idea. He said he would call and check in. He just hasn't yet. Probably because of that, you know, radio silence thing."

The general's gaze darted back to David and my pulse

quickened. His eyes narrowed. "Fine. If he doesn't call by eleven, though, I'll make sure he's contacted. Silence or no silence."

Oh. Crap.

On second thought…staying at Maggie's: bad idea. Very, very bad idea.

General Baker's ruddy appearance darkened as he continued to eat. His plate cleaned, he stood and walked into the kitchen.

Maggie crumpled her napkin as she watched him leave. She scooted her chair back and followed him.

The room's silence intensified the clanging of silverware on the china plates. David's gaze panned to the front door. I placed my hand on his knee, hoping to settle him. We couldn't leave now. It'd look even more suspicious.

Maggie returned, and cleared her father's plate. "Jess, can you help clear the table?" She motioned to the kitchen door.

"Sure."

David stood, and stacked his own dishes.

"Sit, David," Bobby said. "Let the girls clean up. It will give us time to talk."

David's nose twitched, and I tapped his shoulder. "It's that good-old Martinez family upbringing. Everyone chips in, right David?"

He raised an eyebrow. I nodded my head.

"Yes," he said, mimicking my nod. "Everyone helps."

Bobby's jaw dropped, and Maggie snorted a laugh. Their father pushed open the kitchen door and stood in the dining room with folded arms. His jaw set, his gaze on David as we passed.

Yikes. He had that *I'm gonna snap this boy in two* look on his face. I'd seen that expression on Dad way too many times. It never turned out good. Well, not for me, anyway. Had the general figured us out? Talked to my dad while he was in the kitchen?

"Come on, guys," Maggie said, leading David and I through the door and away from the immediate danger.

Her mother followed behind. "I'll take that, David." She took his plates and settled them into the sink. "And thank you for being such a nice gentleman. The rest of them could learn from your good manners."

David bit the inside of his lip. His focus shot toward the back door.

"It's okay, guys," Maggie said. "I told my dad the truth. He knows about David."

Lightening shot through my gut, sending my heartbeat into overdrive. David backed toward the door.

"What about David?" Mrs. Baker asked, scrubbing a pot in the sink.

"That he's not Jess's cousin. He's her boyfriend."

David furrowed his brow. My panic deepened. Having an unknown boyfriend would probably rank worse than harboring an alien in Dad's rule book.

Mrs. Baker rested her hands on her hips. "That explains some things." She placed a stack of plates in the sink. "So, Major Martinez is out, and you were going to spend the night with Jess, is that it?"

David's lips formed a few unspoken words. He looked to me, but I was just as stunned as he was.

"Umm—yes?" he said.

Mrs. Baker shook her head. "I suppose it's none of my business, but I hope you two are using protection."

David straightened. "Protection from what?"

Her brow furrowed, and she turned to me. "Jess, I'm sorry, but I will have to mention this to your father."

Great. Thanks, Maggs. "We weren't going to do anything. David was just going to keep me company until my grandmother gets here tomorrow."

She folded her arms. "He was just going to keep you company?"

David's brow popped up. "What did you think we were going to do?"

Mrs. Baker huffed out a laugh. "My goodness, that surprised look is so genuine I almost believe you." She dried her hands with the towel. "Tell you what, Jess. I won't say anything to Tom, but I want you to tell him. If he's comfortable with David, that's good enough for me."

Relief swept over my body. Temporary respite. "Thanks, Mrs. B."

***

"Yeah, we had dinner. Everything is fine, Dad." I clutched my cell phone to my ear, wishing the general wasn't within hearing range of our conversation.

"All right," Dad said. "I'm glad you're not alone.

Everything okay with Bobby?"

I glanced toward Maggie's father, wishing he wasn't staring me down like a bug he wanted to squash.

"Boyfriends are not an issue. I'll be sleeping in Maggie's room." *Smooth, Jess. Placate two dads in two sentences. Go team me!*

"Okay, well, get some sleep. Call me in the morning before you and Grandma get on the plane."

"You got it. Bye, Dad." I touched the 'end' button and slid my cell into my pocket.

Mrs. Baker handed David a blanket, and General Baker threw a pillow on the couch. He walked out with a *stay down here and don't go near my daughter* look on his face. Do they teach that in dad school or something?

For now, I just hoped he didn't call my dad back. My best chance actually lay in the hands of what I hated most about my father's job—not being able to talk to him on the phone.

I flashed David a smile and followed Maggie up to her room.

"I have an ef-ing alien sleeping on my couch," Maggie said, jumping on her bed. "This is so cool."

I shivered as I laid my blanket out over the floor. Personally, I wasn't all that cool with it. Had they searched my house already? Was David really safe down there all by himself? What if he got cold? I hugged my pillow. So much had happened, and so fast. I couldn't keep track of it all.

David.

His face appeared every time I closed my eyes. His quirky grin, his long lashes, the shape of his shoulders. But none of that was really even him. It was a façade, a costume—but did it really matter?

My hands trembled. Downstairs sleeping on the couch was the epitome of my dreams come true. David had molded himself into exactly what I wanted physically, but it wasn't about how he looked anymore.

He listened. He understood. He didn't judge. I'd never felt so right as I did when he stood beside me. He made everything perfect…or did he? How many of those feelings were real, and how many had he inserted into my brain?

I hugged myself and held my breath. My heart raced at the mere thought of him. My chest heaved and twisted, strangling me with an ache I couldn't swallow away.

David.

I dabbed a tear from the corner of my eye. The second dampened my pillow. He was from another planet, for goodness sake. What was I going to do?

I closed my eyes, begging sleep to take me away for a few hours. A snore rattled the room from the bed above me. A cricket chirped somewhere in the house. The refrigerator in the kitchen below us hummed through the floorboards. Yeah, that wasn't going to drive me nuts. Maggie rolled over, and her bed squeaked. The clock in the family room downstairs chimed at the top of the hour. I yanked the blanket over my head.

The chirping stopped. Maggie's snore melted into deep breathing—and—something else.

A tall broad silhouette moved toward me in the darkness.

I sat up. "Who…"

David, barely visible in the moonlight, placed his finger

over his lips. "Sorry."

"Dude, you gotta stop doing that." I smoothed back my bangs. "What are you doing? If Maggie's dad catches you…"

"He won't. He left a few minutes ago."

"Oh." Knowing I must be a mess, I grabbed my hair and tied it into a speed braid. "Are you okay? Are you cold?"

"No. I'm fine." His fingers wrapped around mine. His touch warmed my skin. "I got the signal."

"Already?" I took in a deep breath, trying to calm my pounding heart. "Okay, so—where do you need to go?"

"Latitude 39-46.505192 north by longitude 074-57.071403 west."

"Wow. I hope you don't expect me to know where that is."

He shifted closer and rubbed his cheek against my forehead. My lips parted, every ounce of me yearning for more contact.

David pulled away. "I know I need to head south. When I get close, I'll feel them. They will draw me to the extraction point."

Strong arms enveloped me. His bandage tickled my neck as he nuzzled my hair. I clutched at his sweatshirt, desperate for his touch.

"I can't ask any more of you," he whispered.

A pain stabbed deep within my chest. "You're not leaving me here. You don't know your way around, and this is my planet. You'll need help."

The moonlight caught David's grin. "You'll come with me?"

"Of course. We've come this far, haven't we?"

He nodded, the most wonderful look of relief filling his

eyes. "We'll leave first thing in the morning. I have fifty-two hours to get there."

Something in my chest sunk and sat on the top of my stomach. Was I really going to do this? The Army was looking for him. What could one teenager do to help?

His eyes melted me. I didn't have to think long. It didn't matter. I only needed to be with him. "Do you know how far we have to go?"

David's sigh filled the room. "No."

"Wake up, idiots," Maggie's throaty voice startled me. "We're not in the Stone Age. Plug the stinking coordinates into a GPS. Now, can we please get some sleep?" She rolled over, trailing her blankets across the floor near her bed.

I smiled at David. More than anything, I wanted him to cuddle up beside me, hold me, make me feel safe. He brushed my cheek with his. The heat of his skin penetrated my sanity and left me witless.

"We'll leave tomorrow morning then." He hesitated, his eyes searching through mine. A smile crept across his lips before he slipped back through the door.

11

Dawn arrived after a long night of staring out the window and studying the stars. I decided to skip the shower, and threw my hair up in a ponytail as I walked down the stairs.

David lay sleeping on the couch, cuddled under the blankets. His long, dark lashes fluttered open as I approached.

"Sorry, I didn't mean to wake you."

"No problem." He sat up, completely alert. I wished I could wake up that quick. "Are you ready to leave?"

"Leave? Now? What about breakfast?"

His jaw tightened. "Okay, but I'm uncomfortable here. I want to get going."

I dug through the refrigerator and found some apples and tangerines in the fruit drawer for David. I cracked open a strawberry-banana yogurt for me and scooped some into my mouth. I hoped Mrs. Baker wouldn't mind us raiding the fridge.

David's turquoise eyes seemed to study me, giving me the chance to lose myself in him. This was it. I was actually going to run with David, defying my father to the umpteenth degree.

I probably needed my head examined.

The right thing to do would be to turn David in. Yeah, that would make Dad happy. Maybe that would make him finally trust me. But his trust wasn't what I needed. Not really.

Helping David was the right thing to do. Dad didn't know him. To Dad, David was the bad guy. The target. The object of his mission. No. Dad didn't understand that David was a person who just wanted to get home.

I fingered the envelope with the cash and credit card in my pocket. Boy was Dad going to be pissed, but I'd probably need this money for something more than clothes.

Maggie tip-toed down the stairs in her pink plaid pajamas and sneakers. Her tangled curls stuck out at odd angles.

"I'm glad you guys are still here," she whispered. "We're in deep dog-doo." She opened up a drawer and plucked out a set of keys. "My mom is on the phone right now. I heard David's name three times."

My heart fluttered. "Who is she talking to?"

"Does it matter? We're toast. We need to leave, like, now." She held her finger to her lips as she opened the front door and led us out.

A crisp, cool morning greeted us. David pulled down on the gray arms of his sweatshirt, concealing his hands within the fleece and rubbing his biceps while Maggie unlocked the car.

"Here. Let me help you." I reached for his hood and drew the soft lining over his ears. A lock of his bangs fell into his eye. I pushed the dark strands away, gently gliding my fingertips across his cheek. Damn, he was beautiful.

"Thanks," he said, tucking his covered hands beneath his armpits. "Why is it so cold?"

I drank in a breath of the invigorating morning air. "It's kind of normal this time of year. It'll warm up in an hour or so."

He grimaced, obviously not sharing my enthusiasm. I guess I wouldn't be too happy either if I were freezing. I opened the back passenger-side door. A woosh of Pine Barrens air freshener tickled my nose. So much for the clean scent of morning.

David's lips tightened as I gestured to the door. He slid inside, resting his hand on the red plush seat as his gaze probed every part of the crimson interior.

I slipped beside him in the back seat. "It's okay, it's just a car."

"Something this small actually moves?"

"Well, it's not a limousine or anything, but it'll drive south."

David eased himself back in the seat, placing his hand on the roof and pressing against it.

I yanked on my seat belt. "It'll probably be a good idea to buckle up. This isn't like space travel, I'm sure."

David watched me click my belt before sitting back and securing his own.

Maggie turned the key in the ignition. "All right fugitives, let's get going."

The engine roared to life.

David cried out and reached for the ceiling. He gaped, his eyes wide with fright.

"What's wrong?" I asked.

"The car is exploding!"

"No it's not."

"Why is it making that noise?"

I laughed. "David, that's the engine. It's supposed to sound that way."

"Are you sure?" Fright shot from his eyes.

"Not completely. Ya never know. Cars do explode sometimes." Maggie snickered, smiling at me in the rear-view mirror.

Troublemaker. I tapped David's knee in hopes of soothing his fears.

My mind drifted to a few nights ago, when a large, silent ship flew over my house, blocking out the stars. Not one of ours… one of theirs. "Your ships don't make any noise, do they?"

"Not that kind of noise, no."

He slowly let go of the ceiling as Maggie pulled away from the curb. Less than a minute into our journey, Maggie stopped the car, exited, and walked over to the passenger side.

She opened my door. "Get out."

"What?"

She opened David's door and motioned to the guard shack down the block. "It hit me that if my mom was talking to either one of our dads on the phone, the MPs may be cued in already. They may be on the lookout for both of you."

David got out and stood beside me. His skin paled.

Maggie was right. We couldn't risk trying to pass the MP's, but the entire compound was surrounded by security fencing, and at a young age, I'd discovered that barbed wire is not your friend. I rubbed the scar on my left arm. Definitely not your friend.

"What should we do?" I asked.

"You can climb the fence beside the Hutchinson's house."

"You're kidding, right?"

Near the Hutchinson's backyard, there was a small break in the barbed wire. A very small break. Kids always climbed over the fence rather than taking the long way around the compound if they'd missed the school bus. That fence was high, though, and I liked my feet on the ground.

Maggie folded her arms. "Stop looking at me like I've split my gourd. We didn't really have time to devise a fool-proof plan."

I nodded. She was right. There weren't many options. I couldn't let my fears get in the way. Not now. "Okay. The fence it is."

Maggie slipped back into her car. "I'll try to drive through the gate. Unless my mom's found me missing, they shouldn't be looking for me. I'll meet you at the corner of Ackey and Adams."

She didn't give me a chance to argue. Before I could compute what was going on, she was heading for the guard shack at the end of the street.

"Where is this *Hutchinson's house*?" David asked.

I shook the confused fog from my head. "Over here."

We scooted down the street and around the block until we came to the Hutchinson's unit beside the western fence. I shuttered, eyeing the sharp barbs lining the top of the enclosure. My scar ached just looking at them.

David chewed the side of his cheek. "There is supposed to be a safe place to climb?"

I shivered, but I didn't think it was from the morning chill. "Yeah, over here."

We circled the Hunchinson's trash cans. Just beside the tree shading their backyard was the two-foot break in the barbs. Shoot. Was that fence always that high?

Something rustled in their back yard. Did they still have that German Shepherd? I prayed not.

David reached up and grabbed the chain links. The fence rattled, and something hit the Hutchinson's wooden privacy fence like a neutron bomb. Their devil-dog barked and growled like someone was murdering his owner or something.

David reached up, and within a second he was perched atop the fence. How'd he do that?

The barbs hung dangerously close on either side of him. The dog continued to cause a raucous as David reached his hand down.

"Come on. Jump up."

Jump up, he says. Friggin' alien Spider-Man. I couldn't just…

The dog hit the fence again, and the wood cracked. Good motivator. I jumped up and David grabbed my wrist, lifting me with ease. He settled me on his lap, and I got a good look at Lucifer, or whatever that big, black, snarling menace's name was. Yeah, he pretty much looked like a big hungry demon. *Not liking this at all.*

Mr. Hutchinson walked out the back door. "Shadow! What's wrong, boy?"

He looked up, and my heart dropped. I mean it really dropped. Something tore, and before I knew what had happened, David landed on the ground with me in his arms.

"We need to go. Now."

I grabbed his hand and we ran. Where would Maggie meet us? Adams and what street?

Dangit. I ran for Adams and prayed for the best.

A siren's howl pierced the morning sky. Boy, were we in trouble. Could that be for us already? What a stupid idea, going to Maggie's house. But where else would we have gone? We were trapped in an enclosed base with the Army looking for David. It was a lose-lose situation no matter what we'd done.

I don't think I breathed or had another thought until Maggie pulled up alongside us.

She jumped out of the car, leaving it running. She waved me to the driver's side. "Go. Just go. You have your GPS, right?"

"You're giving me your car? Are you sure?" I slipped into the driver's seat.

Maggie opened the passenger side door for David, and closed him in. "I'll stay here and provide recon. I'll let you know if they're on your tail of not." She leaned through the window. "Just bring my car back in one piece, okay?"

I wished I could hug her. "Thanks Maggs. You're the best."

She saluted. "Now get out of here before anyone sees you."

Too late. Mr. Hutchinson was probably on the phone already. I hit the gas petal and turned on my phone. One missed call from unavailable flashed across the screen. I dismissed it and called up the GPS app.

"What're the coordinates again?"

"Latitude 39-46.505192 north by longitude 074-57.071403 west."

I pulled up to a stop sign. "Okay, can you slow down a minute there? I can't type fast and I don't want to end up in Maine somewhere."

David repeated the directions at a more type-able speed.

"*Calculating route,*" my GPS said. David lifted an eyebrow.

"That's Michelle, my navigator's voice. She gets me everywhere…or at least she did, when I had a car."

"What happened to your car?"

I flinched, a vision of sirens and ambulances flashing through my mind. "You don't want to know."

David itched a jagged rip on the left arm of his sweat jacket. I hoped he didn't get cut on the barbs. He wasn't complaining, so I figured I'd take a look when we were farther away. Much farther away. The top of my knee poked out from a hole in my jeans as well. I wasn't hurt though, so until I knew we were safe, I'd keep driving and we'd take stock of the damage later.

I pulled out onto the road, passing the entry to the woods and leaving the residential section.

"*Turn right on route sixty-eight north,*" Michelle said.

I glanced at the screen. "It says here, we are about 50 minutes away from your coordinates. We'll be there in no time." As long as the Army doesn't catch us, or the police, or the Air Force. I peeked through the windshield, checking the sky.

"Your father is going to be upset with you, isn't he?"

I thought about the call that I'd dismissed, and swallowed the lump forming in my throat. Upset didn't cover the gamut of emotions that would explode through Major Martinez's psyche when he found out I was missing. He'd set the entire Army loose looking for me. I glanced down at my phone. Last week Dad had called me from work and it came up *unavailable.* If that missed call was him, he was probably rallying the troops already. Dad wasn't one for procrastination.

I bit my lower lip and glanced at David. The panic had finally left his face. There was no use in worrying him with the possibility of pursuit when I didn't even know who had tried to call.

"He'll be fine. I'll explain everything to him once we get you home."

I shuddered, and pushed the thought of Dad scrambling a couple hundred soldiers out of my mind. With all those high tech gadgets at their disposal, how long would it take the army to track us down when they *did* start looking? Once we were close enough to the pickup point, we'd definitely need somewhere to hide.

After changing lanes, I took a deep breath and tried to keep my voice steady. "I guess since we will be there so early we should scope out the place and maybe find somewhere to stay for the night."

"That sounds good," David said, rubbing his arms. "It gets a little too cold here when the sun goes down."

"Sorry. Are you still chilly?" I flipped on the heat and resisted the urge to open the window and let in the fresh air.

"Turn right on route two-oh-six north," the voice sounded from my phone.

David inched forward and looked through the windshield. Stopping at a light, I scanned the sky to see what had his interest, hoping dearly it wasn't a few dozen military helicopters. Thankfully, nothing but fluffy clouds mottled the happy blue backdrop.

"Your sky is such a pretty color," he said.

"Yeah, I guess. What color is the sky where you're from?" I checked for traffic, and continued driving.

He laughed. "I don't know. I've never seen my planet."

"Oh. That's right. I forgot. It must be a lot like being an Army brat, huh? Move from place to place with your parents, never getting a chance to settle down and grow some roots?"

"Yes, I suppose." He craned his neck, gazing through the windshield as a flock of geese flew overhead.

"*Turn left on route two-ninety-five south for nineteen point three miles.*"

I turned onto the ramp, signaling as I merged into traffic. "Okay, so it looks like we will be on this road for twenty minutes or so, and then we take route seventy-three south for ten miles to somewhere called Cross Keys Road…take a left on Watsontown Road, and we're there. Easy breezy."

David stared out the window to his side, and out the windshield once again. It reminded me of a kid seeing Disney World for the first time. But what was he looking at?

Endless lines of trees flanked the highway for as far as the eye could see. Totally boring. Whenever Dad drove on this road, I usually played games on my phone to pass the time. What could he possibly be looking at?

"Are you okay?" I asked.

"Me? Yes." He turned back to the window. "I like all the trees and plants. They're pretty."

"Aren't there trees and plants where you come from?"

"No. Born on a ship, remember?"

"So, you've never seen a tree?"

"Not like these. Is it true they make the air you breathe?"

"Yeah, I think so."

"You *think* so? Don't you know?"

"Yeah, I mean, they do. I don't really know how it works, but yeah, they take all the bad stuff from the air and make more oxygen out of it."

His left eyebrow inched up. "Interesting. I'd think you'd want to know a lot about the vegetation if it's the reason you're alive."

"I know they're important. We celebrate Arbor Day and all. I think it's bad that they cut down the trees, but there's really not much I can do about it."

"You cut down trees? Aren't you worried about running out of air? Why aren't you protecting them?"

I glanced in his direction, surprised by his agitated tone. "I guess we're not all so good about that...protecting the environment, I mean. I hear we're doing a pretty good job of screwing things up."

"That's a shame," David said. "This is a beautiful planet. You should have taken care of it."

My phone rang. Maggie.

"Hey you."

"Jess, where are you?"

I glanced down at my navigator. "We're on 295 heading toward Route 73. What's up?"

"You need to ditch the car—like, now."

12

"Ditch the car? Why?"

"Your grandmother had a conniption when you weren't here. She and my mom called our dads and everyone compared notes. The cat's out of the bag."

"Oh, no." The blood whirled out of my head like someone yanked the drain plug. My hands trembled on the wheel. In one flaring instant, the reality of what I'd done—of what I was still doing, sunk into my bones with the weight of a steamship.

"Yeah, you're not kidding. They noticed my car is gone. You guys are in a heap of trouble."

"Crap. What do I do?"

"Like I said, you gotta get rid of the car, but be careful. I want it back."

"Huh? Oh, of course." I checked the road markers. "I'm almost in Marlton. I think I have an idea."

"Don't you dare leave my car in a ditch somewhere."

"I have something better than a ditch. I'll call you back later."

I tapped *end call* and made my way onto route 70.

"*Recalculating route. Make the next legal u-turn.*"

"I know, Michelle."

The phone rang once again. *Unavailable.* Sorry, Dad.

Cringing, I shut the phone off.

"Don't we need that?" David asked.

"Not right now, I don't. I know where I'm going and I want to save the battery."

I saw my target on the other side of the highway, and eased into the right lane to make the U-turn.

David looked up into the sky, down at the pavement, and over the back of the seat as we passed someone walking a dog. It must have been strange for him, being on a world where everything was new and different from anything he'd experienced before.

I edged to the right, pulling off the road. David leaned back, gaping as we passed the towering Wal-Mart sign. I drove in and out of the rows of parked cars until someone left a spot three spaces away from the front door. "Perfect." I maneuvered the Maggie-mobile between a white van and an old blue sedan and yanked the keys out of the ignition.

"I thought you wanted to hide the car?" David asked.

"Believe me, this is better than hiding it in the woods." I got out and stood by the rear bumper. Shoppers pushing carts filled with bags exited the store, passing me by without so much as a look as they made their way to their vehicles.

A breeze tickled my knee, and I groaned. My jeans were sliced through from the top of my kneecap to mid-calf. Thank you demon-dog for scaring the crap out of me. I knew I heard something rip when we jumped down. I bent my knee and most of my leg came through. What may have been stylin' in the eighties was so not going to fly today, and the chances of finding my size jeans in a Wal-Mart two weeks before school started? Like, nil.

I'd have to use Dad's old duct-tape standby. I didn't have time to try anything on, anyway.

David hadn't left the car, so I rounded the trunk and peered through his window. He still sat in the passenger seat, running his fingers along the rim of the glass. Muddling around, he felt different parts of the door, and finally found the handle. A smile crossed his lips as he lifted the latch and the door opened.

I did my best to hold back a smirk as he stepped out. "You can fly a space ship, but you can't get out of a car?"

His eyebrow arched. "Do you know how to trigger a stagnant preemptory reaction in an overhead visualization module?"

I folded my arms. "How would I know how to do that?"

"Any six-year-old can do that where I come from."

"Well I wasn't born on a space ship."

"And I've never had a reason to get out of a car before."

I smiled. "Touché."

He watched the shoppers unloading their purchases into their cars. "How is this hiding? Everyone will see the car here."

"There are always tons of cars here. No one will notice an extra one." I grasped his elbow, tugging him toward the store.

"Why are we going in there?"

"We need to get a few things."

I led him to the Sporting Goods department, passing

displays of camping lights and sleeping bags before stopping at a peg wall of accessories. I lifted a compass off a hook.

"What is that?" David asked.

I held the clamshell package up and showed him. "This is a compass. The needle always points north. This will help save the battery on my phone." I moved further down the aisle.

"Shouldn't we get one that points south?"

I stifled a laugh. "We'll just go the opposite way."

I chose an army-green backpack from the display and slid the armband over my shoulder before leading David toward the grocery section. His eyes lit up as we rounded the corner of the produce aisle.

"This is incredible. Have you ever seen so much food?"

I picked up a few apples, threw them into a plastic bag, and placed them into the backpack. "Yeah, it's a store. Where do you get your food from?"

"Rations are given to us daily—just enough for my father and I to eat until the next day." He ran his fingers across a display of oranges, his eyes wide. "I've never seen anything like this. How many people will this feed?"

"I have no idea. Whoever buys it, I guess."

"Buys it?"

He placed a hand of bananas to his nose and smiled. I ripped two off the bunch and tossed them into the backpack.

"Yeah, like, pays for it."

"Pays?" He handed me a pack of strawberries.

"No, not those. They bruise too easily." I set the package back on the counter. "Pays, you know, like, money."

"Money?"

I eased closer. "I thought you stole English out of my head," I whispered. "Don't you know what money is?"

"Maybe there's no translation in my culture."

I snatched a handful of green beans and nestled them into a vegetable bag. "But don't you get paid for being a pilot?"

"Paid?"

I slipped the beans into the backpack. "Wow. You don't know what money is, and you don't get paid?"

"I guess not."

"Huh. I don't know if that's bizarre, or incredibly cool."

I snatched a few bottles of cold water out of the deli refrigerator and grabbed a bag of potato chips so we had some real food for me. I tucked it all into the backpack and checked to make sure it zipped shut.

"Okay. I think that's all we need." We headed to the front of the store, and I eased David away from the exit. "No, not yet. We need to pay for this stuff first."

We jumped into a twenty items or less lane. Thank goodness there was a roll of duct tape on the *buy me 'cause you're bored* hooks before the register. I snatched a roll and emptied the backpack onto the counter.

"But we just packed that." The innocence in David's eyes warmed my heart.

I greeted the cashier. "I don't need a bag. We'll just put it all back into the pack, thanks."

David watched with discerned interest as the girl perused each bag and typed codes into the cash register. "Seventy-seven eighty-six," she announced.

Geeze Louise. Three hundred dollars wasn't going

far when groceries were involved. Maybe I should have reconsidered that forty-dollar backpack. I fingered the credit card in my pocket. By the time they traced it, we'd be long gone. Right? Sweat dampened my pits. No. It wasn't worth the risk. I handed her two fifties and shoved the change back into my jeans. Crisis averted. I still had a little over two-hundred dollars to play with.

As we walked toward the door, the big yellow Subway sign called to me. "Let's get a few subs to bring with us."

David's brow furrowed. "What's a…"

"Come on." I drew him toward the line.

The turkey hollered 'eat me' through the glass case. Who was I to argue? The attendant waved me up.

"Give me a foot-long turkey on whole wheat, lettuce and tomato, dry." I perused the choices lined up on the other side of the glass. "I guess you can make another one on whole wheat, and just throw every vegetable you've got on it. No meat."

"You want a Vege Delight?" the attendant asked.

I checked the menu-board and raised a brow. *Vegetarian options…Vege Delight.* Had that always been there? "Yeah, okay, whatever." I waved my hand. "As long as there's no meat or cheese." I added a few luscious-looking chocolate chip cookies to my order, and handed her the money.

One hundred dollars, gone like *that.* No wonder Dad is always complaining about how much stuff costs.

David touched the back of my shirt. "Is there any other way out of here?" he asked.

I unzipped the backpack and stuffed the subs inside. "Just the door by the garden center. Why?" I did my best to zip the backpack closed. The white Subway bag stuck out of the top, unable to fit. David squeezed my arm, stopping my trot toward the exit. My stomach sank when I raised my gaze, and I nearly dropped the backpack.

Near the Wal-Mart entrance, an MP pointed to a photograph, discussing the picture with the door greeter.

Not. Good.

But I didn't even use the credit card. What was Dad, a super sleuth? How did he know to look in a Wal-mart in Marlton of all places?

I backed up so I could see out the front the windows. A group of uniformed men gathered around Maggie's car. One tried to force a flat piece of metal through the passenger-side window.

"This is not good at all," I said.

"Where's the other exit?" David asked.

"We'll have to get past that MP." I gritted my teeth. The door greeter's stand stood right in front of the entrance to Subway, blocking our escape. The MP turned and marched through the front doors, leaving the greeter with the picture. "No way." How did we get so lucky?

"There are still too many outside," David said.

"But we can still get to the Garden Center." We sneaked out of the Subway and back into Wal-Mart, moving as quickly as we could past the checkouts…being careful not to *look like* we were moving as quickly as we could. We came to another entrance, complete with a cheery, pink-cheeked older woman greeting customers as they arrived. A photograph of me in my junior-prom dress was glued to her metal podium. Each time a young girl passed, she looked down at it.

Heart racing, I pointed back into the store. "The garden center door is that way."

David maneuvered me around the greeter and past the stationery department. I pointed in front of us toward the large window-like doors with the words Garden Center printed in bold red stickers.

"There's always an exit in the outside patio this time of year."

"Let's hope it's open."

Mustering up the best 'calm everyday shopper' look I could come up with, I led us past the lawn furniture and hoses, into the warm outer air. David shuffled me behind a display of clearance perennials. Through the leaves, we watched the guy greeting customers at that door. I couldn't see a picture of me posted, but that didn't mean it wasn't there.

A tall man wearing a backwards red Phillies hat asked the greeter a question. The employee smiled, and herded Phillies Guy toward a display of fertilizer.

"That's our chance," David said. His grip tightened on my arm. My pulse raced, pounding inside my head as sunlight touched our faces. Across the parking lot, police cars closed off the area around Maggie's beat-up Ford.

Uniformed men leaned inside the car. One man placed something into a plastic bag. So much for no one noticing the car.

We darted around the side of the building and behind a dumpster. I pressed my back against the warm brick. "Okay. Wal-mart: bad choice." I peeked over the top of the blue metal container, holding my breath against the smell. "How did they find us so fast?"

"Let's not worry about that now. Which way is south?" David asked.

Heart pumping madly, I plucked the compass out of my backpack's side pocket. "We need to go past the police."

"We're not going anywhere near them." He pointed his chin toward the trees behind the building. "Let's head off that way and get heading south as soon as we are clear of all the commotion." He took the backpack from my hand and threw it over his shoulder. "If you don't mind, I'd like to get far away from here as soon as possible."

I held out my arm, stopping David's cadence at the back corner of the building. Near the edge of the tree line, an MP stood facing the forest. A long curve of urine shot into the trees from between his hands.

"Ugh. Gross," I whispered.

The MP turned a little to the left, taking his yellow arc with him.

"Come on," David said, giving me a slight tug.

We sprinted across the blacktop and into the trees. My heart ping ponged inside my chest.

Holy cow, we made it. I checked for the guard.

Crack.

David picked up his foot. A broken pallet lay hidden beneath the pine needles.

"Hey, you. Halt!"

David bolted into the forest. I froze, my gaze meeting the MP's.

He pointed in my direction. "You're Jessica Martinez."

A bolt of terror shot through me like lightening as David's strong fingers wrapped around my elbow. "Run, Jess!"

The MP's cries of 'halt' melted into the breeze. A branch slapped my face, bringing a tear to my eye. My chest constricted. I did my best to control my breathing and not focus on the thought of the entire military gearing up to chase us. Pain inched into my lungs, and I did my best to ignore it, pushing myself faster to keep up with a barely winded David.

We broke free of the trees and into the sunlight, darting across a road and back into the trees again. I slowed, stuck on a patch of thorny bramble. The far off sound of a helicopter became louder. I didn't expect anything less from Dad. Tearing another small hole in my jeans, I pulled free of the bush. David took my hand, coaxing me to run faster.

The throttling helicopter blades overhead jostled the leaves and berated my ears. My throat ached as I panted for more air. My chest seized. They'd found us. It was over.

"This is the military police," a voice echoed above the trees. "Lay down on the ground, and put your hands behind your heads."

The expression in David's eyes sent a clear *yeah, right.*

He skidded to a stop. "Can those things land?"

"Not in the trees. But they can tell the people on the ground where we are."

We bolted ahead, the helicopter keeping pace. What would they do to me if they caught us? Would I go to jail? I glanced at David's back and struggled to keep up. My interrogation would be nothing compared to his. They'd only ask me questions. David, they'd probably dissect or something.

I thought I heard dogs barking and willed my legs to run faster. The blades cut all other sound from my ears. My chest burning, I grabbed onto a tree trunk and looked up into the canopy. I couldn't see the helicopter. I could only hear it. The branches overhead thrashed as it flew past us.

"They can't see us," I said as David moved beside me. "The trees are too dense."

The helicopter started a search pattern.

"Can you keep running?" David asked.

I nodded. "I just need to catch my breath."

More whooting blades cut through the air over our heads. Apparently our helicopter buddy had friends. Lovely.

David perked up, facing in the direction we'd run from. My stomach churned, wondering what he'd heard. "Jess, we need to go. Now."

"Okay." I ran a few paces, but David was already far ahead of me. My lungs ached. I stumbled, but kept my footing.

David appeared at my side, but his eyes still faced Wal-mart. "We're going," he said, taking me by the waist and curling me under his arm like a bag of dog food.

I screamed as we bolted through the forest, bramble and leaves assaulting my face. My stomach jostled in the crook of his arm, and my legs dangled, nearly touching the ground. I couldn't fathom how anyone could run so fast while carrying someone like a sack of potatoes, but the sound of the helicopters seemed to fade, nonetheless. Terrified, I closed my eyes and curled my face down toward my chest. The pain in my stomach waned into a drawn, dull ache as I listened to the sound of David's feet pounding against the Earth.

13

David set me down. My stomach cramped. Each breath I took battered my sore lungs as I stumbled on weak legs. We were alive though, and not caught. I guess that made this a good day. At least that's what I told myself.

The spongy ground bounced under my feet. Years of undisturbed pine needles and leaves left a thick covering beneath us. I swatted a bug away from my face as I treaded through an outcropping of ferns.

I wasn't sure how long we'd been running, but the scratches on my arms and the bruises brewing on my rib-cage told me it was long enough. I looked back in the direction we'd come from, wondering about the silence. If Dad was in charge, those helicopters were still out there. There's no way he'd give up.

David tilted his face to the sky with his eyes closed. "We're coming back to the road."

"How do you know?"

"Can't you hear it?"

No. But I nodded yes.

We came out of the woods behind a strip of stores. The

heat of the sun against the blacktop startled me after the cool walk in the forest shade. I pulled out my compass and waited for the needle to stop turning. The pointer showed north to the right.

"We need to head to the left. We can keep behind these buildings."

"Okay. Maybe we should eat something before we set out?"

"Yes! Thank God." My cheeks heated. "I mean sure, I guess so." Wonderful, Jess. This guy is running for his life and you're worried about food. What a great ambassador for humanity you turned out to be.

We settled onto a curb in the shade. I dove into the potato chips while David grabbed the subs. He handed me the turkey, crinkling his nose.

I offered him the bag of chips. "Do you want some?"

He smelled the opening of the bag. "Is there any nutritional value in that?"

"No, but who cares?" I smashed a handful in my mouth, smiling at his look of disgust. What'd he know? Certain things were totally worth the calories.

Grabbing the duct tape, I unrolled a foot of the blue material, ripped it with my teeth, and mended my jeans. Not a half-bad job if I did say so myself. I ran my finger along the hole in David's sweatshirt. "Are you hurt?"

"Just a scratch."

I looked into the hole. His skin seemed flawless as usual. I ripped off another swatch of tape and glued the fleece back together. What a train wreck we looked like.

David unrolled his hoagie's white wrapper on his lap and lifted his salad-on-a-roll, dusting the crumbs from his bread. He placed the roll in his mouth, slowly biting down. A wide smile appeared across his face, brightening his eyes as he continued to chew. I guessed that meant it was okay.

I unwrapped one end of my sub and gnawed off a bite, alternating between potato chips and sandwich until my stomach stopped complaining.

"Are you sure you don't want to try some turkey? It sure beats lettuce and peppers."

I tilted my sandwich toward him. The glare in his eyes made his answer apparent.

"Okay veggie-boy. Suit yourself." I peeled the rest of the turkey off the roll and stuffed it into my mouth. The roll and lettuce I curled up into the wrapper, and tossed it into the dumpster.

His eyes popped open. "Did you just throw out food?"

"Um, yeah, well, only what was left over."

"Left over? Why didn't you save it for later?"

I reached into the backpack and picked out the bag with the apples and bananas in it. "Well we have all this stuff. I won't need to eat stale, soggy bread."

David's expression remained blank. "But you threw out food."

"Come on. It's not like there's not a Wawa on every corner. I can get another sub any time."

His eyes saddened, and he ran his fingers across the top of his sandwich. What could be so interesting about that roll? His eyes remained down as he took another bite. Once the last morsel passed his lips, he carefully picked up every piece of fallen lettuce from the wrapper, and poked them into his mouth, licking the crumbs from his fingers.

Unease settled over me as I watched him. Eating to him seemed personal, spiritual. I couldn't help but feel judged for the hapless way I'd finished my lunch…and wasted.

David stood, his eyes scanning the south route behind the buildings. Was he avoiding my gaze on purpose?

I eased off the ground, dusting the dirt from my butt. "Hey, listen. I'm not sure what I did, but I'm sorry if I offended you. I mean, I was only joking about the turkey. I'm okay that you don't eat meat and all. That's cool." No response. "Okay, okay. I shouldn't have thrown out the bread, I get it. People are starving in Ethiopia and all that. I'm sorry, but, it's just the way it is, you know?"

David grimaced. "Abundance isn't something you should take for granted, Jess."

"What do you mean?"

His eyes centered on me. Their lack of emotion carved a hole through the base of my throat.

"What?

David shook his head. "Let's get going."

***

As the sun cleared the trees, the stench rising up from the warm dumpsters turned my stomach. David didn't even seem to notice. I did my best to hold my breath as we passed the open containers behind the restaurants. Nasty.

Leaving the longest row of stores, we came out to a huge intersection. The sign above read Route 73 and Route 70.

Shoot. How far out of our way had we gone?

Traffic lined both roads. We waited for the light to change, and ran across the highway, taking quick cover behind the next strip of stores on the other side.

I wiped the sweat from my brow and drew my damp tee-shirt away from my skin. It sprang back, leaving me even more uncomfortable. David continued to walk.

"Come on, don't you ever need to take a break?"

He turned, his bangs rustling across his forehead in the breeze. "I'm sorry. Are you tired?"

I leaned down on my haunches. "A little."

David dropped the backpack off his shoulder. He pushed aside the bags of fruit, and grabbed a bottle of water, handing it to me. The cool liquid slid down my parched throat, easing the burn of our jog across the highway. I leaned back, allowing the water to rejuvenate me, before handing the bottle to back to him.

He looked at the label and examined the water through the clear plastic. Apparently it met his approval. He took a sip and slid the bottle back into the bag.

"You can have more than that, you know."

"Thanks, but that's all I need." He stood and looked down the endless row of dumpsters and loading docks.

It occurred to me that neither of us really knew where we were going. South was hardly a definitive direction. For all

I knew, we could be heading southwest, when we needed to head southeast.

"Can you feel anything yet? Do you have any idea where to go?"

"No. We need to keep heading south." He threw the pack onto his back.

My tired feet trembled in defiance. "You want to go already?"

"Do you need more time to rest?"

Apparently he couldn't take a hint. "I guess not." Sparks shot through my ankles as I stood. My legs begged me to sit back down.

David moved the backpack from one shoulder to another, waiting. If he wasn't going to admit to being exhausted, I certainly wasn't going to come clean either. I had agreed to come with him to help. Becoming a hindrance wasn't an option.

I stretched through a yawn as David loosened the bag's straps.

"Does your shoulder hurt? I can carry that."

He spun his arms in circles. "Nope, it's fine. Maybe that ice you tried to freeze me with actually did something."

I laughed. "I'm sorry about that."

"It's okay. You were only trying to help."

There was that smile again, melting me into a disgusting little bubble of girl-ness. I looked down, awkward under those haunting eyes. He made me feel like an idiot—like a stupid little love-sick girl. I hated it. I was embarrassed for feeling the way I did. If he chose his skin why'd it have to be such a hot one? It wasn't fair. I mentally smacked myself. David chose Jared Linden because he thought it would make me comfortable. He had no idea how *un*-comfortable I'd be, but it could be worse. I could be hiding beside dumpsters with someone who looked like Dad.

We headed down the line of stores, crossed the side-street and entered the Pavilion shopping center. Huge stores and carefully manicured landscaping sprawled out in the overwhelming high-end outdoor mall. The last time I was here was two years ago, with Mom. We didn't buy anything. We just spent the day shopping and laughing at price tags.

David's eyes widened as his gaze fixed on the huge stone statues of old Chinese warriors in front of P.F. Chang's restaurant. Mom and I had actually stopped there for lunch that day. We ordered an appetizer, and they brought out something unidentifiable wrapped in lettuce. We joked about if for weeks afterwards. Days with Mom were always like that. She found joy in everything.

I had to turn away from David and wipe my eyes. I didn't want to explain my tears. They were happy memories, really they were. I just missed her, that's all.

Shoppers in expensive sneakers and designer handbags passed us. I perused my duct-taped jeans and David's matching taped sweatshirt, already sensing the snooty eyes of shoppers on us. I tugged David's arm. "I think we better keep walking behind the buildings."

David nodded and we backtracked around the restaurant, probably adding a half-hour to our walk, but it was better than crossing right through the rich-people-are-us shopping center.

The bandage shifted on David's hand as he pulled the backpack into his arms. Thoughts of the pearly violet skin hidden beneath the sloppy dressing gnawed at me.

My heart kept trying to deny the truth, focusing on David's strong arms and handsome features, while my practical side continued to struggle with the idea that aliens were real. Not only were they real, but they'd been walking around among us, and could be disguised as anybody. The thought creeped me out. How long were they here? Why were they here in the first place?

"Are you hungry?" David zipped open the bag and handed me a pear.

"Thanks." I bit down into the tasty fruit as we kept walking. "So, these people you were signaling, what were they doing on Earth?"

The muscles in his neck tightened, and he hesitated before rifling through the pack once more. "They are scientific researchers. Looking and taking notes I guess." He removed an apple and held it up to the light. He smelled the red skin and smiled.

"So why didn't they tell anyone they were here? Why are you guys being secretive?"

He stifled a laugh. "Jess, your military shot my ship out of the sky without any warning. They didn't say 'Hi how are you would you like to chat'…and you wonder why we want to be secretive?"

I hunched my shoulders. "I guess that makes sense."

"It made sense to shoot me down?"

A twinge of guilt crept over me, as if I'd been the one in

the cockpit of that plane.

The weight of the human race's failings suddenly hung on my shoulders, like I was the one who had to make this right. But how could I explain fear? How could I explain paranoia? I rubbed my temples. Sometimes the truth was the easiest to swallow.

"We have these things called movies and television. They sometimes make aliens out to be the bad guys."

David's pace came to an abrupt halt. He tossed his apple core into the dumpster beside me. "But I wasn't doing anything wrong."

"No, that's not what I said. I mean, they were probably just scared."

He rolled his eyes and continued his gait.

For the first time on our journey, the silence between us seemed uncomfortable.

The woes of humanity spiraled through my mind. We cut down our trees, we pollute our atmosphere, we eat meat, we waste food, and we shoot first and ask questions later when other planets come to visit. What idiots humans must seem like to him.

David remained silent. My stomach flipped, raging against everything I'd eaten. No longer hungry, I stared at the remainder of my pear in disgust, but chewed the soft fruit down to the core, anyway. I wouldn't dare waste it.

A cool breeze hit us, slowing David. "How long until dark?" he asked.

I squinted into the sky, but I couldn't see the sun from our vantage point. I turned on my cell phone. The screen showed

I had a message from Maggie, and another from *unavailable*. I flipped past them both. "It's five o'clock. We probably have about two and a half hours. Let's see how close we are." I clicked on the navigator.

"Calculating route." The circle-thingy spun on the screen. "Go to route 73 south."

I advanced to the next page. "We're actually not that far away from Cross Keys Road. Are you sure you can't feel anything like you said you would?"

"It's too early. They'd be coming tomorrow night."

"That's not good planning, is it? Why don't they come during the day when it's always nice and warm the way you guys like it?"

David raised an eyebrow. "Yeah, a big transport ship dropping out of the sky while everyone is watching would really go over well. I want to be picked up alive, remember?"

A helicopter flew overhead, flying too high and fast to be searching for anyone, thank goodness. I clicked off my phone and tried to think of something to say to brighten David's view of humanity, but he was right. A spaceship would cause world-wide panic. His people were much safer sticking to the cover of darkness.

My fingers tightened on my phone as I began to slip it into my pocket. The thought of the message from *unavailable* constricted my chest. Dad must be going nuts about now.

"David, hold on for a second."

I leaned against the back of the building and turned on my phone. David propped himself beside me and grabbed a banana from the bag. He perused each end. I helped him open it.

He smiled. "Thanks."

I swiped past Maggie's message, touched *unavailable,* and brought my phone to my ear.

My father's sigh tore my soul in two.

"I guess I can't blame you for not answering." A slight hum vibrated the casing against my cheek. "I saw the surveillance footage, and it's pretty obvious you're not a hostage. I can only imagine what he told you to make you trust him." I glanced at David as he chewed his banana. Dad's voice quaked. "Sweetheart, you need to understand that he is a soldier wounded behind enemy lines. He is not above lying to a seventeen-year-old girl to get what he wants." I could imagine Dad pacing the floor, rubbing his hand across his tightly cropped head. "Jess, you've always been like your mother, and I know there's no changing your mind once you've made it up, so I'm not going to bother asking you to turn him in."

He wasn't?

"But what I do want is for you to get away from him. Just wait for him to be distracted and run as fast as you can." I could almost sense him gritting his teeth. "We will find him, Jess. And you know that I'm not going to sleep until you're safe." Muffled voices spoke in the background behind my father's steady breathing. "Please come back. I can't lose you, too."

The call ended, and I powered down my phone. I stared at the blank screen as my father's words bled into me.

I can't lose you, too.

I'd never considered the possibility of anything bad actually happening to me. I was safe with David, wasn't I?

David popped the last of the banana into his mouth and

tossed the peel into the trash beside a loading dock.

What would happen if the Army cornered us? Would there be shooting? Would David protect me, or use me as a shield?

David slipped his hands into his pockets as he strolled back to me, his smile easing any uncertainty.

My conscience fought to call Dad—to let him know everything would be all right, but I knew he'd just try to convince me to come home. I slipped the phone into my pocket.

"Are you all right?" David asked.

I nodded, biting my lip as Dad's voice haunted me. *You know that I'm not going to sleep until you're safe.*

Guilt clawed in my chest, but I knew with every ounce of my being that this was where I needed to be. I closed my eyes and took a deep breath. "We need to find a place to hide for the night."

David nodded. "I agree. Do you have a friend near here?"

"Let me see."

We walked out toward the road. Shielding my eyes from the sun, I scanned the highway. Far in the distance, north of us, several helicopters hung in the air while two others zigzagged in what I guessed was a search pattern. Close, but no cigar, Dad.

I glanced at the sign on the traffic-light pole. *Holiday Inn Express. 1.3 miles.*

"Perfect."

14

A few cars pulled out of the convenience store as we approached. I led David toward the flying-goose logo on the glass doors.

He jerked back, his gaze trailing the signs in the windows. I wondered where he thought we were. I'd never really found a Wawa to be all that scary, but I needed to remember that everything was new to him.

The rip in his sweatshirt flapped in the breeze as he crossed his arms. I needed to replace that duct tape, later. The last thing he needed was extra ventilation.

"I'm sorry it's taking so long to get there." The breeze tickled my skin. Refreshing for me, but David shivered. "Do you want a hot cocoa? That will warm you up."

I held the door until he passed through. The guy behind the counter crinkled his nose. His gaze seemed to drop to my backpack before inching back to my eyes. *Yeah, dude, 'cause we're gonna steal a candy bar or something. Get real.*

I walked up to the deli counter. "Do you have any vegetable soup?"

"Yes." The kid behind the counter pointed to a small monitor next to me. "It's on the lunch and dinner menu." I tapped the display and ordered myself a roast beef hoagie with everything and a vegetable soup for David. I plucked another few waters from the back cases and three single-serving fruit trays from the Grab and Go counter. "Is there anything else you'd like?"

David fidgeted, shoving his hands into his pockets. "What was that warming stuff? Hot something?"

"Oh, yeah." I dropped my selections on the counter, and filled up two hot cocoas. I added milk to mine, and marked it by popping the little button on the top of the lid. Non-dairy boy's lid I left alone.

Pulling two more twenties from my pocket, I made a mental note that we had about a hundred and sixty left. I hoped that would be enough for the hotel room.

So much for those designer jeans I had my eye on.

David helped pack everything but the cocoa and soup into the backpack. I slipped the little compass into my pocket so it wouldn't get lost and sipped my drink.

The sun had begun to drop below the tree tops as we left the convenience store. David's lips formed a solid line as the cool night air hit him. He held the soup and cocoa close to his chest as we treaded back out along the highway.

***

"A hundred and twenty-two dollars for a hotel room?"

The man behind the desk raised an eyebrow and shrugged. "Sorry, that's the price. We take MasterCard, Visa, and Discover."

Crap. Would Dad even remember that he'd given me the card? Maybe he wouldn't think about putting a tracer on it. I laughed at myself. Of course he would. I was skunked. And almost out of money. "I'll pay cash." Thank goodness David was getting picked up tomorrow night or we'd be camping without a tent.

"Very good." The clerk took the money and tapped into his computer.

I gave a fake name. Mary Seivers. Hey, they did it in the movies, right?

"I will need a credit card for the security deposit."

Hashtag: busted. "But I'm paying cash."

"It's only for incidentals. As long as there is no damage to the room, all the towels are here after you leave, there will be no charges against it."

Crap. Crap. Crap. Crap. Crap. Crap. My mental freak-out did nothing to stop the blank stare of the dude behind the counter. There had to be a way out of this. Not everyone has credit cards, right?

A gust of wind assaulted the lobby as another customer entered the building. David trembled, nearly spilling his hot cocoa. I'd have to trust that Dad's card wouldn't be used. I needed to get David somewhere warm. With a deep breath, I handed him the little plastic minion of doom. He glanced at the name on the card. Not Mary Seivers, obviously.

"We're paying cash, all right? We just want to get to our room."

His expression faded. His stare became blanker than before. WTF?

David placed his drink on the counter, and leaned closer to him. "We really don't have time for this. Can we go to our room?"

The man blinked twice. "Of course."

Huh? Did David do that? My alien is a Jedi!

He flipped over my card and swiped it through the reader.

"Wait! What are you doing?"

The machine beside the computer started to print out paperwork.

My hands formed fists. "You said you wouldn't swipe the card."

"I said I wouldn't charge your card. It's only saved in our computer in case we need it."

Oh God. Oh God. Oh God. "So it's not getting sent to the credit card company?"

"No."

Please, please, please let that be true.

He handed me the paperwork, and a plastic card with the company logo on it. "Room 427. Take the elevator to the fourth floor, and head down to the right." He raised his eyebrow, his gaze falling on the backpack—our only piece of luggage. "Have a nice evening."

"Thanks." My cheeks flushed, imagining what was going through his mind, especially with me acting like a complete ass.

I snatched the cocoas off the counter and handed them to David, hoping they'd warm him up. Too bad it's only that easy in fairytales. His shiver deepened as I helped him to the elevator, quaking him hard enough to feel the tremor through his sweatshirt.

The chill had nearly immobilized him by the time we stepped out of the elevator. I took the hot cups from his hands and placed them on the floor with the soup as I fumbled with the credit-card key. Give me a regular metal key like the one for my front door any day.

I swiped the card through the lock, but the door wouldn't open. Flipping the key around, I tried again. After the sixth pass, the little light on the door changed to green, and I turned the handle.

Frigid air from the room rolled into the hallway. David backed away.

What'd we get arctic room or something? You gotta be kidding me.

"Stay here," I said.

Crossing to the far corner of the room, passing the two double beds and the desk area, I found the air-conditioning unit to the left of the glass doors. I switched the dial to 'heat' and opened the sliders to let the slightly warmer air into the room.

I turned to find David behind me, placing the soup on the small table and balancing the two hot chocolates in his trembling arms.

"Here, let me help you." I sat him down and rubbed his arms, doing my best to get his circulation running. His teeth chattered. If I didn't get him warmed up he was going to freeze to death. "I'll be right back."

I opened the closet and found an extra spread alongside the ironing board and spare pillows. I scooted the floral material out of the bag and threw the quilt over him. The smell of stale hotel room wafted from the blanket as he gathered the fabric tightly around his shoulders.

"Okay, let's get you warmed up inside."

I opened the veggie broth and handed him a spoon. David raised his brow and looked at me quizzically.

"It's liquid food. We call it soup. There's vegetables in it and water."

He dipped his spoon in the cup and sipped it. "Mmmmm. It's good. Warm."

"Yeah. Soup always thaws me out in the winter. It should help."

I held my hand over the heater. The little dial was turned to the highest temperature setting, but only a trickle of heat emanated from the metal slats. I dragged the curtain to the side to let some light in. Beyond our fourth-floor balcony, a pinkish glow outlined the tops of the trees in the forest behind the hotel. Despite the coolness of the room, the air coming in the door had become decidedly colder. The door thumped against the frame as I secured the lock.

David held the cardboard container up, pouring the last dribbles of soup into his mouth. "That was great. Thanks." He licked his lips. His eyes lingered on the bag.

"Are you still hungry? I got you some melon and strawberries, too."

I shimmied a fruit tray out of the wrapping and handed it to him. Reaching to the bottom of the bag, I nabbed my roast beef hoagie and set it on the table beside him.

His nose crunched up as I unrolled the white deli wrapping. Ignoring his disgust, I bit into the luscious beefy goodness.

David hunched over his fruit, trembling lightly under the blanket.

"Take another sip of the hot chocolate," I said, handing him the cup. It seemed to warm him for a moment, but the chill soon returned. I lifted the makeshift-mug. "Drink more."

He nodded, shaking the cup within trembling fingers between sips.

"All right, I guess I need to think of something else."

I stood and rubbed my face. Whenever I had a chill, cuddling up in bed always felt the best. I rolled back the covers from one of the mattresses and helped David get in. He huffed and grunted beneath a shiver as I tucked the sheets and blankets around him.

Why wasn't the room warming up?

At a loss, I glanced over to the other bed. I certainly wasn't going to be cold with the heat running all night. I stripped the second bed, throwing all the covers onto David.

No dice. He still shook like a nickel in a truck's change tray.

I sat on the edge of the bed. A ball formed in my throat as I felt the vibration of David shivering through the mattress. I needed to find a way to warm him up.

Body heat.

I groaned. "Okay, Maggie, you win."

The heavy, warm blankets weighted me down as I snuggled up behind David. Spooning, Maggie would have called it. I wrapped myself around him, holding tightly to counteract his shaking. As the trembling subsided, David's breathing leveled off. I listened for a moment before relaxing my hold.

A content smile formed on my lips. I guess the whole body-heat thing was a good idea after all. I rubbed my cheek against David's sweatshirt, enjoying the quiet cadence of his breathing.

He smelled like pine trees and dirt, and a little like Dad's cologne. I snuggled closer, pressing gently against his back. His muscles flexed at my touch, but his breathing remained steady. I wondered what he'd think if he were awake. Would he be mad that I held him so close? Would he enjoy it? Would he pull me into his arms?

A tear formed at the corner of my eye. It didn't matter what he felt. It didn't matter how either of us felt. Tomorrow night he was going home.

I tried to push the thought from my mind and concentrated on the compass in my back pocket as the sharp metal clip cut into my butt. My cell phone poked my hip in my front pocket as well. Despite the pain, I didn't move. David was warm and asleep, and I didn't want to wake him.

Well, that wasn't entirely true. The real reason I didn't want to wake him was because he might move away from me. I savored the sensation of him breathing, letting everything that was David seep into my pores. Shame fluttered through my chest, but I didn't care. Laying so close to him felt too right to be wrong.

I did manage to shift slightly to avoid leaning on my

phone. I hadn't turned it back on since listening to my father's message. My chest tightened, imagining Dad sitting behind a desk somewhere, dragging his fingers across his scalp, worry riddling his features. He wouldn't sleep. He'd stay beside a phone—or maybe he was out there looking for me...Maybe even in one of those helicopters searching the trees. I wished I could call him, but I'd have to wait and explain when this was all over—and ready myself for ten years of being grounded with extra chores.

Bending my knee, I was surprised to feel the drag of rubber against the sheets. My sneakers were still on. I hadn't taken off David's either. My mom would have had a cow. I contained a snicker. Here I was, lying in bed with a boy in a hotel room, and I'm thinking that Mom would have been mad about our shoes? Seriously, *our shoes*?

I smiled, thinking about my mom and enjoying the comfort of being so close to another. Every muscle in my body relaxed, encompassing my frame in the same sense of calm that caressed me whenever David was near. Real or feigned, I couldn't tell, but it didn't matter.

Exhaustion fingered its way in, making my lids heavy. Sleep wasn't far behind.

***

My eyes fluttered open. A panicked rush of heat throttled my body as I realized David wasn't cuddled up next to me.

I reached across the bed, moving my hand along the warm sheets. Why was I alone? The prickly fingers of fear edged up my back as I sat up. "David?"

He stood in dark silhouette beside the closet, standing flat against the wall. He held a finger to his lips and pointed to the floor.

My heart fluttered. I choked back the pang of terror building in my throat as I peeked over the mattress. A small black tube snaked across the floor, slithering further into the room from beneath the only safe exit. A white light emanated from the snake's tip—just like in the freaking movies.

I got out of the bed and grasped David's hand. I held him close, like we were lovers, and stepped over the tube, easing him toward the sliding glass doors. "They're watching us," I whispered, leaning close to his ear. "That's a camera. As soon as they pull it out of the room, they'll break in."

David nodded and unlatched the lock on the glass door behind me.

My heart thumped rampantly. Please, Lord, tell me he's not going to…I peeked over the balcony to the lighted parking lot below. We were on the fourth floor. What if they…

The camera zipped back under the door and disappeared. David slammed open the glass sliders, and his grip tightened around my waist as he jumped over the railing. The sensation of my stomach falling out from under me seemed to last for minutes. My ponytail flapped in the breeze before my body jolted to a painful stop when David's feet hit the asphalt.

My lungs emptied. I gasped for air, grabbing my throat.

"Halt!" A voice shouted.

"Stop right there!" Flashlight beams blinded me. My vision blurred. Someone wrenched me out of David's arms as streetlights and flashlights whirled through the darkness.

"David!"

My heart raced as I heard a man's voice cry out. The flashlight nearest me hurled through the air. It wasn't until it hit the base of a streetlight that I realized it was still in a soldier's hand, nearly twenty feet away. The man crumbled to the asphalt.

"Jess!" Dad's voice boomed over the confusion as a horrid cracking sound resonated through the sound of a scuffle. Another MP fell to his knees.

My gaze shot to the balcony. A blurry vision of Dad hung over the edge, reaching toward me. The whites of his eyes came into focus; huge and imploring. I took a step back and stumbled into the man holding my wrist.

"Don't move!"

A rifle poked out of the darkness, pointed at David. I didn't even think. I lunged forward, throwing myself between David and the gun. I held up my shaking hands, my gaze centering over the shotgun—into Bobby Baker's eyes.

"Get out of the way, Jess."

I shook my head. Above, Dad pounded the balcony's rail and darted back into the room. David's fingers slipped into the back of my jeans. I felt his hold tighten over my belt-loops.

"Jess. Move." Bobby grinded his teeth, his face twisted in a sneer.

"No way. You don't understand."

David's other hand slipped to my waist, and a bolt of

assurance wafted through me. I leaned against him and kicked as hard as I could, shoving the gun upward. The weapon shot into the sky.

Bobby cursed under his breath.

Shouts began anew as David spun me around, at the same time punching another soldier, sending the man flying off his feet. I didn't see him hit the ground.

David grunted, and his grip on me slackened. I slammed against the pavement. My head throbbed, the world becoming a blur again. Soldiers barked orders. A mound of men piled on the spot I last saw David.

"I got you, Jess. You're safe. It's okay." Bobby's voice didn't comfort me.

He yanked me to my feet. My ears rang. Steadying myself, I struck his chest. "You have to let us go. You don't understand!"

"Jess!" Dad's voice echoed through the mayhem. "Baker, what happened?"

"Dad?"

Bobby straightened. "I think we've lost her, Sir. It looks like that thing has her under its control."

I twisted in Bobby's grip. "No one has me under anything. Dad, you need to let me go!"

Dad's face came into focus. He stared into my eyes as if maybe he thought I wasn't really in there. He gripped both my wrists, gentle, but firm. He grimaced. "She needs to be detoxed and debriefed."

"Detoxed? What the heck does that mean? I'm fine."

Dad's brow furrowed as his lips tightened to a straight line. He released me as Bobby pulled my arms behind my back.

Bobby began to back me away from him.

"Dad?" I stumbled a few steps. "Dad!"

He turned from me, and approached the mountain of soldiers trying to hold David down. Bobby pushed me into the back of a police car and closed me in. I scrambled for the door handles and rattled the grating that separated me from the vacant driver's seat. Nothing budged.

So this was it. Caught. Some friend I turned out to be. I promised to help David, and instead my psychotic father tracked me right to him. Dammit!

I slammed myself against the back seat. Bad idea. My head started to pound again, the pressure mounting and slamming like a bludgeon against a locked door.

The windows blurred. The car's interior spun twice before my world faded to black.

15

I held my head as the car jiggled around a corner. The haze coating my vision slowly faded. The fog eased from my brain.

Damn, it wasn't a dream.

I grabbed the grate in front of me. Two men in Army fatigues sat in the front seat. Our headlights illuminated a huge, metal box-on-wheels traveling down a road lined with trees on both sides. The megalith in front of us must have been some sort of armored car—probably the only thing they could find that would hold David. At least three, maybe four jeeps travelled behind us, and probably two helicopters from the sound of the blades cutting through the evening sky.

"Where are you taking me?" Their silence pissed me off more than being taken against my will. "Where's David?" I slammed the grate with my fist. "Where's my dad?"

The soldier in the passenger seat flipped through papers on a clipboard. "There's no need to hurt yourself, Miss." He didn't even bother to look up. "You might as well just…"

The armored car swerved left and then right. My heart

jumped into my throat as the sound of screeching brakes broke the cadence of the helicopters above. The sound of metal crunching replaced the failed brakes, followed by blinding light and a deafening boom.

Our car swerved as flames flashed across our windshield. The cacophony of changing images swirled in front of me as my head hit the roof of the car, then crashed to the ground again before slamming back toward the roof.

A loud hum overtook my world. Splayed across the floor of the car, or rather flat across the ceiling, I spun like a calliope, only faster and without the horses. The seatbelts hung from the seats above me like oxygen masks on an airplane.

But we weren't flying, right? Were we upside down?

We continued to spin, one second seeing dark forest, the next seeing flames and confusion. Everything I ate in the last year threatened a reappearance.

And the heat. So much heat.

And screaming. And yelling. Lots of yelling.

The scene blurred to nothing.

Mom? What's going on? Where am I?

A green pasture appeared around me. One solitary tree stood in the distance. As I walked toward it, thousands of birds took flight from its branches. I reached for my camera.

Click.

Beautiful. The perfect photograph for my portfolio. I raised the lens for another shot, and a gong vibrated through the waving grass. I glanced over my shoulder, but there was nothing but meadow for miles. Another bang resonated through me, as if I were in a small, enclosed space.

"Jess!" David's desperate voice boomed from above.

Had he left already? Was he on his ship?

I turned and ran, looking into the sky. Another metallic clang reverberated, and a hole ripped through the clouds. Fire and heat howled through the aperture.

"Jess!"

My daze slipped away as the opening widened and a gray, fleece-covered arm shot toward me. I cried out as my body slid through the hole and into chaos incarnate. Flames sprouted from cars and jeeps. A helicopter lay on its side along the far tree line, the windshield smashed.

Behind me, the car Bobby had shoved me in lay on its roof, the rear door splayed open like a can of cat food. Two dark figures hung upside down in the front seat.

Hashtag: nine-one-one.

Someone grabbed my face. "Jess, are you okay?"

"David?" His blurry outline loomed before me. Was I still dreaming?

"Hold it." Dad's voice froze me.

Night became day. A helicopter's blades added to the roar of the fire as it aimed its searchlight on us.

David gripped me from behind as we faced a man holding a gun.

My vision slowly focused, bringing the man into view: my father.

"Let her go," Dad said. "You don't need her."

David snorted behind me.

Oh my God, he was using me as a shield. Maybe Dad was right about him.

A curse sounded from the overturned car. Someone kicked against the glass. Apparently my escort had just come to. Yippy freaking ha.

The world fuzzed around me. My head pounded as it rolled to the side.

"Wake up, sleepy head," Mom said, opening the blinds in my bedroom. *"How about we save the world today, one shopping mall at a time?"*

A jerk brought me back to chaos. I was standing alone facing the car. Both Army dudes kicked at the doors, trying to get out. The helicopter above spiraled out of control, the searchlight scanning the scene like a game-show spotlight until it disappeared from view.

Dad stood inches from David, backing away with his hands in the air. The gun lay on the ground a twisted, broken shape.

I stumbled forward to David's side. "That's my father."

David didn't break the stare between them . "I know. That's why he's still standing."

"Please," Dad said. "Just go. Leave her, and go."

I grabbed David's arm. "I promised I'd help him. He just wants to get home."

Dad shook his head. "That's not what he wants, Jess. This is a lot bigger than him."

David grasped my shoulder as he backed up. He pointed at Dad with his other hand. "Don't follow."

"You know I'm not going to promise that. That's my daughter you've got there, and I'm not giving her up. Not now, not ever."

I stumbled. Nausea returned. "Dizzy," I whispered.

David lifted me into his arms. As he carried me past the car, the windshield crashed to the pavement.

"Halt," one of the men called, crawling out.

Dad started running after us, but David had already picked up speed.

The light and heat from the flames faded to the darkness of the forest. The breeze whipped my cheek and blew hair in my face. I buried my eyes in David's neck as he ran. How much help was I to him when I could barely stand? He should have left me.

I shuddered. He'd placed me between himself and the gun. He'd done exactly what Dad said he would—a soldier, wounded behind enemy lines. Was that all I was now, a shield? Would he continue to use me to get past my father?

His grip tightened on me as he leapt over something. Protective. Caring. He held my head close as he whisked us between patches of dense overgrowth.

A sense of calm eased through the pain throbbing above my brow—a sense of security. David would never hurt me, and he would never use me. He took me because he cared, because I had helped him.

Or was it so I couldn't tell them what I knew? I shifted my weight, feeling my cell phone still in my pocket.

The coordinates. I had the coordinates on my cell phone of where we were going.

Maybe I *was* a risk to him if I got caught.

Flickers of moonlight continued to flash across my face. By the time we slowed, my head threatened to break in two.

David set me down and leaned on his knees as he caught

his breath. My arms, neck, and back seared in agony as I stretched my aching muscles. Crickets and frogs chirped, echoing nature's song through the woods, but nothing more. No sirens, no helicopters, no soldiers shouting orders. How far had we come?

"Are you okay?" David asked.

"Yes." Whoa. That was a bold-faced lie. I held my throbbing temple. "How about you?"

"I'm fine." He rubbed his arms.

I moved closer. "Are you sure? Because what you did back there, that was crazy. I mean, I'm not completely sure of what even happened. Did you actually knock two helicopters out of the sky?"

He shrugged. "Inferior technology. Nothing to be proud of."

No thoughts of the people who may have gotten hurt in those misley pieces of inferior technology?

Come to think of it, there had been an entire caravan along with those helicopters. There were not too many people left standing by the time we left. Had he actually killed anyone?

David rubbed his arms. His lips formed a straight line.

"You're cold, aren't you?"

He rubbed his hands together. "I was okay while we were running, but not anymore. How long until your sun comes up?"

"Sunrise?" I pulled my phone out of my pocket. Three text messages. I flipped to the next screen. The low-battery icon flashed incessantly. 4:15. "It will probably be about two hours." I shut off the phone and plopped it into my pocket. "I guess running for two more hours is out of the question?"

David laughed. "I wish I could." He chewed his bottom lip, his eyes scanning the dirt at our feet. "Jess, I need to sleep, but I can't take this temperature."

Shoot. I gawked, probably looking like a blithering idiot, which wasn't far from the truth at that point. But this was why he wanted me with him—to help. I certainly couldn't start a campfire. I could barely do it as a girl scout, not to mention it would turn into a giant beacon that said *here we are!*

I closed my eyes, and firmed my resolve with a deep breath. "Okay. Body heat."

"What?"

"I'm going to keep you warm. Lay down." He settled on the ground, curling into a ball. I laid beside him, and wrapped my legs over his, covering his body as much as I could with my own.

His breathing settled to a normal cadence.

I wished I could calm so easily. It would probably be days if not weeks before I'd be able to sleep again, trying to sort out reality from fantasy. There had been so much destruction. How could one person, even one alien, take on the Army? "David, what happened back there?"

"Not now, Jess."

"Yes, now. It looked like World War Three out there."

He trembled under my touch. "They put me into a vehicle with no windows. I didn't know where you were, or where I was going. I broke out."

And then some. Incredible Hulk-style. "Did you hurt anybody?"

His back tensed against me. "Jess, I'm tired."

"Did you hurt anyone?" The adamancy in my voice startled even me.

The moonlight caught his eyes as he turned toward me. "I had no idea where you were, or what they'd done to you. I wasn't going to let them hurt you for helping me. Yes, I saw some people bleeding. A lot of them weren't moving. I didn't stop to check."

Holy cow.

"Don't look at me like that. What did you expect me to do?"

Good question. I had no idea, but not killing people would have been on top of my list. I mean, Batman never left a body count behind him. Then again, he only had the Gotham Police to worry about, not the entire US military. Not that David was Batman or anything, but there should have been a way.

I shivered. Welcome to the real world, Jess.

"Thank you," I whispered, "for not hurting my dad."

He turned completely toward me, leaning up on an elbow. His other hand cupped my cheek. "It wasn't my intention to hurt anyone. I don't belong here. If they'd just let me go…" He rubbed his palm across his face.

"Dad said this is bigger than you. Do you know what he meant by that?"

David's eyes widened with a big old *yes*, but he shrugged. I was beginning to hate that shrug. "I have no idea. I'm just trying to get home." His eyes narrowed, searching deep into mine. "You believe me, don't you?"

Of course I did. But then again, I didn't have a choice. Or did I?

"My father thinks I'm under some kind of mind control."

"What do you think?"

"I think that I can't say no to you. I think that I trust you, even though I know you just lied to me. I think I should run back to my dad, but I have this overwhelming need to stay here and keep you warm." I slapped my hand against my forehead. "Oh my God. I *am* under your control."

He took my hand and kissed it. "No you're not. I promise you, the only thing I did was give you a suggestion to trust me. Everything else you're doing on your own."

Could I trust him? More importantly, should I trust him?

Two questions you should have asked before you became a fugitive, Jess.

I pulled him closer and cuddled against him. All I had to offer at the moment was temperature control. "Let's try to get some rest."

He tightened his grip on me, as if he feared losing me while he slept.

16

A dull ache bled through my brain, feeding the pulsing soreness that strained my entire body. I stretched; squinting as the sunlight gently poked me from between the trees.

Trees. Dirt.

Outside.

I bolted upright and brushed away a twig that stuck to my cheek. Last night's Terminator fest flashed through my mind, but how much of it was real, and how much delusion? I rubbed the tender top of my head. The car accident, at least, was real. Which meant David destroying the convoy was probably real, too.

And Dad.

My face fell into my hands. What had I gotten myself into?

David crouched beside me. "Jess, what's wrong? Are you hurt?"

I pushed him away. "Of course I'm hurt. Yesterday I jumped out a hotel room window, got in a car accident, and ran away from the United States Army." I hopped to my feet.

"No, I am not okay."

He was back beside me within a blink and pulled me into his arms. I let him. He was the cause of all this, but part of me didn't care.

"We could have died yesterday. You know that, don't you?"

"But we didn't. We're okay."

Tears pooled in my lashes. "Are we?"

A shiver ran across him. "Now that it's getting warmer, yes, we are."

At least for now we were okay. But where was the Army?

Looking for us, of course. It wasn't like they were going to let David go just because they were afraid he might bust up some more government property.

Yikes. Was I an accomplice to any of that? Was I on the wrong end of a one way ticket to traitorsville?

It was August. I should be sitting by a pool somewhere, shopping, being lazy like everyone else. "This is so not how I expected to spend my last week of summer vacation."

David lowered his eyes. "You wanted to be with *him*, didn't you?"

"Him? Who him?"

"Jared Linden, the boy you were thinking about when we first met." He touched his cheek. "The boy with this face."

A giggle burst from my lips. "I don't know him. He's an actor. I've never even met him. I just think he's cute."

"Cute?"

"Yeah, like, attractive, you know?"

His eyes twinkled. "So, you find me attractive?"

"Maybe—when you're not ripping off your fingers or

freezing to death."

Or tearing apart cars with your bare hands, beating people up, or getting me chased down by the Army.

Ugh, when did my life become fodder for a cheap science fiction novel? I could see the teenage girls flittering about it already: super-cute alien, stupider-than-thou heroine and a bigger than life story with no chance of a happy ending.

My heart fluttered. *No chance of a happy ending.* Was that the kind of story I was in? Was all this running and hiding all going to lead right back to Dad and handcuffs?

Probably, because one of us was *so* not super hero material. I was a mess. A stinking mess. David should have chosen someone else.

I glanced up, expecting to see a condescending glare. Instead, his deep turquoise eyes melted me. Although I was the one trying to comfort him last night, the sensation of his body next to mine, the safety I felt, the security of having him so close...Dammit, no matter how hard I tried, I still longed for him, for everything about him. I still didn't know if this childish attraction was a result of that mental mojo he did on me, or just Jared Linden's face, or the sweet, quirky way he acted. At this point, I'm not unsure it really mattered.

The sweet insecurity in David's eyes drew me closer, closing the gap between us as I fought the desire to pull him back down to the forest's dirt floor and cuddle into his arms.

I set my fingers on his chest. He didn't protest. One point for my team.

Venturing even closer, I breathed in the essence of earth and mild musk. So normal. So human. So right.

My shoulders tensed as my gaze sought his. Did he think I was pretty? Did the trace of my fingers make him tingle, like his touch did to me? My cheeks heated as David's gaze dropped to my lips. I should have looked away, but I couldn't. I didn't want to. If he was thinking about my lips, I needed them right where they were.

The trees and bushes faded into the distance, leaving nothing but us. I leaned toward him, opening the door to what I wanted. He didn't step through, so I gave him the customary two seconds to turn away before I settled my mouth over his.

Part of me died as the softness of his lips consumed me. I reached behind his neck, tangled my fingers through his hair, and drew him closer. My tongue burned delightfully as I glided over his lips, shooting a tickle through my core that settled into my toes—until I realized he didn't kiss me back. A lump formed in my chest, and I moved away.

David's eyes opened like saucers. "Why'd you do that?"

I backed against a tree, abashed. "I'm sorry, I thought you wanted me to."

"Why would I want that?"

My gut shoved up into my chest, and I burst into tears. "I thought you liked me."

"I do. What's wrong?"

I covered my face with my hands. No matter how hard I wiped my eyes, the waterworks continued to flow. The emotion of several days swung in and hit me like a hammer, and I couldn't stop its release.

"Jess. I'm sorry. Geeze, I don't even know what I did."

"I kissed you, and you, you..." I lost my words in a sob.

"I don't even know what a kiss is." He clawed at the hair near his temples. "Jess, please, I have no idea what just happened."

I gulped down my sob and did my best to steady myself. "Didn't you feel anything? Anything at all?"

Frightened eyes drained to lost defeat. "Jess, please. I don't understand. It was nice, I guess—the kiss thing. But it took me by surprise. I didn't know what to say. I do like you."

I uncovered my face and wiped my cheek on my sleeve. "You do?"

"Of course. Here…" He leaned down and plastered his lips against mine. It had all the passion and sincerity of kissing a cereal box.

I couldn't help but laugh.

"I'm sorry." He sat back on the ground and slumped his shoulders. "I've never done that before. I really didn't mean to hurt your feelings." He picked up a rock and chucked it at a tree. Hit it dead on. "I am screwing everything up!"

I bit down on my smile. "You're not screwing everything up." The furrow of his brow told me I hadn't convinced him.

Color me stunned. He was serious. He'd actually never been kissed.

The fabric of my Dad's sweatshirt stretched over his hunched shoulders. My heart skipped a beat, remembering the taught, hard lines of his back, the lean lines in his stomach, and the cute little dimple in his cheek when he smiled. He was beautiful. Absolutely beautiful. I shook my head.

"I can't believe you've never kissed a girl before. I mean— look at you."

He held out his arms and examined himself. "Is there something wrong with me?"

I snorted a laugh. "No, your gorgeou…I mean, I think a lotta girls would be interested in you."

He tapped his chest. "Remember, this is Jared Linden. This isn't what I really look like. Besides, girls don't really care about your appearance where I come from."

I settled beside him. "No? Then what do they look for?"

"Accomplishment. Someone they can brag about." David pursed his lips. "I'm the one who downed his plane on a simple communications mission. I'm the complete and utter failure."

"I don't think you're a failure. I mean, you're nice. You care, and you…I don't know…you're brave."

"Brave? When was I brave?"

"Well, you saved me twice last night. You could have jumped out the window and left me in the hotel, and you could have left me in the car when you broke free. I'd probably be under hot lights being questioned by now."

"You'd probably have been better off. Instead, you're out here, hungry and freezing to death."

I ran my fingers through his silky dark tresses and wondered if Jared Linden's hair could possibly be as soft. I smiled to myself. His hair was as soft as I always imagined it would be, because David was everything I'd ever dreamed of. He was a dream. My dream. How could I be better off without him?

"David, there is nowhere else I want to be. If I wasn't here last night, you might actually have frozen to death." I moved closer.

"I owe you a lot, you know." David shifted his shoulders

shyly. "If you want, you can do that kiss thing again."

I smiled. "You don't have to. I'm sorry I even tried it. I feel like an idiot."

"Actually I kind of liked it. It was…warm. Nice."

"You're all about being warm, aren't you?"

"You'd be too if you spent most of your night shaking in a frozen dementia." He smiled and rubbed his cheek gently against mine. "I liked it Jess. I just didn't understand what you were doing. My people don't…*kiss*."

I cleared my throat. "Okay. We can try it again."

He leaned down and mashed taunt lips against mine. I laughed, and pushed him away. If he were from this planet, I would have thought he was making fun of me.

"Stop."

"What? Did I do it wrong again?"

I bit my lip to keep from laughing, and held him back. "Tell you what. Relax. Don't be so stiff. Concentrate on the way it feels, and when I open my mouth, you open yours. Follow my lead."

"Umm, okay."

I licked my lips and eased closer. His lips brushed against mine, and I gently closed my mouth over his. David parted his lips, and I slid my tongue between them. The heat of his mouth enticed me, like drinking cocoa that had cooled to the perfect temperature—only sweeter. A gentle suction drew my tongue further from my mouth as his glided across mine. My body fell into a whirlwind of senses, spiraling beyond control and screaming for more. His hands moved behind my back, drawing me into his warm embrace.

His touch drove me nuts. I wanted more. I needed to touch him. I shimmied my hands beneath his sweatshirt, and trailed my fingers down his spine, delighting in the twinge of his tight muscles under my touch.

David broke our kiss and looked down, lips still slightly parted.

Damn. Definitely not bad for a first try.

I sipped in a slow breath, savoring his taste still on my lips. There was no way Jared Linden would kiss that good. David's expression seemed uncertain, though.

"Was that okay?" I asked.

David nodded without raising his eyes. "It was nice. Really nice. It's, well, we're alone, and it didn't seem right. You don't really know me, and that felt kind of…intimate."

"That's what a kiss is. It's intimate."

Confusion crossed his features. "Why would you want to be intimate?"

My heart sank. My stomach turned over and pinched from within.

David's eyes saddened. "I said something wrong again, didn't I?"

I swallowed down the pain building in my throat. "I like you David. Can't you understand that?"

"I like you too, but I don't get you. I offered you first friendship, and you pushed me away, and then you start helping me, and now this? Why are you messing with my head?" He closed his eyes and held his forehead.

I gave him a moment to calm down. "What do you mean, first friendship? When did I push you away?"

"In your room. Sitting on your bed." He dragged his fingers through his bangs. "You were pretty plain in your rejection."

Whoa. But wait. That hadn't felt at all like a pass. At least at the time it didn't. "David, I don't get it. What are you talking about?"

He held up his hands. "You took care of me, and I offered you first friendship, but you denied me."

My eyes narrowed. "You're going to have to tell me what first friendship is, 'cause I have no idea what you're talking about."

David hunched. His gaze trailed to the tree trunks. "I held you and brushed my cheek against yours. It's a sign of mutual…" He blinked. "It doesn't matter. You pushed me away."

I stiffened, remembering the awkward chawing in my gut…and yes, I'd pushed him away. "But I also told you that you could put your arm around me, remember?"

His gaze fell to the forest floor. "But you made quite certain that more was unacceptable." He stood and ran his fingers along the bark of a tree. "And then you start taking care of me again—and then this." He raised his hands in the air. "I have no idea what you want."

I jumped to my feet. "Okay, I think we are experiencing a little culture-shock here. I had no idea that you brushing your cheek up against mine meant anything. I guess it was a pass, but…"

"What's a pass?"

"A pass is when you are interested in someone, and you want them to know it."

David's lashes fluttered. "Then maybe it was. I don't know.

You have me so confused I don't even know what I'm doing anymore." He forced his eyes shut, as if steadying himself. "In my world, a female taking care of a male is a show of interest."

I suppressed a giggle. "So you thought I was making a pass at you when I gave you blankets and food."

"Yes, and not just that. Everything else. You've been taking care of me since we met."

I struggled against a smile and eased back to the ground. "Okay, I get it. Go on."

He sat beside me on the forest floor. "It was proper for me to acknowledge what you'd done by offering first friendship—a brief touch, and a brush of the cheek."

I straightened. "Okay, so that's where I screwed up, right?"

"When you pushed me away, you denied first friendship, which meant our relationship should stop. I've been very confused ever since, because you were acting like…"

I lifted up to my knees, and knelt in front of David. He tensed as I placed my hands on his chest. "I like you David, and I'm sorry." I brushed my cheek against his.

He smiled, and ran his fingers through my hair, sending a shiver of delight through my spine. His other arm slipped behind my waist.

Soft lips pressed against mine. David's mouth opened slightly. His tongue teased, forcing a moan from somewhere deep within as he slowly leaned me back into the grass. I reveled in the firmness of his body pressing against me, light but strong and oh, so perfect.

His lips formed a smile when they left mine. "You are forgiven."

I struggled for breath beneath the riveting beat of my heart. My skin felt empty, lacking, as he drew away from me. I reached out to pull him back, but instead he grasped my hand and helped me to my feet.

He looked into the trees, seemingly unaffected by the kiss that had stolen all sense of reason from my being. "We need to get moving."

Moving? Oh, yeah. Army after us. Spaceships to find. South to walk. Got it.

I worked hard to keep from stumbling on knees made of jelly, before an embarrassing gurgle emanated from my stomach.

David's eyes widened. "Did your body just make a noise?"

I laughed, easing away the last tremors from his kiss. "I guess I'm a little hungry."

"I wish we thought of grabbing the backpack before we ran."

"Food wasn't quite the priority at the time."

David sighed. "Maybe we should start walking and see what we find?"

"Okay." I grabbed my phone. Still two messages. The battery flashed low. I clicked on the navigator. "Crap. David, you ran in the wrong direction. We are about 25 miles away."

"Sorry, you had the compass. I only wanted to get us as far away from your dad and his friends as I could."

Compass. Good idea.

I pulled the plastic container out of my back pocket and opened it up. "Okay, according to the navigator, we need to go that way." I pointed into the woods. "We need to keep the compass pointed in this direction, and we should stay on course."

"Will the compass run out of power if we leave it on?"

I raised my eyebrow. "I'm pretty sure it's powered by the planet, so I don't think so."

I clicked local search on the navigator, and typed *fruit*. A smile crossed my face as the local listings appeared. "Perfect. And it's on the way."

"What's perfect?"

"Come on. We're getting breakfast."

17

I broke through the rough brush. *Conte's Farm. Private property.* The red-lettered sign blazed in warning as we approached the edge of the woods.

An itching burn crawled from the base of my throat into my ribcage. My eyes settled on the farmhouse in the distance… the normal entrance. Something in the recesses of my mind cautioned me to keep away despite the angst building inside me.

"What does the sign say?" David asked, his fingers trailing across the hand-painted lettering.

"It says welcome."

I guess pulling the English language out of my head didn't include the ability to read it. Lucky me.

"Let's wait a few minutes." I scanned the field, watching a cloud of dust kick up on the far side of the farm. A tractor rolled out of sight behind some trees. "Okay, let's go."

We wiggled through some deep brush into a field of low-lying greenery cultivated in perfectly straight rows. Tall weeds grew between the rounded plantings, leaving me to believe this part of the farm had been abandoned for the season. I brushed aside the leaves, and found a huge, red strawberry. Jackpot. I plucked the ripe fruit and lifted it from the plant. Turning the berry over, worms and small, crawly black bugs scurried for safety.

"Yuck." I dropped the fruit and wiped my hands on my jeans.

David's brow inched up. "I thought you liked to eat living things."

I wanted to punch the smirk off his face. Instead, I smiled. Maybe he could be taught sarcasm after all.

"Not the buggy kind. I don't like to share my food." I shielded my eyes and scanned the field. "We need to find what's in season."

We started walking in the direction the tractor-cloud had been. Lines of corn formed a wall between us and anything that might be edible. I stepped within the stalks and searched for ears, but they'd been stripped clean.

Rows of sword-like green leaves swayed in the breeze as I passed. They relaxed me with their gentle motion, until I realized I was alone.

"David?" The silence sent a stab of panic into my chest. Green stalks swallowed me on all sides, blotting out and consuming everything. Even the sun. "David!"

A hand reached out of the greenery and David appeared. "You really can't see through these things, can you? I was standing right there."

I hugged him, letting my panic subside in his warmth. "This corn is making me feel caged."

David ran his fingers up one of the stems. "I like it. It's confining, safe."

"Confining is safe?"

"I guess you have a different perspective when you've been inside a fixed space all your life." He looked up. "The last time I felt this relaxed I was in your closet."

I rubbed my arms. "Well, I don't like it."

David sucked in his bottom lip, then smiled. "Does this bother you?" He wrapped his arms around me, easing me to his chest.

I couldn't help but cuddle in to his embrace. "Now this I kind of like."

"But I'm confining you."

"But in this case I want to be confined." *Like, forever.*

I leaned up, and this time he took the bait. His lips brushed across my cheeks, and his tongue eagerly sought the parted space between my lips. The heat of his body shot through me, sending a ricochet down to my toes and back until I tilted my head with a sigh. His cheek came to mine, and I was sure to return the gesture, becoming surprisingly entranced as our chins touched.

"Wow," I whispered. Warmth swirled around us—attraction transcending anything I'd experienced before.

David's eyes sparkled and saddened as he stepped back. "I'm sorry. I shouldn't have done that."

The pain in his eyes echoed what I already knew, and it slapped me back to reality. He wasn't human. It didn't matter how either one of us felt. It could never be. I turned away in hopes of warding off embarrassing tears.

The rumbling of the tractor saved our awkward silence. I pushed through the stalks until the fields opened up before us. Dust billowed above an outcropping of trees.

"Come on. Whatever's in season is where the tractor is." I took David's hand and led him out of the corn.

His fingers instantly squeezed around mine as he stepped back into the air.

"It's okay," I said.

I followed his eyes up the branch of the tree beside us.

"What is that?" he asked, pointing to a cascade of red fruits clinging to the tree branch.

"No way." I reached up and grabbed the largest specimen, yanking hard to dislodge the stem from the tree. The half of the fruit shaded from the August sun still held a slightly green hue, and a white spotty dust shaded its skin. I rubbed it in my shirt until the fruit shined. "This is how apples grow. It's just like what we bought from the store." I took a bite, and grimaced at the bitter taste. "Ugh. I guess they're not ripe yet."

"Can I try it?"

I nodded, and handed it to him. The fruit crunched in his mouth. He turned his nose, but took another sample despite the taste.

I took it from him before he could take a third bite. "This is not the best Jersey has to offer. Let's go see what they're picking over there."

We moved through the trees and around a corner, coming out to the rear of a long, railed flatbed attached to a tractor.

A mother helped a few younger children down a rickety ladder beside the rear wheels, as other people holding buckets sauntered away from the wagon.

"Come on," I said.

I reached up and swiped a basket from the back corner of the flatbed. Walking as innocently as possible, I guided David beside me to join the group moving about the trees.

"If you keep to this side," the driver said, "you will get the ripest fruit."

The crowd split up. David and I joined them, moving into the field and ducking under low hanging branches. My heart throttled my chest as I did my best to blend in with the group.

"I thought we were trying to keep hidden," David said.

"Don't worry. Who'd think to look for an alien in an orchard?" I reached up, and plucked a plump fuzzy peach from a branch above my head. I held it to my nose, and breathed in its luscious scent. I bit into the fruit, and closed my eyes, allowing the sweet nectar to roll across my tongue. I handed it to David. "Here, try it."

He turned the fruit over and pressed his thumb against the skin, releasing the juice. A smiled crossed his lips as he licked his finger. Taking a large bite, he closed his eyes and mmm'ed as he chewed. It took forever before he finally swallowed. "That's the most unbelievable thing I've ever tasted."

I smiled. "You should taste their strawberries. They are out of this world—well, in June they are—before the bugs get at them."

His eyes shined brilliantly. "The trees bear fruit at different times?"

A smile graced my lips as I nodded. "Yeah. Strawberries come early, blueberries in July, and peaches at the end of the summer. It's so we don't get bored with our fruit. There's tons of other stuff, too."

The tractor geared up and drove down the path, leaving the customers to play farmer to their heart's content.

"Didn't he forget the people?" David asked.

"No, silly. He'll come back to get them later. I guided him further into the orchard, away from the other patrons. I picked another peach, and placed it into the bucket.

"Can I try?" David asked.

"Sure. Reach up and pull one off."

David laughed when the stem popped off the tree, allowing the peach to fall into his hand. "Is this where all your food comes from?"

"What, you mean, from trees? Well, some of it. Other things grow on bushes and stuff, or in gardens like the buggy strawberry before. Why? Where does yours come from?"

David shrugged. "It comes from the people who deliver it. I know they grow it in special places on the ship, but we're not allowed to go there." He grasped another fuzzy orb. "This is incredible." He rubbed the surface of the peach, his eyes seemed to study each hair on the skin.

A warm sensation settled into my chest. "It must be so cool, experiencing all this stuff for the first time."

He brought the peach to his nose, closing his eyes as he inhaled the scent. "You have so much. You have no idea."

"Yeah. I guess it's cool. I never really thought about it. It's just always been here, ya know?"

"No. I don't know. I've never had a planet to call home."

I sucked in the side of my cheek. Guilt panged beneath my

ribs. For what? Having a planet to live on? "I guess it's hard, being out there, huh?"

"No. Honestly, I never even thought about it. I didn't know there could be anything else." His gaze centered far away. "Now I understand."

I snatched a few more peaches from the tree, and placed them in our bucket. David lifted the handle, and we made our way back to the group. Our quarter bushel paled in size to the overflowing buckets lining the trail, waiting for the driver to return.

"Let's try picking over there," I said, much louder than necessary.

I motioned David to follow. We dashed into the next set of trees, re-entering the woods. I stopped on the edge of the forest and looked back. My chest stung, strangling my heart as my gaze fell over our bucket of peaches.

"What's wrong?" David asked.

"I just stole. I never stole anything before."

"What does that mean?"

"There's no word for stealing in your language either?"

"I guess not."

Hmm. Part of me started to think his world seemed like a pretty cool place. "Stealing is when you take something that doesn't belong to you. It's wrong."

"Can you un-steal?"

I fingered the credit card in my pocket. I could go back and pay for the peaches. An itchy feeling in my stomach told me not to. I turned my face up to the sky. "I'll pay for it when I get back, okay? I swear." The sun poked out of a cloud, and shone through the treetops, warming my cheeks. "I'll pay for it. I promise," I whispered, wiping a tear from my eye.

"Who are you talking to? Are you sad again?"

"No," I said, breaking out the compass. "I just miss my mom sometimes."

He wiped my cheek clean with his thumb. "Me too."

I sank my teeth into a peach as we walked deeper into the woods. "So your mom really is dead?" I asked.

"Yes. Why would I lie about something like that?"

"I don't know. To gain my trust?"

"I've never lied to you, Jess."

"You didn't tell me you were an alien."

"You didn't ask."

He had me there. Note to self: next time you meet a cute guy in the woods, check to make sure he's not an alien.

"So, your dad really is ticked off at you?"

"Now that I crashed a plane and ended up lost on an alien planet, I'm sure he is." David slowed his pace. "I was an embarrassment before. I can't even imagine what he's thinking now."

"What happened between you two, anyway?"

"I had this crazy theory." The muscles in his cheek twitched. "At least everyone else thought it was crazy. I spent three years formulating it, and testing the hypotheses. I know it would have worked."

"What was the theory?"

"Do you know what terraforming is?"

"Like in Star Trek? Making a livable planet out of a dead one by flipping on the Genesis Project or something like that?"

He raised an eyebrow. "Do you have a way to do this on your world?"

"Ah—no. It's from a movie."

His gaze lowered to the bucket of peaches. His eyes seemed to linger on each piece of fruit, as if memorizing the imperfections on the skins. "My theory was a dead planet could be revived if it once held life. If I could tap into a natural water table, if it still existed…that I could bring the water back to the surface."

"They didn't like your idea?"

"That's an understatement. They laughed at me. They said even if it were possible, it would take too long." He shook his head. "I don't agree. I know I could do it."

"So, I guess your dad didn't stick up for you, huh? That sucks."

"He was ashamed. His rejection hurt me, you know, here." He touched his breastbone.

I lowered my gaze. "We call that a broken heart."

He nodded. "Yes. I felt broken."

For several moments we listened to the chirping of birds and the sounds of the wind blowing through the trees. I thought about Dad, and how he didn't think I could make it as a photographer. He didn't believe in me as much as I believed in myself. It wasn't far off from David's relationship with his own father.

I moved closer to him. "I was wondering why you were piloting a ship if you're some kind of smart scientist-like-person."

"Losing my father's favor killed me inside. I would have

done anything to get it back. So I joined the military and studied to be a pilot." David rubbed his eyes with his fingertips. "He was so proud. He was there at my inaugural flight. He smiled and waved as I took off."

"And what happened?"

"I never returned. I crashed on my first mission, and here I am." He quickened his pace. "When I get to the extraction point, I'm going home in shame. My father will probably never talk to me again."

A pang of emotion balled up in my chest. After all that had happened over the last few days, would my own father react the same way? Would he disown me for helping David and never speak to me again?

"I'm sure that's not true. He's your dad. He has to love you, right?"

David stopped and set the bushel of peaches on the ground. "You don't get it, do you? I'm going home to be ridiculed and loathed for the rest of my life. I've had two chances. I won't get more. I'm done."

I stepped back, surprised by his tone. "You could stay here."

He huffed. "Yeah, what a great life I'll have here." He spun toward me, his eyes darkened. "They are hunting me right now. What do you think they'll do if they catch me?"

I sucked both of my lips into my mouth. Dozens of movies came to mind—dead Martians floating in liquid ooze, alien experiments, and torture among other uncomfortable scenarios. "You're right. You can't stay here. I'm sorry."

I looked down, and he gently lifted my chin. "Jess, I'm sorry. I shouldn't have been like that with you. I'm tired, and I have to admit, I'm scared. We're not even sure how close we are to the pick-up location, and I'm running out of time."

"All right. Let's see." I pulled out my phone, surprised to see it still lit up.

Smooth move, Jess. The navigator was still on, so the phone didn't automatically power off. The phone had been on the entire time in my pocket. Battery power: five percent. Wasn't that just great.

"We have about ten miles to go. We're still on the right track, but I don't have much power left."

A text message popped up.

Maggie: I hope U don't read this. Don't use UR cell phone. They can trace it. They R waiting for U 2 turn it on.

The words scorched my eyes, slowly sinking in. My cell phone had been running, with the navigator on no less, for at least an hour. David would be lucky if he didn't have a bullet in his back by nightfall.

"Oh my God!"

"What?" David checked over both shoulders.

I shut off my phone, turned in the opposite direction, and threw it with all my might.

"What are you doing?"

"We have to go."

I handed two peaches to David, took two for myself, and left the bucket.

"What about the rest of them?" David asked, slipping the fruits into the pocket of his sweatshirt.

"Forget the peaches. They know where we are. We need to run."

18

I tugged his elbow and bolted into a sprint, hopping over brush and fallen trees, doing my best to stay focused on one direction. My chest stung with each breath, but I concentrated on keeping my respiration steady. I could do this. David needed me.

The sound of barking ping-ponged through the trees. We both skidded to a stop.

"It's probably dogs fighting," I said.

"Are you sure?"

"Umm…yeah." The crinkle in his brow told me I had a lousy poker face. I choked back the pain filling the base of my throat. We'd come so far, and I'd screwed it all up with my dumb phone.

David centered his eyes on me, and ran his palm across my cheek. His touch reached through my skin, injecting courage where mine had faltered. Strong hands settled on my waist, and he lifted me at the hips and into his arms. I wrapped my arms around his neck, and crossed my ankles around his back. Not very lady-like, but I was beyond caring about appearances.

"Okay," I said, tightening my grip. "I'm ready."

David broke into a sprint. My hair flew behind us like a banner as he increased speed. The trees blurred together, and my stomach flopped. I closed my eyes, clinging to him for dear life—not mine—his.

The barking dogs advanced, their cries encircling us from several angles. Was it just an echo, or were they closing us into a trap?

David slowed, his heartbeat quickened beneath my grip. Sweat dripped down my sides.

"Jess?"

I shivered, slipping to the ground. There was no denying it anymore. The dogs were getting closer. "I hear them."

David's gaze darted from side to side. The barking continued, until a rumble and high pitched squeal turned our attention behind us. The sound grew louder, muffling the yapping dogs.

What now?

The roar came closer, the ground trembled.

"Hold on," David said.

I wrapped my arms around his neck as a set of German shepherds broke through the brush, the MPs following close behind.

"Hey," one of them called, pointing.

"David, go!" I tapped his back.

He lifted me and darted ahead. The MP placed a whistle to his lips as we left him behind, the dogs snarling and pulling faster than the man's legs could carry him.

The roar and rumble reached deafening heights. I struggled

to see what we were running toward. As we broke through the trees, David stopped, jolting me. A screech shattered my eardrums, blotting out everything.

"What is it?" David yelled over the sound.

I twisted my face to the right, eyes wide as a raging locomotive barreled toward us. "It's a train!"

David backed away from the tracks. His muscles constricted beneath my clenched fingers He seemed to struggle to keep himself from being sucked into the engine's backdraft.

The dogs breached the trees. I dropped my feet to the ground, but he pulled me closer.

"No. Hold on," David bellowed into my ear. He turned toward the train, bracing himself.

"Oh, God. David, please don't." I wiped the sweat from my temple with trembling hands before weaving them back behind his neck.

His feet left the ground and my stomach lurched as we rocketed through the air. My world became an onslaught of sound and throttling wind. I gritted my teeth against the shriek building inside me, praying with all my might as we slammed against the side of the speeding train.

I buried my head in David's neck. Tears streamed from my eyes and flew through the air—never having the chance to dampen my cheeks as they ripped into the wake of the speeding train. David's knuckles wrapped around a metal bar on the side of the car. We swung manically, bobbing up and down across the cold steel. My bones slammed against the molding, skin and muscle unable to protect them from the tremulous onslaught of flesh banging against metal.

"Hang on!" David growled as we jolted and rocked. Our bodies flailed away from the train before barreling back toward the rigid steel. I lifted my face, my skin prickling and tearing from the airstream's merciless bite.

I struggled to open my eyes against the pressure of the wind. David hung to the side of the locomotive with one hand while the other clutched my back, holding me aloft. Another jolt sent us smashing back into the metal frame. David groaned, taking most of the blow.

I could do nothing but pray as my tear-filled eyes struggled to focus.

Two of David's fingers shook from the metallic edging. A rumble sprang from his lips and his hold on me tightened.

This was it. The end. I was going to die on this train. And Dad would never know why.

David sputtered as he lost his grip. He wrapped his arms around the back of my head and held me tightly. Our bodies flew through the air as one, slamming once against the side of the train before hurling away and bouncing on the dry, grassy ground. I wheezed, searching for air that forcibly expelled from my lungs as we rolled away from the tracks.

David's blurry face moved into my line of sight, I felt his hands on my face. "Jess? Jess are you okay?" His voice sounded hazy in the vacuum of the train's roar.

"Stay where you are," someone hollered over the rattle of the locomotive. David helped me to my feet.

A helicopter hovered overhead, a uniformed man hanging out the door with a gun pointed at us. Two Zulu Cobras dropped out of the sky and hovered behind David. The gunships dwarfed the smaller helicopter. The Marines. Crap.

I trembled in time with the whirling blades and raised my hands in surrender. *I'm sorry, David. I tried.*

A black smear flew before my eyes and imbedded in the dirt at my feet. The base feathers of a dart stuck out of the ground. I squinted up toward the gunman. Bullets would have been more effective, but apparently they wanted us alive.

"Come on!" David grabbed my hand, and tugged me toward the train.

"You're not going to—" My arm wrenched from its socket as David jumped back toward the locomotive.

He landed on the platform between the last two cars.

I didn't.

My body slipped along the steel until my fingers caught the molding on the edge of the railing. My hips slammed against the unforgiving metal framework. My sneakers dangled mere inches from the churning wheels. A scream spewed from my lips, lost beneath the roar of the locomotive and the helicopters now following above.

David leaned down from the platform, gritting his teeth as he stretched toward me.

My fingers burned as they slipped. "David!"

"Don't let go. I'm coming!" He wrapped his knee around a metal plate, and thrust his hand toward me, grasping my arm below the elbow. "I got you."

I dared a breath, and released my grip. My muscles contorted and ripped. My bones whimpered in agony, my senses rejecting any more pain as he lifted me into his arms.

"Oh my God. Oh my God. Oh my God." I buried my body

into his, scrambling onto him, trying to become part of him.

"I've got you, Jess. You're okay."

I sobbed into his sweatshirt, struggling to get a breath into my lungs. The world whirred, unreal around me. What reality I could find blurred into a haze of uncertainty.

WHHRRT. A black dart slammed against the glass window behind us. I shook my head, struggling to find focus that refused to come. David yanked on the door, but it didn't budge. He released my hand, using both to struggle with the handle, but the clasp wouldn't release.

The train jolted, and I staggered backward. "David!"

A strong hand steadied me. My heart thumped madly as I pawed at him, seeking security he wasn't able to give.

WHHRRT. A dart passed between our faces.

"We've got to get out of here." David's head turned back and forth.

I palmed the door, desperately searching for a hidden feature that would open the lock and save us.

WHHRRT. The dart ripped the edge of David's sweatshirt. Our luck would run out sooner or later. David drew me closer. "I need you to trust me." His lips formed a straight line.

Sweat soaked the nape of my neck. "David. What…?"

"Promise."

I nodded. "Yes, I promise."

"Hold on to me." He folded my head into the crook of his neck.

I sniffed, tears welling in my eyes. "What are you going to do?"

"I'm not sure yet."

A dart clanged against the metal floor plate to the right of us. Another bounced off the door to the left. I crossed my arms around David's neck. Hiding my eyes in his collar made me feel safe. Well, as safe as I could feel on the back of a speeding train car, with three helicopters hovering overhead, and a guy trying to shoot us.

I stole a glance upward. The metal ceiling provided little cover from the gunships speeding above. The massive spinning blades blurred the sky as they kept perfect pace. I wished I had my camera to catch the beautiful symmetry of the haunting image, but even if I had it, I doubted I'd be able to do much more than clutch David in absolute terror. Maybe I didn't have the courage to be a photojournalist after all.

David's left hand slid down my waist and cupped my rump. If it were Bobby, I would have slapped him, but David's grip felt solid and reassuring rather than groping.

"Ready?" he asked.

I grunted in response, clinging with all my might.

"When the time is right, I'll go."

Go where? I didn't bother asking. I tucked my head in. My lips whispered in silent prayer as my hands tightened around his neck.

The train's howl muffled for the briefest of seconds, and David sprang into the air. I had the sensation of hanging, like a slow-motion movie cut, before we slammed to a sudden, brutal stop. I shrieked, my hands smashing against a hard, jagged surface. My kneecaps buckled and crashed, jarring every muscle in my body. My fingers reflexively untwined, and both David's arms wrapped around me as we plummeted—bumping and dragging down a rough, tearing surface.

David cried out and lost his grip on me. My rear slammed into the rocky ground before I slumped onto his chest. I threw my head back, trying to get my bearings.

A thick cement overpass shielded us from the sun. Gravel pinched and cut beneath me. My sneaker lay against the edge of the tracks.

The train sped onwards, shaking the rail against the base of my shoe. The helicopters kept pace steadily above the locomotive until they all turned into the tree line and out of sight.

David grimaced. He pushed away from the cement wall, his hand rubbing the back of his neck. Was he hurt? For that matter, was I hurt? How were we even still alive?

Wincing, I righted myself. My left knee dripped with muddy blood, while the other ached beyond reason. I hugged David, desperate for reassurance we were okay. He rubbed my shoulder, hauled me up from the gravel, and checked the direction the train had gone.

"We need to go. It won't be long before they figure out we're not on there anymore." He put my hands around his neck. "Come on. I'll carry you."

I furrowed my brow. "You can't possibly be not hurt."

"I'm sore, but I'm fine."

But I wasn't. I'd just jumped off a moving train. A freaking moving train!

He turned toward the trees. "Which way do we go?"

My hands shook as I pulled the compass from my pocket. The needle wobbled until it decided on north. "That way." I pointed across the tracks.

I limped a few agonizing steps. Who was I kidding? I didn't have a fake skin to rip off. My injuries were real. Pain wouldn't stop me, though. I stepped over the rails and hobbled toward the trees.

David grabbed my arm and tucked that one annoying stray hair back behind my ear. I shivered as he touched my cheek.

"You're hurt. It doesn't make you weak. Let me carry you."

I didn't answer, but he lifted me into his arms anyway. My right knee twinged in protest, the ache deep and severe. I put my hands around his neck, for the first time seeing my bloodied knuckles. I bit my lip, refusing to let the pain in. I was not about to let him down. He was right. I felt weak next to him. I was embarrassed. For what? Being human? All I wanted to do was cry. Instead, I choked back the tears and clutched his sweatshirt.

The sounds of the helicopter got louder. We were out of time.

"I'm ready. Go."

***

I leaned my head on David's shoulder. The sight of trees passing my eyes at high-speed lulled me into a stupor. As he slowed his pace, I woke suddenly, my hands throbbing from my death-grip around his shoulders. My fingers cramped as David eased me down.

A small private plane flew overhead, slightly shadowed by the setting sun. David didn't react. He rested on his knees, breathing heavily.

"David, the sun is setting."

He raised his face. "I saw. Maybe we'll get lucky and it will be a warm night?" The cool breeze answered his question. We hadn't had a warm night in a week.

"Should we keep going? Maybe we can find another hotel."

"Yeah," he puffed, "because that worked so well last time."

I flung my hands in the air. "Well, I'm open for options. I'm trying to keep you from freezing to death, jerk."

Smiling, David wrapped his arms around me. His cheek brushed against mine, and my body tingled in response. It calmed me instantly. How did I ever not recognize that for the affection it was?

David kissed my forehead. "It was a joke. I'm sorry."

The remainder of the exhaustion-fed anger swirling inside me slipped away, and for a moment everything became right again. "I'm sorry too. I shouldn't have snapped. This has all been crazy, you know what I mean?"

He nodded and rubbed his injured shoulder. "Definitely not what I'm used to."

My brow furrowed. "You *are* hurt, aren't you?"

I moved behind him and ran my hand across his back. A long rip in his sweatshirt exposed most of his right arm. I slipped my hand inside, my fingers probing a huge slice in his skin.

"David you're cut. You're really cut bad!"

"I'm fine. I'm just a little shaken."

"No, you're going to need stitches. Lots and lots of stitches—or worse." I stood, frantically looking from side to side. For what, I didn't know.

He smiled. "I'm fine. It's not my real skin. Remember?"

Oh yeah. Alien. Fake skin. Color me sheepish.

I bit my upper lip and set it free. "So, umm, why are we stopping?"

He scanned the forest. "We're here. The extraction point."

A raking pain ebbed into my chest, settling over my heart. "Oh, already?"

He nodded. A word shaped on his lips, but he turned away without speaking.

A knot formed in my throat as I faced the agony of our inevitable farewell. I placed my hand on his shoulder. What did I want to say? Everything, and nothing. I'd only known this boy for a week, but he'd become part of me. How could I ever say goodbye?

The breeze tickled my cheek. David tensed. What was going through his mind? He seemed conflicted, like he didn't know what to do. Would he stay with me? Could he, if he wanted to?

I pushed away the ridiculous thoughts. Dad was on our tails, waiting to grab David and do God knows what to him. There was no choice. David had to leave.

"How long until they come for you?"

"Not soon enough." David turned, centering his gaze on me. "Would it be too much to ask you to hold me again tonight? For warmth, I mean." His eyes betrayed a need for more than his words let on. Could he be as afraid of saying goodbye as I was?

I placed my hand on his chest. "I would hold you even if it wasn't cold."

He moved toward me. The power and certainty in his eyes devoured the dread that had been building in my heart the closer we came to this unavoidable night—blotting out the fear of dogs and helicopters and dart guns, leaving nothing but us. Swirls of limitless emotion tickled through me, easing and caressing as I inched closer. The world became nothing but a backdrop to the all-encompassing certainty of my need for him.

He gently stroked both my cheeks with his fingertips and touched his forehead to mine. I soaked him in, rubbing my cheek along his. The heat from his skin burned, but I couldn't break the contact. I needed to feel him more than I needed to breathe. I needed to be with him, in him, sheltered and protected from everything that scared me. Was that so much to ask? To freeze this moment? To live in his arms forever? To pretend that everything was okay?

David's hands wove through the back of my hair. His eyes, deeper and bluer than I'd ever seen them, gazed into mine, consuming me and leaving me breathless. Was it possible he felt the same way about me? Did he need my touch as much as I needed his?

His gaze dropped to my mouth, and his lips parted slightly. I drank in his scent, my mind swirling in musk and earth.

Aliens didn't kiss, but he was thinking about it. I knew he was. Had he enjoyed the feeling of my lips, my tongue? Was he afraid to tell me?

I moistened my lips and brushed them over his. David's reaction was instantaneous, and gave me my answer. His arms folded around me, his lips searching, his tongue finding. My body succumbed to a whirl of pleasure and need. I sunk into him, became part of him, opened myself in ways I never dreamed possible. This is what I needed. This is what I wanted. Nothing mattered but his touch.

I gasped as he pulled away. My body arched, yearning for more.

David licked his lips and turned from me.

"David?"

He wiped his kiss from my lip with his thumb and stared at his finger. The sadness in his eyes cut through me. "It's getting cold," he whispered, as if speaking to his fingers. "Maybe we can make a bed out of some of these leaves and stuff."

"But David—"

"We can't do this, Jess." His eyes blazed. His words sliced through me like a knife. "I'm going home. Tonight. Nothing can change that."

How could he cut it off like that? I could've stayed in that embrace forever, lost in a bliss I never even imagined possible.

For some reason—the way he clung to me when we kissed, the way his hands stroked my skin, or maybe the way he was avoiding my gaze—I knew he felt the same way.

But that didn't really matter, did it?

I pulled myself together, reminding my stupid heart of who he was, and who I was—and why we were out here. The tickles of attraction and need receded, losing themselves in a wave of practicality. I sighed, missing their warmth.

David was leaving, and my current job was to keep him warm. Period. Nothing else mattered.

After ruffling through the underbrush, I found a rut covered with moss beneath a large log. At least it would be soft. David tossed the log aside, and we worked together to line the crevice with soft ferns and other forest plants.

By the time the sun sank behind the trees, David had already started shivering. I helped him into the makeshift bed, and tucked the leaves around him.

"Are you comfortable?"

A rattle-like giggle ebbed out beneath his shiver. "I guess as best as I can be."

I eased myself down and covered his body with mine, cuddling as much as I could on the uncomfortable ground. Both of my knees began to throb, pulsing against my jeans. I ran my fingers over my scraped knuckles. It seemed like an eternity since we'd jumped off that train.

David shuddered beneath me. "I have a feeling this is going to be a long night."

I grit my teeth as the temperature fell, praying David's ride would come before he froze to death. "You're going to be fine." The words sounded rehearsed. Forced. Were they to make him feel better, or myself?

He reached up and ran his fingers through my hair. "It shouldn't be too much longer, Jess. I can feel a pull in my stomach."

I looked up. "So, like, they're here? Can they pick you up before—"

He placed a finger over my lips, silencing me. "They're

not here yet, but they're close." He closed his eyes and took a deep breath. "They are very close."

"So, they're like, calling you? E.T.-phone-home or something like that?"

"I guess. What is this E.T. thing, anyway?"

"Just an old movie. Maggs called you E.T. and it stuck in my head."

"So, was this E.T. tall, strong, and dashingly handsome?"

I snorted a laugh. "He was definitely cute."

"How...how...d-did it end?" He stammered with a chill.

I tightened my grip around David, choking back a sob. "E.T. gave the little boy a hug, and he went home." Tears gathered in my lashes.

"D-do you think we're going to havvvve a happy ending J-Jess?"

I pressed my cheek against his. "Yes. Definitely." I only wished I felt as certain as my words.

19

A twig snapped, jolting me awake. I leaned off David and tucked back my hair. A sweet piney scent filled my nose as the song of crickets answered a cool breeze rustling the trees.

David's body quaked beneath me. His lips quivered, and he moaned. A pang of guilt seeped into my gut, cutting a painful hole with the realization that my body's heat wasn't doing enough. I cuddled around him. "Come on David, warm up."

Crack.

Silence.

What had happened to the crickets?

The underbrush rustled. I tensed, holding my breath. Wind swished the trees above. A car horn honked far off in the distance.

The muted evening air clung about me as if someone had pressed a pause button. Why was it so quiet?

I screamed as two hands came out of the night, their fingers digging into my flesh. The moon sank behind the clouds, darkening the forest and hiding my captor. My body lifted into the air. My lungs struggled against an overwhelming pressure against my ribs. Held from behind, I struggled and kicked. "Let go!"

My feet dragged across the forest floor as someone hauled me further from David's shivering form. I twisted and tugged. Another set of arms shot out of the dark and clutched my hands, tying my wrists together with a coarse rope before drawing me into the air.

The pressure against my sides subsided, and I drew in a deep breath. My shoulders throbbed from the strain as my captor maneuvered my hands over a tree branch and hung me like a Christmas ornament. "What are you doing? Let me down."

I trembled as the cloud cover shifted. The trees, like sharp shadows, seemed to reach toward me, watching. A large broad man walked away, his bobbing gait somewhat familiar. A woman adjusted my bindings, her face partially covered by a fuzzy-edged hood.

"What do you want?" I asked.

Her silence hung in the air like a veil. She either didn't hear me, or didn't care that I'd spoken. Sweat ran down my temples as she turned and joined her friend. I writhed in my bindings. Was this the end? Had we come so far, only to be caught by… who? Crazies? Drug dealers? Who were these people?

My jailers brushed the dirt with their hands before gathering something from the woods, stacking it on the ground.

"Please, let me go. I didn't do anything."

The continued their chore.

The man raised his hand. I flinched as a high-pitched noise

blasted my ears. A flash seared my eyes. Orange spots obscured my vision, blotting out what little I could see in the darkness.

Heat rolled over my cheeks, and I blinked repeatedly. The orange spots receded, revealing my wardens standing opposite a large, roaring campfire. My jaw dropped, dumbfounded.

The woman pulled back her hood and shook her head. Long, golden curls spilled on her shoulders. She turned from the fire. Her thigh-length brown jacket rustled as she walked toward David.

"I need to get to my friend. You don't understand. He's freezing."

The blaze gained in height. I turned toward my shoulder, trying to shield my face from the heat. The woman knelt on the ground. Beside her, the broad guy tugged at David's sweatshirt.

"No! Please don't do that. He needs to be warm."

The man swiped back his black hood. Light hair flew up from his head in static wisps. He rubbed his cheek, smudging dirt across his wrinkled skin.

A sinking feeling drew my fear deeper within as I recognized the crazy old man in the coat that I'd seen in the woods a few days before. Stunned, my gaze moved to the woman. Her features flickered in the light of the flame. Recognition sent a shiver through my bones...the crazy guy's daughter.

I struggled to breathe as my heart worked to beat out of my chest. "Please don't hurt him."

The girl lifted David's head into her lap, and brushed back his bangs. Her cohort leaned close to David's face and turned to the side as if to hear his breathing.

She whispered a few words, and the man harrumphed.

He lifted David from the ground, and carried his limp body toward the flames.

"Stop! Don't." I struggled. The braided strands around my wrist dug and ate away at my flesh. "Let him go."

The man dropped to one knee and laid David beside the fire. I released the breath I hadn't realized I was holding, and searched for any movement from the boy who'd become more dear to me than I ever imagined possible. The light from the flames flickered across his still form.

Please be okay, David.

The woman knelt beside them and withdrew a pencil-sized silver rod from her pocket. The metal glistened in the firelight. She tapped the edge, and the pencil lit up.

What was that?

A line of yellow light shone across David's face, and scrolled down his shivering form like a price gun at a supermarket.

"What are you doing to him?"

My captors murmured to each other. Their heads bobbed in nods and shakes before the man stood and unzipped his jacket. He spread the coat over David, wafting the fire in my direction.

The blond woman watched, nodded, and turned to me. Her gaze locked with mine as she approached.

Her eyes…so blue. No, not blue—turquoise, like David's.

She slipped her hands into her jacket pockets. "His temperature has dropped twenty degrees. He's dying. If you could keep quiet, I might be able to save him."

My heart skipped a beat. My lips formed letters, but words didn't follow.

Her eyes narrowed, as if gaging my reaction. She crinkled her nose before gliding back to David's side.

Her partner sat by the fire, holding his hands close to the flames. My eyes widened. The old man didn't have any pinky fingers.

"You two are the scientists, aren't you? You are the people David was signaling before his plane crashed."

The woman tucked the jacket around David and looked up. "This is the pilot?"

My gaze flicked between her and David. "Yeah."

She raised her eyebrows. "Well that explains some things."

"*Curz cum qhoz puellima est*," the man said. His eyes remained fixed on the fire. His lips thinned to a straight line.

The woman's gaze trailed to me. "*Nonz scirb est.*" She removed the old man's jacket from David, speaking more words I couldn't understand.

My chest twisted into a pretzel as the man rose to his knees and placed his palms on David's chest. The woman squeezed David's cheeks, forcing his mouth open. A clear vial caught the firelight as she tilted it toward his lips. A drop formed along the rim before disappearing into his mouth.

David choked and sputtered. Dark liquid ran from his mouth in an incessant stream, staining his lips and cheek.

"Oh, God! Is that blood?"

The man grumbled and leaned down on David's ribcage.

"Stop it. You're hurting him."

David's body arched. Dull, emotionless eyes sprang open. They stared in my direction, but held no sense of memory, no sense of recognition, no sense of David.

My heart sank, swirling into recesses further than oblivion. "Oh, God. Oh, God, David!"

He kicked madly, thrashing toward the fire.

The man bellowed in his own language as the woman fumbled for David's legs. David's foot flailed, kicking her in the face twice. Dark fluid ran from her nose, pooling in the crook of her mouth. The older man grabbed David's ankles, pulling him from the edge of the fire.

"*Opules ahsah qanon rezpoadena est,*" she said, reaching into her pocket. A blue vial sparkled in her hand.

The old man shouted back at her in their own tongue.

She mumbled in response. Her fingers squeezed David's mouth open again. His body struggled against them. Vacant eyes glazed past me.

"Please, David, please…" I whispered.

A drop touched his lips. The woman stopped the vial and shoved it back into her pocket. David's eyes blinked twice, before rolling into the back of his head. A deep gurgle erupted from his throat, and the shaking ceased.

The man stood. The woman ran the light pen over David's forehead and smiled. She murmured a few words to the old man, who mumbled and sat near the fire, his back to me.

The woman tapped David on the forehead and replaced the jacket over his torso.

I twisted and tried to get a better view. "What happened? Is he okay?"

The man spat foreign words carrying a menacing tone.

The woman looked up. "He wants you to be quiet."

"I'm sorry. I just want to know what's going on."

The man abruptly stood, but his friend grabbed his arm and wrenched him down. His eyes bored through me, daggers piercing my skin. I backed as far away as the ropes allowed. Unanswered questions swirled in my mind, but for the first time in my life, I kept them to myself. My gaze settled on David as I leaned back against the tree and waited.

***

Cranky-silver-haired-guy grumbled and picked up a piece of fruit from the ground. He rubbed his thumbs across the tender flesh, smelling the fuzzy skin.

"That's called a peach. David and I picked them before we…"

He gnawed off a bite of the fruit.

"Wait. That's all we have!"

Cranky stood and approached me. He leaned close and took another bite, purposely crunching the fruit in my ear. I scowled at him as he swallowed.

He tilted his head to the side. "You covered him with your own body," he said.

Huh? "Wait, you speak English, too?" I adjusted my weight, giving my left foot a rest.

He didn't answer me.

"Of course. I tried to help him. He was cold."

"Why do you care?"

"Because he's my friend."

Cranky laughed. "He's not your friend."

I squirmed in my bindings. "Yes, he is."

He spit out part of the peach skin. "And what makes you think he's your friend?"

My gaze trailed to David. "He cares about me."

Cranky slapped his knee. His laugh echoed through the night. "He cares about you? Now that's riper than this piece of fruit." He turned to the blond girl. "The base, rudimentary reactions of these creatures disgusts me."

Blondie tucked the jacket around David's shoulders. "But we have seen high levels of intelligence."

"Intelligence does not equate to sentience." He threw the core of the peach into the woods. "Their animalistic nature makes them no better than the vermin infesting the cartilage tubing in our ship."

"We're not vermin," I whispered.

He walked toward David, and stood over him. "No? Then why would you be so blinded by our young pilot, I wonder?" David turned in his sleep. "He's handsome, isn't he? You find this form attractive?"

I fought against the ropes. "I don't know. I hadn't really thought about it." *More than 1,000 times.*

Cranky placed his hands on the edges of his tattered blazer. "Here I chose a form of an elder, one I thought would evoke feeling of knowledge and warmth, and I received nothing but sneers and disdain. He takes the form of a young, virile male, and finds a pathetic, affection-starved little girl to help him. Smart boy."

"I'm not pathetic."

"You're entire race is pathetic."

I tugged on the bindings, but they gashed deeper into my flesh. "David cares about me. He does."

Cranky stood. "And such devotion! This pilot must be a master at manipulation." He walked toward me. "He doesn't care about you."

"He does. I know he does."

Cranky leaned close to my ear. "He used you."

I shook my head. "No."

"Oh, yes, he did."

"I'll never believe that."

"What's easier to believe, that he's using you, or that someone that looks like this..." he pointed at David, "would actually be interested in the pale, sniveling likes of you?"

Tears welled in my eyes, my lungs constricting my breath. "Stop it."

He turned back to Blondie. "You see? They'd rather cling to impossible hopes than face reality." His fiery eyes returned to me. "Want to know the truth, little girl? He's going to get on that ship, and not even think of looking back. We are going to fly to safety, and he won't even shed a tear when the scourge takes you."

A pain tore through my chest. "The what?"

The woman pulled Cranky back. "Leave her alone."

He chuckled, and they both sat by the fire.

"What's the scourge?" I asked again.

Blondie looked away. "It's nothing to worry yourself about."

Cranky huffed. "I'd be worried if I were her."

Blondie shot him an angry glance, and returned her gaze to the fire. The flames continued to flash shadows across David's sleeping form. I hung on my tree, arms too numb to feel the pain.

Complete darkness surrounded us. The firelight didn't seem to reach the neighboring trees. No smoke rose from the flames. David turned in his sleep. A smile touched his lips. He looked no less menacing than the night he slept in my closet.

Cranky was lying. David would never hurt me.

I shifted, testing my ropes again. The movement sent a stinging jolt through my knee, and my scraped knuckles throbbed. "Please let me down. This really hurts."

Cranky grumbled as he stood. "I'm done listening to this talking rodent." He opened his sport coat and extracted a long silver instrument. "In the name of *science*, I'm going to see how long it takes her to bleed out." He lunged for me, the sharp silver object twirling in his fist.

I screamed and recoiled as the point spiraled toward my eye.

20

"**N**o!" I cried.

Cranky grunted, and I looked up. The old man stood before me, fist and blade still poised and pointed in my direction. His lips curled back in strain, as he hissed through clenched teeth.

A hand held his arm in mid-swing…a bandaged hand with four fingers. Cranky twisted and growled as he fell to one knee.

David hovered over him, his fingers indenting the skin on the older man's arm. "Let go of it," he ordered.

Cranky's lips formed a sneer, before the blade fell to the ground. David kicked Cranky's chest, sending him on his backside. Smoothing the hair from his eyes, David plucked the instrument from the brush, and pointed the object at the older man. "Stay down."

Cranky flared his nose and turned away. Blondie sat by the fire, snickering.

Warmth circled me as David rubbed the silver-thingy against my ropes. The severed bindings slid to the forest floor. Relieved beyond belief, I threw my hands around his neck.

"Are you okay?" he asked.

"Yeah. I'm so glad you're awake." I clung to him, reveling in the safety of his arms, allowing my fear to fall away.

"Look at that," Cranky said. "How touching. What's your name, boy?"

"David."

Cranky's lip curled. "That's a human word. What is your *real* name."

I blinked and looked up at David. It never occurred to me that he had a real name.

"David," he repeated.

Blondie rolled her eyes, and Cranky chuckled. "Suit yourself. So how did you get that annoying creature so devoted to you…or is it simply carnal attraction to the form you chose?"

David tightened his grip on my arm. "You obviously wouldn't understand."

Cranky snickered. "Please enlighten me."

David stared him down. "She helped me. She has a good, kind heart. Human beings are a strong, thriving race."

"The Caretakers would disagree."

"The Caretakers haven't been down here. They haven't experienced life with them. We have."

"Yes, we have, and I see no reason to counteract the timeline."

Blondie lowered her eyes and shook her head.

"You can't do this," David said. "You need to tell them what we've found."

Cranky sneered. "By this time tomorrow, it won't matter."

I turned to David. "What is he talking about?"

Cranky smiled, folding his arms. "Yes David, what *are* we talking about?"

David's gaze fell to the forest floor. The light of the fire cast a sparkling glow about his raven hair.

"David?" I put my hand on his arm. "What's going on? What's the scourge?"

David's eyes darted fierce anger across our camp. His chest rose and fell in deep, careful breaths.

"This is going to be good," Cranky said, his grin nearly touching his ears.

"Can we have some privacy, please?" David grasped my hand.

"No," Cranky said. "We need the heat of the fire, and I don't want to miss a second of this." He sneered. "Go ahead, David. Tell her why we're here. Tell her about the scourge."

Blondie threw something into the fire, sending sparks into the air. "Leave them alone, Cassum Ael."

"David, what's going on?"

The confusion in his eyes frightened me. He slid my other hand into his. "Okay...I told you I was born on a ship."

"Yeah. Alien. Got that."

"Everyone in my generation was born on a ship, and I think most of the generation before us as well. Our planet became unlivable some time ago, and we had to leave it. Ever since, we've been searching for somewhere else to live. We came across several planets, but they were inhabited, like yours. So, we collected data from them, and moved on." David's gaze trailed to the fire. "We came across the fourth planet in this system. I studied it. There are enough building blocks from its previous life to bring it back."

"Which one is that?" I asked.

"The red one. You can see its glow in the morning and early when your sun sets."

"That's, umm, Mars. So, you're going to terraform Mars? That's actually cool. We'll be neighbors."

David's nose flared "No. The Caretakers rejected my proposal. They said it would take too long to warm the planet enough to support our race."

"Okay, so, what does that mean? Can you use Mercury or Venus?" David tilted his head. "I mean the other two planets that are pretty close to us."

David blinked. "No. They are both *too* warm. It is easier to harness the power of a sun to warm a planet than it is to fight a sun in trying to cool it."

"I guess that means you'll have to look for another solar system?"

David closed his eyes, and inhaled. "The reason they won't wait for the terraforming project, is that we are low on fuel and supplies. The planet won't be ready before our people start to starve, and we haven't found another planet close enough."

My stomach sank. "What does that mean?"

David rubbed his face with his hands. "We're not monsters. We've been waiting for years. Your planet was getting warmer. You were destroying yourselves, and fixing the climate for us all at the same time. So we sat back and waited for your natural demise."

"You mean that global-warming thing everyone talks

about? You just sat there and watched us ruin the planet?"

"Yes, until the ozone layer started to repair itself in the past several years. The Caretakers decided to scourge the planet before the climate had a chance to recover more, so we'd be able to warm it faster." David chewed his lip and looked at the ground.

Why had he turned away? "David, what-is-the-scourge?"

He grimaced, before slowly raising his eyes. "A scourge is the removal of an offensive life form...before colonization."

I leaned back. "Offensive life form. You mean humans?"

"Yes."

My hand darted up to my lips.

Cranky laughed. "So, is your boyfriend still the man of your dreams? Do tell."

I steadied myself, doing my best to push aside the thought of global annihilation. "Okay, wait. They are picking you three up, so that means you won't survive this scourge thing either. Right?" Their uncomfortable glances gave me my answer. "Then we can stop it. Just don't get picked up."

David placed his hand on my arm. "No, Jess. Three lives are not worth risking our entire race. The scourge starts at sunrise, whether we've been extracted or not. By noon tomorrow, it will be over."

Rage throttled through me with the force of a seven-forty-seven. I slapped his hand off me. "So that's it? I'm supposed to stand here and let you kill us?"

"Jess..."

I shoved him with all my might. "No, David. I'm going to stop you. I'm going to tell someone."

I turned and tore into the woods, intent on putting as much space between me and the aliens as possible. Where I was going or who I would tell were lost thoughts, but if the Army was still looking for us, they had to be out there somewhere. I had to find them. They could stop this. They *had* to stop this. I swallowed down the painful ball of dread building in my throat. Dad was right. David was using me. How could I have been so stupid?

Strands of hair stuck to my tear-dampened cheeks as I ran deeper into the trees. The sky above loomed, devoid of stars. Was the ship already there, waiting to do whatever the scourge was to my planet…to wipe us all out? I quickened my pace. There had to be a way to stop this.

David stepped out from behind a tree in front of me. I plowed into him at full speed.

"No!" I said, propelling off of his chest. I ran in a random direction, no longer sure which way I should go.

David appeared from behind another tree. "Please can we—" I stopped short, dirt and plants piling at my feet as I changed course. I managed ten steps before a firm grip jolted me backward.

I pounded my fists into David's chest. "I hate you. I hate you!" I repeated between my sobs. "Cranky-guy was right. You were going to leave me here to die."

He slipped his fingers around my face. His hands were gentle but strong, immobilizing me. "No, I wasn't. I never intended to leave you."

"Yes you were. Cranky guy said—"

"I have never met that man. He doesn't know me. He

doesn't know anything about me. He doesn't know anything about *us*." He closed his eyes and took a deep breath. "I'm not leaving you. I was never going to leave you."

I wiggled out of his grip, and wiped my nose. "You weren't?"

"No. I need you, Jess. I was going to bring you in front of the Caretakers. I was g-going to prove to them that you're s-s-sentient."

"That we're what?"

"Sentient. A th-thinking, developing and emotional race— s-something worth saving."

A light breeze surrounded us. David began to tremble. Part of me wanted to watch him freeze. Part of me wanted to wrap him in my warmth.

"Really? And that would make them stop?"

The cool night air tickled my damp cheeks. David ran his fingers down my shoulders, his hands shaking.

"I don't know, b-but it's the best chance we have. And if it doesn't work, at l-l-least I know you'll be safe." He stroked my cheek with his.

My body tingled, my pulse quickened. Could it be that easy? "I'm scared."

"I'd never let anything happen to you."

I fell into his embrace. A swirl of energy spun through me, radiating from his warmth and encompassing my entire being. Comfort, safety, love, a gamut of emotions reached inside and injected themselves into every sense, filling every void with a small packet of joy. My head tilted back, and a sigh escaped my lips. So warm, so perfect. So…

I pushed him away. "Wait. How do I know you're not lying

to me again?"

"I never lied to you Jess."

"But you didn't tell the whole truth, either." How many of my friends had fallen victim to a handsome face and a mouth filled with lies? I refused to be one of them.

Pain reverberated from his eyes. "Jess, I'm not lying. How can you think that after I just gave you my affection?"

Affection? "Wait. The feeling that was just inside me—did you do that?"

David shrugged. "I gave you my affection. Didn't you like it?"

I moved closer, part of me desperately yearning for the tenderness of that touch, that insane feeling of intimate connection, but reason prevailed. I stepped back. "Yeah, so, how do I know you're not faking it?"

David cocked his head to the side like a sorry puppy. "You can't fake affection. You can either give it, or you can't. I don't understand."

"You mean, you can't fake liking someone?"

His eyes widened. "No. Can you?"

I gritted my teeth. "Actually I can. That doesn't take me off the sentient list, does it?"

He blinked. His eyes held no emotion. "I thought I felt something like affection when we kissed. Did you fake your affection for me?"

"No. Of course not." I put my arms around him and buried my face in his chest. His muscles were tense, taut rocks, slightly quaking with a chill. "You're freezing. Let's get you back to the camp."

***

Cranky laughed as we returned to the fire. "She came back? You certainly are a master, boy. You will need to teach me your secrets."

"Shut up." David held his hands up, rubbing them near the flames.

"What are you going to do with her?" Blondie asked, pointing her chin in my direction.

"She's coming with us."

"A pet?" Cranky asked.

"Proof." David rubbed his hands on his jeans. "All we need to do is show her to our people. They will stop this once they meet her."

"Her?" Cranky chuckled. "Humans are nothing, and she's a poor specimen of a dying race. You're wasting your time."

"How could you have lived among them so long and not interacted? You are scientists. You should have been studying them. You should be as convicted as I am right now."

Cranky stood, pointing at his chest. "I am convicted." His eyes shook, nearly bulging from his human skin. "I'm convicted that our race is superior, and if a choice must be made between our people and this feeble, deteriorating, gluttonous race, than I say let them die."

"Why can't we live together?" I asked.

A snort escaped Cranky's nose. "So naïve."

My chest burned with rage as my fingers wrapped into a fist. David raised his arm between us. "She's coming back with me. Period."

"Suit yourself." Cranky stood and zipped his recovered jacket closed. "I'm going to scout the perimeter and make sure your little friend didn't compromise our location."

As Cranky's silhouette blended into the night, Blondie poked the fire with a long branch. The flames reflected golden circles in her turquoise eyes. Her gaze periodically fell on David as if contemplating him, before she dropped her branch alongside the fire and scooted beside us.

"Before, you spoke of terraforming. You are Tirran Coud Sabbotaruo, aren't you?"

David glanced in her direction before returning his gaze to the fire. "What of it?"

An uncomfortable tingle simmered through me. His alien name seemed so…alien, but his touch seemed so human, so right.

"I read your work. Your theories are sound."

David pursed his lips. "You're probably the only one who thinks so."

"Did you ever consider melting the ice at red planet's polar caps?"

David held up his hands. "It would only diffuse in the atmosphere."

"Not if you do it at the middle of the process, and not the beginning. If you give the elevated atmosphere time to solidify, it will retain the moisture and you will have a basis for precipitation before you drill for the water beneath the planet's crust."

David leaned toward her. "If it's already raining…"

Blondie smiled. "The soil will be better prepared, and the water bodies will fill faster."

"If we puncture the crust in the enlightened hemisphere, the ocean will fill in half the time!"

"And become a natural mirror."

David's hands flew to his temples. "Which will rebound off the existing atmosphere and warm the planet faster!"

His hands flew to the sides of her face, drawing her to him as he kissed her lips. A pang of jealousy rattled my toes. Blondie sat back; eyes furrowed and mouth gaping. She wiped her lips with the back of her hand and stared at the moistened skin, grimacing.

"I guess this is all good stuff?" I asked.

David jumped to his feet and raked his fingers through his hair. "It's fantastic. I can warm the planet in half the time."

Blondie stood. "It is still only a theory, and the chances of it warming before the fuel runs low are slim. It would be difficult to convince the Caretakers."

"No it won't. They'll listen. They'll have to listen."

Blondie grasped his hands. "You are very young, Tirran Coud. I'm not sure you—"

He yanked away from her. "I'm not that young."

She smiled, her head tilted to the side. Mom used to do that, when she was about to tell me what I didn't want to hear.

"But you *are* young. *Anotaboaoliter iuvenes aouod impligendizx est.*"

"Speak in this planet's language. Jess deserves to know what's going on."

"Fine," Blondie said. "You are brilliant, but not quite yet

a man."

"I'm old enough."

"But you still have not learned to handle your emotions."

I folded my arms. "Awe, crap. You're not like a bunch of Vulcans, are you?"

David looked in my direction and smiled.

Blonde's eyes narrowed. "I believe Cassum Ael was wrong. I believe you do care for the girl."

David made a motion to speak, but closed his lips and turned to the ground.

"You need to be clear why you will make the decision before you. Do you do it because it is right, or do out do it out of affection for this native?"

David met her gaze. "Does it matter?"

"I think it does. The girl hinders your concentration. She can be used against you."

"No. I am clear."

"Maybe, for the time being, but when faced with the pressure of the Caretakers? When facing a council that will notice your feelings for her? Who will be disgusted with you over emotions they will be repulsed by?"

David paled and looked away.

Blondie stepped past him and leaned close to me. "When he nears you, he warms. Even now, his muscles strain in preparation should I try to hurt you. You have compromised him, when he must be focused."

I moved away from her. "I, umm…"

Blondie pointed at me, her eyes never leaving mine. "And you, as well, are too young to understand what lies ahead."

She paced around the fire, tapping her fingers to her lips. Her steps circled twice before stopping beside us. "I have been here six months. I've lived among these people. I've seen acts of charity. I've seen rational behavior. I've seen love. Granted, I have seen many inexcusable things, but it is not our place to judge another culture. These people are sentient. Scourging this planet is wrong."

David nodded. "You don't need to tell me that."

"This is going to be difficult, Tirran Coud. Far too difficult, in my opinion, for one so young. But what you lack in experience, you have in knowledge. I believe in your theories. I believe, with work, that the red planet will thrive. I can give the Caretakers the emotional balance they require."

"What does that mean?" I asked.

She turned toward David. "If you can find the courage to stand before the Caretakers, I will support your theories. I will stand at your side."

David straightened. "Do you think they will back down?"

She bit the inside of her cheek. "No—but we have to try. It's wrong to stand by and do nothing."

A rush of hope filled me, overwhelming my fear. "How will we..."

David moaned, and his back arched, craning his neck up toward the treetops.

"David, what's the matter?" My hope drained away into a pool of fear. Beside him, Blondie stood frozen in a similar pose. Their faces pointed toward the stars, their eyes closed, their breathing slowed. My heart worked to beat out of my chest. "What is it? What's going on?"

A gentle breeze swept around us, not cooling, but warm. The fire crackled, snapping a few sparks into the air while the animals of the wood remained silent.

Blondie shook her golden locks and rubbed her forehead.

David blinked, turning to me. A gentle smile crossed his lips. "It's time."

"What? They're here?" I craned my neck to the sky. A starless night greeted me. "So, like, do they beam us up or something?"

David guffawed. "I'm not going to pretend I know what you're talking about."

Blondie stroked my cheek, smiling. "Are you ready, little one?"

"I guess." I steadied my stance to support my shaking knees.

She tapped David on the back. I'm going to go find Cassum Ael."

Cassum Ael? Oh, Cranky Guy.

The wind blew through my hair. "Are you going to be okay if we leave the fire?

David smiled. "Do you feel it?" He raised his arms, lifting them to the sky.

The breeze spiraled around us, warming as much as the flames.

"They're sending us heat. We'll be fine." David drew me from the fire.

"Where are we going?"

We stepped into the darkness. "This way."

"This way to where?"

David pointed up.

My stomach plummeted. Saving the world sounded good and all, but leaving the planet? I didn't like to fly in an airplane. The last thing I wanted to do was get on a spaceship.

David's eyes warmed as his gaze returned to mine. My heart fluttered, my body filling with a sense of whole-ness and purpose. David's affection? No. This time, it came from within *me*. I was doing the right thing. I was taking a stand, even though I was terrified.

A loud hum mixed with a bug-zapper-like buzz rattled the silence.

"Was that your ship?" I asked.

David dragged me down into a crouch. "No. Our transports don't make noise."

"Then what was…"

Cranky jumped out of the woods. "Hide! The humans are here."

"What? How?" David asked.

"I don't know. Nemitali Carash is dead."

David's grip on me tightened. "Dead?"

Blondie?

"She made it to the extraction point, and this planet's military hit her with some sort of huge, intense light. It stripped the human skin right off her. She's gone."

David grabbed his collar. "Are you sure?"

"Well, I didn't stay to inspect the body." He shoved David away.

"Where are the humans?" David asked.

Panic stretched the wrinkles in Cranky's skin. "The landing site. It's crawling with them."

21

We peered through the branches, doing our best not to be seen. A long strip of asphalt lay within the clearing of trees before us. Lights imbedded in the pavement illuminated the ground, forming straight lines stretching far in either direction. They looked like landing strips. It must have been some kind of small airport.

David held his finger to his lips, pointing toward the right, where a line of tanks towered behind rows of armed troops. A jeep drove across the field and stopped beside a circular search light five-times the vehicle's height.

"That's it," Cranky whispered. "That's the machine they lit up Nemitali Carash with. It melted the skin right off her."

A man stepped out of the jeep. I gasped and ducked as he scanned the tree line with his binoculars. The gray highlights in his tightly cropped hair sparkled as the searchlights grazed over him.

Dad? I stooped back down, despite being well hidden in the bushes.

David gave me a forced smile. "It's all right. We'll be okay."

"You don't have to try to sugar coat this. We're in big trouble, aren't we?"

"We aren't in trouble," Cranky said. "They are." He pointed toward the tanks. "Two pumps of a cagier spiral and they're all dead—and we walk out unscathed."

"What? That's my father out there."

David put his hand on my back. "We're not a belligerent people. We won't attack unless provoked."

Cranky chuckled. "No, we're very peaceful—but we have no problem with obliterating her entire race because they're in our way." His snicker cut through the darkness as he jostled out of the bush. "I'm going to check a little further down the field."

David lifted a limb and looked out over the runways. His eyes darted toward the sky twice.

Tremors ran through me, and I swallowed down the pressure building in my throat. "I can't believe that you were part of this, that you would have let them kill us."

He shook his head. "No. I wouldn't have." He turned to me. "We were lied to, Jess. We were told the primary species on this planet was uncivilized and hostile. We were told you were lower entities, incapable of emotion or intelligent thought." He allowed the branch to pop back in place. "We've passed fourteen perfectly good planets because they had intelligent life on them. It's not our way to take what isn't ours."

"But that's your plan now…to take Earth away from us."

"Haven't you been listening? My people don't know you're sentient. Once they see the truth, they won't let it happen. It's not who we are."

"So your government lied to you."

David's eyes glassed over, and he blinked. His face turned upward. "They are here."

My heart rattled. "What's going to happen?" I clutched at his arm. "How do we get to them?"

"Let's wait and see what they do."

My father moved away from the jeep. His binoculars dangled from a strap around his neck as his gaze focused on the sky. I couldn't see a darn thing up there from beneath the stinking bush.

David's skin prickled. The hairs on his arm poked the palm of my hand. "Are you cold again?"

"Shhh." He looked up. "They're insane. There's no way. We'd be too easy a target if…"

Cranky leapt from the bushes about fifty feet from us, and ran into the middle of the field.

"No!" David shouted, standing.

I yanked him down. "Don't."

My father ran backward several steps, and the giant searchlight beside the jeep switched on. Three soldiers turned the massive beacon toward Cranky's advancing form, illuminating the alien completely.

Cranky turned toward the beam and hollered at it. He raised his hands to the dark heavens. The sky mottled and moved toward him. A dark mass crept out of the night like a black-gloved hand reaching out of a shadowy closet.

Dad shouted orders across the field, and the giant search light changed to a bluish-green stream. An ear-shattering tone reverberated through the clearing. Above us, the black glove receded into the sky.

Cranky recoiled as the blue searchlight hit him. His body shook and reeled. His feet held firmly to the ground. His hair turned to smoking tendrils of light before fizzling away. What were they doing to him? His body lurched back, as if being pulled forward by invisible hands. His face changed, distorted.

My jaw plummeted, exposing my tongue to the warm air and the taste of acrid smoke. Cranky's face rippled, buckled, and slipped from his body. David wrapped his hand over my mouth, and I realized I'd screamed. I grit my teeth to keep from crying out again as pieces of Cranky's skin drew away from his form, melting as they flew through the air, sucked in by the light. I gagged on the putrid stench.

Cranky fell to his knees. The light changed from deep blue to clear, illuminating his alien form as clearly as if in daylight. David released me and we both inched the branches further apart. Cranky remained down, his chest shifting rhythmically in a constant stream of deep breaths.

He stood slowly, allowing his four-fingered hands to fall to his sides. I knew it was probably an illusion, but freed from his human disguise, Cranky seemed taller. Deep violescent skin covered a lean, muscular body. Large spots of darker purple decorated his form in a mottled pattern. His head, naked, glistened with what appeared to be perspiration.

A low hum emanated from above, lasting not longer than five seconds, but rattling those below.

"What was that?" I asked.

David shivered. "A warning—but that doesn't make any sense. It sounded like a battle ship, not a transport."

Cranky inched toward the light.

"Stop," a voice called over a speaker. "Lie down with your hands on the pavement."

Cranky continued to walk.

"What is he doing?" David whispered.

"Put your hands on the pavement, now!"

Cranky sprang into a jog, bolting toward the light.

"No," David cried, throttling through the bush.

I wrenched him back. "Don't do it, David."

Gunfire rattled the forest. Cranky shook with each impact and fell to his knees.

"Why?" David whispered. "Why would he do that?"

Cranky edged forward on his knees. Two more pops reverberating in the night slowed him. A sinking dread encompassed me as he fell to the pavement, face-first.

"This isn't good," David whispered. "We have to get out of here."

He backed out of the bush. I followed on my hands and knees. David yelled, and I heard something hit the ground. "David?"

A hand reached inside the bush and hauled me out by the hair. My scalp burned as a shot of panic engulfed me.

"Let go, Jerk!" A flashlight blinded my eyes.

The hair-yanker forced me to my feet. David lay on the ground, a noose around his neck attached to a long pole held by an MP.

A soldier approached.

"Look, sir." An MP grasped David's hand, showing the officer the exposed alien flesh left after melting his skin on my stove.

The officer drew a small flashlight from his jacket. "Good. Let's test him and make sure this thing works." He rolled up the arm of David's sweatshirt and shined the light on his wrist. David's face twisted as the pink flesh melted away, revealing the pearly lilac hue beneath. "Bingo," the officer said. He turned to me, light in hand.

"Get away from me with that thing, you jerk. I'm human."

"Gotta make sure." He raised the light.

"Wait!" A voice cried. Maggie's brother circled around a guard and stood in front of me. I'd never been so happy to see a familiar face in all my life, even if it was my ex. He leaned close to my face. "Who am I?" he asked.

"Bobby, it's me, you freak! Tell these idiots to let me go."

He smiled. "This is Jessica Martinez. She's the missing girl."

Officer Jerk advanced, light-thingy in hand. "We still need to test her."

Bobby moved between us. "But I know her."

"We can't be sure that's not a stolen skin."

Bobby grimaced, and nodded. The officer pointed the light at my face, but Bobby shielded me with his hand.

"Do it somewhere where it won't scar."

"Like where?"

Bobby gently lifted my arm. I tried to pull away.

His grip tightened. "Jess, hold still." He held my left pinky steady, while the jerk shined his light on my fingertip.

My skin tingled. Pressure built until a searing red burn appeared. I whimpered, flailing and lashing against the restraint, and finally howled as a blister rose and burst.

"Let her go," David grumbled. "I'm the one you want."

"She's clean," the jerk said, dropping the light in his pocket. He turned toward David. "Let's get Martian Manhunter here back to General Baker."

I stared at the welt bubbling from my skin and bit back my tears, pulling against the guy holding me as they heaved David to his feet. The MP handling David's leash pressed a button, and David's body convulsed as if he'd fingered an electrical socket. A groan escaped his clenched teeth.

"Leave him alone," I shouted.

The jerk pointed at me. "Take her too."

Mr. Pull-My-Hair cricked my hands behind my back, and cold metal touched my wrists. The click sent a shiver up my spine.

"I'll take her." Bobby's warm fingers brushed against my hands, taking the icy cuffs. "Make this easy on yourself, Jess. They think you were in cahoots with that thing."

"I *was* in cahoots with him. He's trying to help."

Bobby tensed. "You're not yourself right now."

"Yes I am." I leaned back and whispered, "Bobby, you need to listen to me. The aliens are invading. David is the only one who can stop it."

"You're talking crazy."

"No, I'm not. If David doesn't get on that ship, we're all going to die."

Bobby gently nudged me. "You've been compromised, Jess. These things can get into your head...make you believe anything they want. It's not your fault."

"No, it's not true." At least I hoped it wasn't true.

The airstrip lighting glowed through the bushes to my left. Cranky had crawled up to his knees, and the man with binoculars around his neck stood above him.

Dad.

Bobby gave me a mild shove, and I stumbled forward. I pulled at the handcuffs, craning to see through the bushes where Dad pointed a gun at Cranky's face.

"Dad, no!"

The resonance of the gunshot bore through my chest as painfully as if the gun had been pointed at me. Everything that made me human wailed in anguish as Cranky fell to the pavement, lifeless.

"Dad! No. Dad!" I struggled against Bobby's grip.

"Jess! Thank the Lord." My father's voice froze me.

I stopped struggling, my eyes filled with tears. "Dad?"

My father stepped out of the forest. Relief swept over his face. I twisted to see over my left shoulder. The man hovering over Cranky's body holstered his weapon and marched toward the jeep. *It wasn't him.*

"Get those stinking handcuffs off my daughter." Dad pushed Bobby back.

Officer Jerk intervened. "We found her with the alien. She needs to come in for questioning."

Dad snatched the keys from Officer Jerk's side. "She'll cooperate. You don't need the cuffs."

A click and a gentle tug freed my hands. I rubbed my wrists, warding away the suffocating feel of the metal from my skin.

An ominous hiss bounded through the forest, followed by a ringing that ricocheted inside my skull. I pressed my hands against my ears.

David's eyes searched the sky. "Oh, no."

"What is it?" I called over the noise. "Are they landing?"

"No, it's much worse."

A black mass skipped across the treetops as the hiss soared overhead. A low-toned *Whomp* thumped my chest.

Officer Jerk fell to his knees, clawing at his ears. "What the fu…"

The jeep that carried binocular-guy rose into the air, hovering for three seconds before exploding, showering the landscape with sparks and fire.

I held my arms up to shield my eyes from the light, and ran to David. "Is this the scourge?"

Another ship passed overhead.

"No," David said, panic riddling his face. "It's my father."

"Your what?"

My eyes darted to Cranky's lifeless body, illuminated by the flickering flames from the explosion. The Erescopians expected to pick up Cranky and Blondie together, and David all by himself. What would David's father do if he thought his son was dead?

The man with the binoculars ran from the debris and falling flames. A hiss and a mottled black shadow appeared out of the night, enveloping him. He screamed, shaking and convulsing. The veil closed over him like a mouth. His feet left the ground as the shadow rose and began to fade. The man's form dissolved within the dark mass and disappeared within the diminishing apparition. His screaming stopped.

"What was that?" I grasped David's arm.

The MP yanked on his collar, dragging David from the trees.

"Let him go," I pulled David back. Another soldier knocked me forward and I fell, buckling my kneecaps against the ground. So much for chivalry.

I wiped the hair from my eyes as a dark oval fell from the sky and hovered mere feet above the runway.

A dull thud echoed through the forest. The reverberation struck my heart, tingling my chest until the ship darted straight back into the sky. The giant searchlight-alien-skin-stripper burst into flames. The heat battered my face despite the padding of brush. The tops of the trees overhead disappeared into a maddened blaze. My flight reflex fought against my need to stay with David. My legs ached with the desire to run.

Far above, rattling automatic weapons told me our planes had joined the fight in the sky.

I searched the confusion and found my father barking orders into the air while soldiers swarmed around him. I clutched at his shirt. "Dad, you need to let David go. He can stop this."

He grabbed my shoulders. "Jess, you need to understand that what you're feeling isn't real. It's made you believe what it wants you to believe."

"Dad, you're wrong. David's not like them. He wants to help. He wants to tell them to stop."

"You can't be sure of that."

"But I am. Dad, you need to believe me. You don't know what we've been through. David is real. We can trust him."

He set his jaw and turned away.

"Dad, if you can trust me once in your life, it's gotta be now. Please, help me."

His eyes darted to my left. David knelt, noose around his neck. Officer Jerk had a gun pointed at his face.

"Stop," Dad said. "What are you doing?"

An explosion lit up the sky, shaking what was left of the trees above.

"They killed the other one, didn't you see?" The Jerk's finger shook on the trigger.

"Stand down," Dad held up his hands and walked cautiously toward him.

The Jerk spun, pointing the weapon at us. "No. You stand down. This thing was in your house. How do we know *you* aren't compromised?"

Dad huffed and punched him in the nose. He disarmed the jerk before he'd even hit the ground. Bobby took the gun from Dad and tucked it into a pouch.

I dropped to my knees and tried to remove David's noose, but Dad stopped me. "We can't let him go, Jess."

"Why not?"

"Right now, he's all the leverage we have."

A hum like the loudest train engine *ever* blasted us from above. Our eyes shot to the treetops. A plane, whose I couldn't tell—fell from the sky. Branches melted like butter before the ship slammed into the woods. Fire shot out, consuming the trees and singing our faces…pinning us between the intensity of the crash-sight and the explosions rocking the airfield.

"Dad, you need to listen to me."

His eyes hardened. He held me from David.

Another blasting crescendo raged through the forest, ending with a rippling explosion. The ground shook beneath our feet.

Dad thrust me into Bobby's arms. "Get her out of here." He turned to the soldiers. "Fall in. You there—" The commotion engulfed him as he continued to bark orders.

My gaze found Bobby's. "You said you cared about me, right?"

"Not really a good time, Jess."

"I need you to trust me. David is the only one who can stop this."

Bobby shook his head. "I have to follow orders. I can't let him go."

I punched his chest. "Wuss!" I shoved him away and flung my body through the bushes. Brambles snagged at my shirt. A branch whipped back and gashed my face. I reached for my cheek and pulled away blood-stained fingers.

Fear found me as I fell to the asphalt. The hard surface of the tarmac scraped my hands. I struggled to catch my breath, alarmed by the heat and flames shooting out from the remains of the jeep and searchlight. A tank moved across the far side of the field, shooting into the sky. A second lay on its side. The bodies of five soldiers littered the ground at the machine's base.

Another dull thud droned through the air. The intense sound tingled my skin. The air quivered and hazed before the airport's re-fueling tank erupted into a howling ball of flames. I held my hands over my head. My skin burned as the heat rolled over the blacktop. The hairs on my arm curled and fell away as I shielded my eyes from the billowing cloud.

This had to stop. It just had to stop!

I raised myself from the hot runway and ran into the center of the field, passing Cranky's body and what remained of the alien-melting searchlight. Smoke filled my lungs, choking me as I reached the small grassy area separating the two landing strips.

Black shimmering ovals zoomed back and forth over my head. The air rattled above as another base tone resonated through the night. The tank firing into the sky left the ground and exploded into a shower of metal and fire. I ducked. A melted piece of a door clanged to the ground not more than a yard from me. I stared at it, transfixed, allowing the heat to singe my face.

"No more," I whispered.

I stood and waved my hands in the sky. "Hey! Hey you up there! David is okay! He's fine." I pointed toward the trees. "He's in there. Please, you gotta stop. Please!"

A huge ball of fire zoomed past my face. What was left of the airport's tower teetered and fell across the field, crashing atop the one-story building at its base. Soldiers scurried away, looking for cover that no longer existed.

One of the long, black floating ovals slowed and hovered above me. The glossy exterior spun, silent amongst the ensuing commotion. The surface rolled. Its hull shined like the patent leather shoes I used to wear for dance class.

"Hey," I waved my arms. "You up there. Come out. David's over here!"

The hull shimmered. The ship's underside molded itself

like animated play dough, teasing and kneading into a myriad of shapes. Light filled a hole centered in the flexing clay. Thousands of stars shifted and coalesced inside, forming into one solid sparkling band. My lips formed into an "O", my mind allured by the light's beauty.

"Oww!" A blinding pulse shot from the ship. I shut my eyes, but it hardly seemed to help. When my lashes fluttered open, swirls of white effervescence imprisoned me. My gaze trailed upward, and I grabbed my throat when I realized I couldn't breathe. A piercing screech blotted out all other sound, filling my ears with brash resonance. I opened my lips to cry for help, and whimpered as what little air inside my lungs sucked out, stolen…propelled toward the light source.

I fell to my knees, holding my neck, struggling for a breath of non-existent air. The tarmac gravel bit into my cheek, and I realized I'd collapsed. The light became transparent and turned orange. Through its pulsing screen, hazy visions of soldiers falling and clawing at their chests seemed distant, unimportant.

My cheeks heated. My back stung. My body shook. Dread beyond measure wrenched a hole in my heart.

I'd failed, and as punishment, I would be the first victim of the scourge.

22

A heavy weight pressed me to the ground. Out of air, I had no energy to fight it. My mind whirled.

My first time horseback riding. Mom laughing on the Snow White ride at Disney World. Dad telling Grandma I never think of anyone but myself. Driving down Route 42 before waking up in the hospital. Mom laughing at my third-grade play. The look on Dad's face when he told me she was dead.

My cheek scraped across the gravel. My body lifted, and strong hands flung me onto my back.

"Breathe, Jess!" David's voice filled my mind, circling and weaving around memories of camping in Delaware when I was eleven. "Breathe!"

I opened my lips and inhaled. My lungs filled. I blinked, and the world came into focus. Soldiers littered the runway, scrabbling, crawling—trying to escape the lights. The pressure continued to hold me down.

"J-just k-keep br-reathing." David's face came into focus above me. His lips stretched in a grimace.

I reached up to touch his cheeks. My hands singed as the

orange sheen touched them.

"No," he said. "K-keep under m-me."

I drew my hands back, and placed them on his chest. David trembled, holding himself over my body, shielding me from the light. Dark fluid seeped from his ear, and dripped to my face.

Tears blurred my vision. "David, is this the scourge?"

His lips formed a straight line. Fear, terror, and pain coalesced in his eyes, igniting a dread inside me far more horrible than anything the suffocating light could manifest. He clenched his teeth, straining against a scream.

His body shook. His eyes glassed over, becoming less blue.

I choked back the fist of terror punching through my chest. "David! No, David!"

The weave of his sweatshirt liquefied, raising into the air and disappearing into the light. The remaining fabric from the front of his shirt fell into my hands. My mother's necklace, free of the sweatshirt, fell down and dangled near my chin, the etching of the cross glinting in the light.

David glanced up, grunted, and returned his gaze to me. His left cheek smoldered, pearly lilac skin showing through a melted elliptic hole in his human skin.

His eyes opened wide, horror dripping from them as his gaze focused on me. "I—I'm s-sorry, Jessss." His eyes faded to gray.

"No!"

The searing buzz around us ended in a resounding bass thud as the orange light disappeared. David collapsed on my chest, wheezing.

I reached my arms around his neck and touched damp heat. Steam rose from his exposed violet skin. I lifted my hand and shuddered. Indigo fluids dripped from my fingers.

"Is that blood? David, are you bleeding?"

David closed his eyes. The oval of exposed Erescopian skin glinted on his left cheek, the surrounding human skin hung in melted waxy globs. He groaned and leaned off me.

"David? David!" Tears streamed down my face.

I smoothed back my hair, my gaze meeting Bobby's at the edge of the runway. The trees behind him cast an eerie glow from the fires both on the field and within the brush. His blank expression remained fixed on me as the pole and noose that had held David cascaded from his hand and bounced on the pavement.

Despite orders, Bobby had let David go, but the hurt in his eyes riddled my heart. He told me once that he'd always love me. I never believed him until that very moment.

David moaned, and I touched his cheek. "David, please…"

Holding my fingers over the burned flesh on his jaw, I brushed his other cheek with mine and kissed his forehead.

"David, I'm here."

Bobby's eyes lowered as he backed into the trees.

"Bobby, wait!"

I leaned up, but David stirred beside me.

"David?"

His eyes fluttered open. Blue. They were blue again.

"Thank God." I kissed his cheeks, his eyes.

He smiled at me, straining as if it took the last of his energy. "Are you okay?" he asked.

"You saved me." I brushed the hair from his forehead.

"Yeah, well, now you can call us even."

I leaned away, grabbing my forehead. "I thought we were dead."

David frowned and turned up onto an elbow. "I don't know why we're not." He ran his thumb across my cheek. "I promised I wouldn't let anything happen to you."

Strong fingers reaching from behind lifted me to my feet.

Dad's arms enveloped me inside a hug. "I thought I lost you again."

I relished his embrace, not remembering the last time he'd held me. "I'm okay, Dad." I wiped my cheeks with the back of my hand and turned. "Dad, this is David."

Officer Jerk dragged David to his feet. David winced, not fighting him at all. The jerk's swollen red nose caught the light as he lifted the noose toward David's head.

"No." My father snatched it from his hand.

"What are you..." Officer Jerk gaped as Dad broke the noose over one knee.

Soldiers crawled out from the smoldering wreckage throughout the field, all eyes fixed on the sky.

David stumbled to my side and placed his arm around my shoulder. I braced myself, holding his weight as he leaned on me. The edges of his human skin along his back steamed, glistening like hot wax before it dries. His alien skin, now exposed, wept dark shiny ooze. I shivered, knowing he'd nearly sacrificed himself to save me.

My father threw the pieces of the noose to the ground, and hesitantly approached.

He stared at David for a moment. "You look like you've seen better days, soldier."

David laughed, and his chest buckled with a wince. "That's a bit of an understatement, sir."

Dad put out his hand. "Thank you for saving my daughter." David glanced at my father's hand, his expression blank. "You're supposed to shake his hand," I said.

"Sorry." David reached out his left hand, and shook the back of my father's fingers rather than grasping his palm. Dad pretended not to notice.

A deep hum filtered through the airfields. The trees shook as dozens of huge, gleaming black ovals descended. They hovered, sparkling in the lights shining on them from jeeps and hand-held spotlights below.

I cowered beside David. "Are those nice, friendly, pick-you-up kind of ships, or mean nasty blow-us-up kind of ships?"

David flinched. "Those are the blow-you-up kind."

"Great Lord in Heaven," my father whispered, moving closer to me as more vessels appeared.

The ships hung like huge molten raindrops in the sky, as if someone had melted millions of black pearls, poured them into oblong lakes, and then rendered them weightless. The amorphous, liquefied masses contorted until slow waterfalls of shiny ebony drizzled from each craft, shifting and shimmering in the moonlight. The glinting and flexing cascades solidified as they touched the tarmac. Each filled into a dense rectangular pole, attaching respective liquescent masses to the ground.

A slice of light burst from the base of the first waterfall, followed by another and another. The landing strip pulsed in their amber glow as golden lights drew upward, illuminating the waterfalls and spreading until each pole shone brighter than a lighthouse beacon.

David's grip on me tightened as dark figures appeared inside the lights. Long, lean, lavender Erescopians glided from the ships one at a time. Each held a silver saucer not much larger than their hands. As they touched the blacktop, they raised the instruments, pointing the shiny disks outward.

Across the field, human soldiers scrambled, readying weapons and taking cover behind any debris they could find. Dad stood beside David and me: tall, secure and serious. Major Tomás Martinez calculated the situation, while the man I knew as my father reached out and slid a comforting hand around my wrist.

David leaned toward my ear. "Stay beside me. No matter what, you don't leave my side."

More ships disseminated above the field, dropping black waterfalls below them.

My stomach tingled while my heart fluttered. "Where would I go?"

The aliens scattered themselves around us. They seemed to take no heed to the crouching and hiding soldiers. Their forms glided with each step, almost majestic in their gait. Violescent from bare head to toe, their bodies showed darker purple splotches in indiscernible patterns that seemed unique to each being.

My grip on David's arm tightened as a few of his people came closer. While quite manly from a human perspective, I couldn't tell if any of them were male or female. A tremor ran down my spine. The skin where their legs met seemed smooth and devoid of sexual organs. Glancing at David, I couldn't help but wonder: did they have sexes where he came from?

One of the aliens touched his turquoise gaze to mine before turning his attention back to the ships as another Erescopian stepped out. The being appeared no different from the rest, but his bold carriage held him above the others as he moved past his predecessors. His eyes fixed on us. His gait quickened as silver-disk-carrying alien soldiers flanked him.

"What's so special about this guy?" I asked.

David tensed. "He's their commander."

The being stopped less than a foot from David. Grimacing as he arched his back, David tried to stand taller. The commander's bottom lip quivered before he reached out and pulled David into his arms, muttering something in a melodic dialect.

"*Oagnaribysso, oxhamata, est.*" The sound of David's voice speaking the strange words startled me.

The alien touched David's back. Dark liquid stained his hand. He showed the bloody tint to David.

A slight shrug brought a frown to David's face as he uttered another series of words in the odd tongue.

The commander's eyes quavered before he clamped David into another embrace. He whispered into David's ear. The gesture seemed extremely intimate, even for an alien culture. The two closest Erescopian guards looked away, almost as if giving them privacy.

A flush of understanding overcame me. Could this alien be David's father?

David leaned away. *"Xaqnon oxhamata. Oate zeplurs opoluus zmecit est."* He pointed at my father before rattling off another series of foreign words, his eyes both pleading and hopeful.

My mind whirled, taking in their musical speech. The entrancing tones enlivened my senses, while the curious side of me itched…wishing I knew what they were saying to each other, especially when David's tenor became anxious, unsure, and panicked.

After a brief interchange, David shook his fists and spoke with a harshness I'd never heard from him.

The commander's eyes narrowed. The being's gaze fixed on me before his hand darted out and snatched my wrist, hoisting me into the air.

My skin burned beneath his touch. "Ouch!"

Dad reached for his gun. Eight silver disks rose in Erescopian grips and shined on his face.

"No!" David raised his hand. "Jess's father, please put your weapon away."

"What is he doing?" Dad asked.

A hiss escaped David's father's lips as he shook me. My shoulder stretched, threatening to pop from its socket.

"Stop hurting her," Dad screamed, moving toward us.

David yanked him back. "They don't believe you are a thinking, feeling race. You need to prove it."

The burning deepened. I imagined my muscles tearing. "Daddy?" I said, unable to force out another word.

Dad's face contorted. He holstered his gun and dropped to his knees. His gaze lowered. "Please. Please don't hurt my daughter. I love her, I need her, and I don't know what I would do if anything happened to her." He raised his eyes. Tears streamed down his cheeks, carving a crevice into my soul. How long had it been since I'd seen him cry?

My toes hit the ground, releasing some of the strain on my arm, but the commander's grip remained firm. He reached out with his other hand, and brushed a tear from Dad's cheek. He rubbed the dampness between his fingers. All I could do was pray that tears had the same meaning in their culture.

David fell to his knees beside Dad and whispered a string of harmonious words. His eyes softened, pleaded, yearned for acceptance.

I balanced on my tip-toes, trying to find sure footing. Struggling for any positive sign, I held my breath, both terrified and encouraged by the hopeful yet acquiescent expression on David's face.

The grasp on my wrist slackened, and I slipped gently to the ground. Relief charged me as I reached for my father and helped him to his feet. I hugged him, burying my face in his neck.

His grip tightened around me. Warm emotion coursed through our embrace. This kind of affection had been lost between us since Mom died. I slipped deeper into his hold, realizing these feelings had always been there. We just needed to reach for them.

One of the saucer-holding aliens approached, mumbling in their musical tongue.

The commander's short-bridged nose twisted. If he were human, I would have thought it a sneer. He tapped a finger to his lip as if contemplating before raising his voice, shouting in his foreign speech. His words sliced though the silence.

Several of the Erescopians holding the disks lowered them. The remaining glanced to their comrades, wide-eyed.

My mind whirled. What had he said? Was everything okay? Were they calling off the attack?

One of the human soldiers left his hiding place behind a mangled metal plate and moved toward an alien with a lowered disk. The Erescopian, probably just as nervous as we were, turned quickly, raising a glowing circle in his palm.

"They're attacking," the soldier yelled.

"No," David screamed, but the deadening boom of the soldier's rifle had already shattered the silence.

A slice of dread cut through me as the Erescopian's head whipped back. The disk shot an amber glow in a circular pattern as it flew from his hand. The device clanged to the blacktop a second before the body of its owner hit the ground.

The world moved in slow motion as a beam of light from the fallen disk shot into the soldier's abdomen. The man howled, clutching his stomach as he fell. His rifle bounced once on the asphalt beside him.

I drew in a slow breath, tensing as every prayer I could think of sped through my mind. Dozens of the Erescopian's silver disks rose to eye level, changing colors as they swirled.

"No!" David flung his body on top of the wounded human soldier. The lights from his own people's weapons shone on his bare human skin and caught the etching in my mother's necklace. The oval glinted, sending rays of light in all angles. David's blue eyes sparkled, changing in hue as the amber rays illuminated them.

My breaths became slow, calculated. My body remained rigid, my mind reeling over the calamity about to ensue over such a simple misunderstanding.

The human soldiers advanced, forming a wall behind their wounded comrade. Terror raged in their eyes as the aliens mimicked them. Ranks formed two lines. Disks and rifles pointed at each other in shaking hands.

"*Xaqnon zrhaimittam est,*" David's father called. "*Aountenzrzhere est.*"

"Stand down!" Dad ordered, but the humans remained locked on their targets.

David held one hand out toward his people. He rattled off words in his own language, the desperation in his voice enunciated by the terror in his eyes, but his words seemed to have no effect.

He kept his palm raised, and looked back toward the human soldiers behind him. "Please, listen to Jess's father. Stand down. We do not need to fight here."

An endless silence riddled the field. My pulse throbbed through my temples as humans and Erescopians stared at each other, distrust flaring in their eyes.

"Stand down!" My father's voice echoed through the field. "Everyone—lower your weapons. That's an order." Across the tarmac, firearms hesitantly lowered, the soldiers casting uneasy glances toward the aliens.

The saucer pointed at Dad's face turned back toward its handler. David closed his eyes and exhaled.

"*Xaqnon zrhaimittam est,*" the Erescopian commander bellowed, and the remainder of the disks lowered to his people's sides.

Relief-filled tears blurred my vision as my father helped David to his feet. "I don't know what you said kid, but whatever it was—that was pretty brave."

David smiled and unsuccessfully tried to cover a wince as he moved his arm. "I wasn't so sure it would work."

Two guards flanked David's father as he approached.

Dad held out a hand to the slightly taller alien. "Can we have peace?"

The commander tilted his head to the side. He obviously couldn't understand what Dad had said.

David stepped between them. "Let me translate." He placed two fingers on Dad's outstretched hand. "*Apacem zrahpetiit, evfronossimezrah est.*"

The commander nodded before turning toward Dad. "*Aet inter zeplurs scirrf crestmiglova.*"

David smiled. "My father says that we can learn from each other," David tugged his father's palm toward Dad's. Relief flooding me, I helped them place the correct hands together for a proper grasp.

Dad tilted his head slightly, shaking the alien's hand. "Well, I guess that's a step in the right direction."

I released my breath in a huge puff. "We did it. We actually did it!"

Dad gripped my shoulder in a reassuring hug. "At least for now. There's a long road ahead of us."

David's smile warmed me, giving me the last spark I needed to finally relax. Careful of the broken skin on his face, I leaned close to him and brushed his cheek with mine.

A shrill noise robbed us of our tender moment. A lighted beam cut through the black waterfall below the center ship. The last of my relaxation ebbed away, lost in the fading darkness and the agitated, ever-changing movements of the Erescopian soldiers. I held my breath as a form filled the light and a wide, much taller alien strode out and treaded toward us. The Erescopian soldiers lowered their eyes as he passed. Commander-Dad adjusted his footing, and followed suit.

"Why is your father bowing? I thought he was their leader?" I asked.

David's eyes trembled before he bowed his head. "He is only a commander. Everyone bows to the Caretakers."

23

The larger alien ambled past the commander and grabbed David by the neck, raising him into the air.

"Hey, stop!" I shouted. My father grasped my arm, holding me back.

The Caretaker's eyes seared into David. He spat out words in the alien tongue with a sense of hatred and authority, completely lacking the musical tone of David or the commander.

No one in the assembly moved as David reached for the hand around his throat. His nails dug unsuccessfully at the larger man's grip.

A tear fell from David's father's eye, but the commander stood back, watching his son struggle for breath. His lower lip quivered slightly before he pressed his lips taught.

No freaking way...we've come too far. I bent my knee and kicked backward, nailing my father in the shin. His grip slackened, and I bolted toward David.

I reached above my head to slap the solid lavender arm that held David aloft. "Let him go!" I hung from the huge alien's arm, feeble, staring into David's swollen eyes.

"*Aet oate.*" The alien spat.

His free hand plucked me from his arm and constricted around my throat as more brash alien words tumbled from his mouth.

I rose from the ground. My ears pounded. My brain throbbed.

A glint of metal caught my peripheral vision as my father raised his gun. "Put her down."

"N-no," David struggled against the chokehold. "D-don't shoot. You'll…prove…bad…." David's eye's fluttered, and his head lulled. The alien continued to hold him aloft, sneering at David's unconscious form.

Dad struggled to keep his gun straight, sweat pouring down the sides of his face. "Please," he whispered. "Please put her down."

The commander moved to the Caretaker's other side, his head still in a bow. He raised his eyes slightly, and his gaze locked with my father's. "Doont shoooot," he said, drawing out his vowels.

My father's eyes widened. He hesitated, before his gun lowered to his side.

The commander focused on the Caretaker for the first time, his eyes seemed expectant and hopeful as he spoke several melodic words, but the larger alien only sneered in return.

The huge being's grip tightened about my throat. I lost the strength to fight back. A dull haze blanketed my vision. My hands and toes started to tingle. Who would cook for Dad when he got home late from work? Would Mom be there to greet me? The fog deepened, as if I'd fallen into a cloud.

The commander's blurry form eased back, and one of his feet rose from the ground and slammed into the side of the Caretaker's chest.

My forehead smashed onto the blacktop before I could move my hands to protect my face. I pushed up enough to turn my cheek and ease the lightning bolt of pain zigzagging through my nose.

One difficult breath filled my lungs before David's unconscious body fell beside me. His ribs swelled. Relief washed away the pain shooting through my face. I pulled myself up, ignoring the cries of muscles ready to surrender, and gathered David into my lap.

His father stepped between us and the Caretaker.

"*Aoet dexlioxnate ab aofiliuxm meum est,*" the commander said, raising his arms.

An amused expression crossed the larger alien's face as he rubbed his chin with the back of his hand. Two nonchalant brushes with his other hand cleaned the debris from his chest as he advanced, grumbling in his harsh Erescopian tongue.

The commander pointed across the field and spoke to his soldiers. Part of me struggled to understand what he said, but most of me channeled what strength I had to hold David squarely in my lap. He groaned in my arms, and a pang of hope shone through my fear.

Dad knelt beside me. "I don't suppose you know what they're saying."

I shook my head, my eyes remaining on David.

Dad touched David's forehead. "He's running a fever."

"No, his body temperature is higher than ours."

David's eyes fluttered, stamping out the dark cloud around us as they opened. He reached up and gently ran his fingers down the side of my face.

"Thank God," I whispered, tears trickling down my cheeks.

The Caretaker spat a series of words toward the crowd, startling us.

David blinked and sat up. "Xaqnon." I helped him to his feet. He stumbled toward his father's side.

The commander's gaze lowered to the tarmac as he spoke a phrase to David in a hushed tone.

"No!" David seized his father by the shoulders. Desperation touched his voice as he shouted to him in Erescopian.

"*Xaqnon sioxtelcs est,*" the Caretaker spat, pointing at David's face.

My mind reeled. Every time I thought it was over they started shouting again. What were they saying? What was going on?

David turned from the larger alien and raised his voice, addressing each Erescopian within view. The violet-hued soldiers began muttering amongst themselves. David turned toward his people behind the Caretaker, calling more desperate-sounding words into the air. I crossed my arms, trembling— praying for the happy ending like in the movies. The aliens shifted their weight, glancing at each other. Whatever David had said to them seemed to be sinking in, but even I could tell they were hesitant.

David's nose flared. "*Hoic xoteqt crlederx debes est.*"

The Caretaker reached out and wrapped his large hand around David's face. A single, stern word passed his clenched teeth.

David's feet kicked as he rose into the air. My father jerked me back as I dove to help him.

In a fluid, graceful movement, the commander took a disk from the nearest Erescopian soldier and pointed it at the Caretaker's forehead. An orange glow swirled, and centered into a beam of concentrated light.

The larger alien hissed. "*Oaminaris dum xontemniq?*" He turned to the soldiers beside him. "*Aproheqe sme.*"

The Erescopians raised their disks, pointing them at the commander.

David's father didn't flinch. His gaze remained strongly centered on the Caretaker as he spouted words even I could tell were a threat.

The larger alien sneered in return, spitting a word at him as his eyes burned angrily.

I couldn't understand what they were saying, but I knew a standoff when I saw one. My heart throttled within my chest. The Erescopians stared at each other. Several dropped their weapons.

The Caretaker threw David to the ground. His head bounced on the asphalt. "*Adixi eum oxqidere.*"

An alien helped David to his feet. I wiggled out of Dad's grip and ran to him. David winced and held his head as I drew him into a hug.

"What's going on?" I asked.

David swallowed hard. "The Caretaker ordered my father to be executed."

Five Erescopians stood between the commander and the Caretaker, their weapons lowered. Three more approached from behind, their weapons at their sides.

"What are they doing?" I asked.

David smiled. "Disobeying a direct order."

The Caretaker's jaw set. He folded his arms.

David's father circled around the mass of alien soldiers now protecting him. "*Asi meum qnovam stexllam, oportet euxm in est.*"

"What did your father say?" I asked.

David gaped. "He wants them to let me try to terraform your fourth planet."

David stood taller despite his injuries. His face changed. The features of the meek, unsure boy I'd met in the woods faded, replaced by someone more confident, mature.

The Caretaker's nose flared. He attempted to walk through the growing mass of Erescopian soldiers, but they squeezed closer, forming a wall around David and me.

The huge alien growled, followed by a string of angry words that seemed to overlap each other. He turned, clenched his fists, and trudged back to the ship.

The Erescopians cheered as the Caretaker disappeared into the yellow light. I released David, allowing Commander-Dad to embrace him.

I grabbed the sides of my head. "Will someone please tell me what's happening?"

David smiled. "We're going to be fine, Jess. We have until sunrise to prove your race is sentient."

"And what if you don't succeed?" Dad asked.

A brief hush hung in the air between them.

"I will succeed. You have my word, sir." David brushed his fingers through my hair, and kissed my forehead. "We have a lot to do in the next few hours."

I shuddered. "That orange light. When I was trapped and couldn't breathe. Was that the scourge?"

The color in David's eyes deepened. "Don't worry. Once my people see you are sentient, they will stop the countdown."

My father placed his hand on my back. "But right now the countdown is still on?"

Panic returned when David hesitated. So we weren't safe? They were still going to blow us up?

"Yes. That's why I'm taking Jess." David grasped my hands. "You need to meet them publicly. Once they see you, they'll stop this insanity."

Dad leaned in closer. "Are you sure?"

David didn't acknowledge my father. His lips pressed together. His hands shook. "Jess, we need to go. Now."

My stomach twisted and dropped to my toes. David wasn't sure. He didn't know if he'd be able to convince his people to let us live.

Dread coated my heart. Leaving was wrong. I needed to be here with my people. With my dad. "I'm not going with you."

David tensed his jaw. "What? You have to."

"No, I don't." I waved my fingers toward the aliens surrounding us. "All these guys saw what happened. They know we're not a bunch of stupid animals. Bring them. Let them tell what they saw."

"Jess, I need you to come with me. I want to show you to them. I need to make sure you're safe."

"Why? In case you lose? In case they wipe out humanity anyway?"

David closed his eyes. His muscles tightened. "I need you with me."

I backed away. "No, David. You're not sure you can stop it, and that's why you want me to come with you." The terror in his eyes confirmed my fears. The only way I could make sure he fought for my life, was for my life to actually be at stake. "I'm staying here. Where I belong."

"But—"

"No but. You promised you wouldn't let anything happen to me. I'm trusting you to keep that promise."

His eyes reddened. "Don't do this. Come with me."

"No, David. If I'm here, I know you'll work your hardest to keep me safe."

"You'll be safe with me up in the ship." Tears dripped from his lashes.

His jaw quivered as I took his face in my hands and kissed him. His lips gently stroked mine. Salty tears fell from his eyes, invading our moment of tenderness with the reality of separation. I held him close, burying myself inside his touch. I'd never wanted anything as much as I wanted him. I relaxed, secure in his embrace. Content.

"Come with me," he whispered.

I glanced up at the black waterfall. It would be so easy to leave. David would make sure I was safe, no matter what. I needed to be with him. I wanted to be with him.

David smiled, took my hand, and backed toward the ship.

His eyes consumed me. Love flowed freely through his touch, warming me, making everything in the world okay. He looked like Jared Linden, but his eyes were what truly attracted me. They were his most striking feature, and they were real. I walked with him toward the ship and held him tightly as we approached the amber glow emanating from the waterfall. I reached out and ran my fingers through the liquid metal. A cool tingle met my skin, as if washing my hands under a cold running faucet.

"Are you ready?" David asked.

I smiled. He returned the gesture, leaning toward me. His mouth covered mine, sending a beautiful tingle through my nervous system. I parted my lips, drinking him in as his arms slipped around me. My body trembled in his embrace, longing for more of his warmth…for the protection and love I knew he offered.

A swirl of affection coated me—a sensation so deep, so real, my body seemed to split in two before reveling in the wonder of coming together again. David echoed through me in a shimmer of omniscient glory—taking, but giving at the same time. Nothing else existed. Nothing else mattered.

Deep in the recesses of a world swirling with ecstasy, I sensed my body moving closer to the ship, closer to the light and permanent, unending bliss. The glow of amber filled my eyes, but I blocked it out. All that mattered was being lost inside him, to feel his power within me. Forever.

But such bliss wasn't meant for only one. The debt was far too great.

My bones shook. Anguish crushed me as I fought for control. Cold overcame, thrashing me with the shock of a freak winter storm as I severed my thoughts from David's.

The instant we lost touch, pounding need drove me back to

his mind's intoxicating embrace. Nothing could keep me from him. My unconscious beckoned to return, to be bathed in his undeniable encompassing delight once more, but deep within, a snap jolted me back.

Tears streamed from my eyes as I pushed him away. "Save my planet, David. Keep me safe."

Shock touched his expression. "Jess, no."

I wiped dampness from my cheeks and stumbled back to the arms of my father. The cells in my body revolted, twisting inside me, yearning to return to the arms of the boy who'd coated me in a stupor of unadulterated ecstasy. I dared to raise my gaze, and shook when our eyes met. The only thing that mattered was returning to his arms, returning to the envelope of perfection that he'd created for me, returning to that dreamlike state of pure joy. But I couldn't. What David offered wasn't enough. I needed my father. I needed my planet.

I choked back a sob. "I'll be here waiting for you... Tomorrow night. I'll bring the blankets, okay?"

The tremor in his jaw and the panic in his eyes told me he wasn't sure there would be a tomorrow night. My hands shook as terror overcame me. I didn't want to die, but I couldn't leave everyone else behind. This is the way it had to be. It was the only way.

"Save me, David," I whispered.

Agony welled in his eyes as I let my father guide me away from the ship. David held his hands out to me, his eyes begging me to return. I fought the incessant urge to give in to him, and gulped down my tears.

David's lips parted, and he closed his eyes. Another

Erescopian placed its four-fingered hand on David's arm, and led him into the ebony waterfall. The blazing amber engulfed them, distorting my view for a moment. The alien wiped his hand across David's chest and neck and followed across his face. David's human skin disintegrated, falling into the blazing light, leaving striking violet magnificence behind. My mother's necklace hovered before him and slipped from his neck. He seized the glimmering charm, and gripped it to his chest. He blinked twice, his arresting turquoise eyes now free of the unnatural human covering. Sparkling, majestic, knowing, and oh, so vulnerable.

He looked at me—a tentative, frightened crease in his pearly lavender brow. No longer Jared Linden, but so unbelievably right. David. Just David.

My lips perked up in a smile, and relief fell over his beautiful violet features. He ran his fingers in a circular motion around his cheek. It warmed me, the Erescopian version of blowing a kiss. I made the same gesture with my own fingertips. David smiled, raised his hand, backed into the light, and disappeared.

The commander's gaze fell on me. His large blue eyes discerning, questioning. He shook his head, and strode toward the ship.

Leaving my side, my father jogged after him. He grabbed the commander's arm, stopping the alien's retreat.

I inched up slowly. The tension between the two of them boiled in the air as they stared at each other.

Dad cleared his throat. "Your son. You should be very proud of him."

The commander tilted his head to the side.

"Dad, he doesn't understand English."

My father pointed toward the waterfall David had disappeared into. "Your son, David."

"Tirran Coud Sabbotaruo," the commander said.

"Okay, Tirran." He pointed toward the commander's chest. "You." He placed his hand on his own chest, and lifted his head high. "Proud." He pointed at the waterfall. "David—err, Tirran."

A smile touched the commander's lips. He nodded "Tirran Coud. Prooud." He placed his hand on his chest, mimicking my father.

Dad put his arm around my shoulder. The commander turned from us and continued toward the waterfall. Before stepping through, he spun and returned.

He pointed at my father's chest. "Yoou." He placed his hand on his own chest. "Prooud." He pointed at me. "Jesss."

Dad's lips quaked. His face burned crimson before tears cast glistening trails down his cheeks. "*I am* proud of her. I always have been."

I threw my arms around Dad. My own tears dampened his jacket. "I love you, Daddy."

His grip tightened around me. "I love you too, *pequeña*."

My father's warmth filled me. For the first time, he saying *I love you* meant something. I felt his adoration, and I savored it.

The commander bowed his head and backed away. The light engulfed him, shimmering until he disappeared behind the liquid metallic stream. The ebony waterfall shifted, and began to flow upwards, retreating into the craft until the

FIRE IN THE WOODS

shiny oval consumed the extraneous molten mass completely without any sign of the gateway ever existing.

The ship spun, its smooth, glassy surface shining. I clutched Dad's chest, afraid if I let go, our unexpected tenderness would end.

Around us, the last of the Erescopians disappeared into the lighted gateways, and the remaining dark vessels rose to meet the ship David and his father had entered. Their surfaces flexed, changed, and puddled across the night sky. Their fluid essence combined, becoming one massive floating pool of liquid ebony.

"Amazing," Dad whispered, his eyes reflecting the glassy surface above us.

The puddle drew itself in, forming one huge black orb in the sky. It twisted and settled into an enormous gelatinous oval.

A jeep appeared from behind a floodlight. It circled around the remains of a tank before stopping beside us. Maggie's father stepped out and adjusted the rim of his hat.

Dad saluted. "General Baker, sir."

Maggie's dad returned the gesture. His gaze settled on the wounded soldier David had protected. A paramedic helped the private to his feet and led him from the field.

The general glanced at the sky casually, as if the massive ship above us was an everyday sight. "What's your report, Tom?"

Dad relaxed his stance. "I'm not sure where to begin, sir. Apparently they weren't friendly, but Jess did something to make them change their minds."

The general turned to me. One hairy eyebrow arched up

under the brim of his hat.

"They were gonna kill us," I explained. "They need a planet. But they didn't know we were people. It's okay, though. David's going to make them stop the countdown."

"David?"

I tensed, uncomfortable under the sudden scrutiny. "Yeah. He's my friend."

The general's nose flared. "You can make friends with a cobra, even call it your pet, but it could still turn around and bite you."

I raised my chin. "David would never hurt me."

A soldier approached, saluting the general. "Sir, we have set up a base for you. We can begin reporting at any time."

He nodded. "Tom, get Jess out of here. This is going to be a long night."

Dad's grip tightened on my arm. "No. She stays. She's had more contact with the aliens than anyone else, and I want her here."

A dull hum emanated from the ship above. The general grimaced. "Just keep her out of the way."

24

We walked across the landing strip, past the smoldering debris of the gas tank. The blacktop indented and smoked, sunken and melted from the explosion. The heat in the ground seeped through my sneakers.

As we neared what was left of the small airport's control building, paramedics lifted two soldiers from the tarmac onto gurneys. A sheet covered one of the soldier's bodies.

"Unnecessary losses," the general grumbled.

My chest heated. "What do you mean? If you didn't attack them, David would have gone home and everything would be fine."

The general turned and pointed to me. "You seem to forget, missy, that there is still a ship carrying enough firepower to wipe out a planet hovering over us. We've seen what these things can do. I think you have too much faith in your little purple friend."

Dad tugged my arm, keeping me back a few steps. "Just keep quiet, Jess. Stay out of the way." He placed a gray sweat jacket around my shoulders. I hadn't realized until it surrounded me how cold I'd become.

We followed General Baker beneath a large khaki canopy. Dad sat me beside one of the tent poles and joined Maggie's father. I zipped my jacket and shoved my hands in my pockets to fight off the chill.

"Why haven't they left the atmosphere?" Dad asked.

The general tossed a paper report on the table in the center of the tent. "Because there is still a shiny green planet here, ripe for the picking." He turned to the man at his side. "Are our people at the ready?"

"They are in the air, sir."

"You're not going to attack them," Dad said. "That's suicide."

"Suicide is sitting here and waiting."

A slight radiance edged up behind the trees to my right, illuminating the sky with a hazy pink hue. The fallen control tower cast an eerie presence with the bright glow behind it.

Sunrise.

The soldier working the communication station lifted the headphone from his ear. "Sir, we are getting reports from Jacksonville, Florida. The ship above their city is moving."

"Is it leaving?"

"Negative. It appears to be rolling, sir."

I peeked out from beneath the canopy. David's ship remained still.

"Reports from New York and South Carolina are the same, sir. The ships are rolling."

"Are they taking the stance we saw in Zone One?"

"Negative, sir. They are just rolling."

I pushed into the conversation. "What's Zone One?"

The general darted me an angry glance.

Dad moved between us. "What happened in Zone One, Jack?"

Maggie's father threw his hat on the table. "As far as we know, it's not there anymore."

Dad backed away. All signs of color drained from his face as he joined the others in staring at the liquid ship above. A twinge of doubt settled into my chest as Maggie's father joined mine. The general nodded as Dad whispered something into his ear.

I rose from the chair and slipped my hands in my pockets. Just sitting there and waiting was driving me crazy. I strode a few feet from the canopy for a clearer view of the black, swirling lake hanging above us.

As I approached, a guy in a white lab-coat lowered some kind of laser-thingy he was pointing in the air and backed away from me, his expression grim. He blinked twice, and headed toward General Baker's tent.

They didn't understand. David was going to save us. They had nothing to worry about.

A cool breeze shanghaied leaves from the surrounding trees, funneling them across the field and dropping them onto the tarmac. Simple, ordinary nature. Dawn approached as it did every day. Nothing special. Unless we looked up.

The communications officer beneath the canopy stood from his chair. "Sir, Florida and New York are both reporting tilt."

"No," Dad said, moving to the man's side. "It can't be."

A woman at a computer screen turned. "Visual confirmation from Jacksonville. Their ship has tilted."

I ran beneath the tent and leaned around the general. The screen flickered with a staticky video of a ship similar to David's. The gelatinous form spun and arched, the oval tilting perpendicular to the Earth.

Dad hauled me back from the screen. I startled, finding Bobby standing beside him, his eyes reddened.

"Jess, I want you to go with Bobby. He's going to get you out of here."

"What? No." I folded my arms. "What happened to me staying with you?"

"That was when I thought David had a chance."

"Why are you giving up on him?" I pointed at the sky. "Look, our ship isn't moving."

"Jess, please. I need to know you are…"

"Sir, Jacksonville is reporting activity."

My father's attention flung back toward the screen. The base of the Jacksonville ship mottled. A luminescence appeared. A painful pang coalesced in my throat as the glow turned from amber to orange. Blinding light flashed from the screen, illuminating the tent before leaving static in its wake.

"We lost the feed, sir."

"Sir, New York is reporting heavy casualties. Massive damage. The Marines are engaging."

"Jess," Bobby said. "Come on, let's go."

I dug my heels in. "No. I'm not leaving."

"Sir, South Carolina is reporting tilt."

The general slammed his fist on the desk. "Tell the Marines

to engage. Call out the Navy. And we are evacuating now. Someone get me the President!"

A dull moan filled the air, and the breeze shifted. Sunlight cleared the treetops as the massive ship above began to spin.

"Bobby, get the civilians out of here!"

Chaos ensued as the people below the craft grabbed essentials and made for the waiting lineup of jeeps. Bobby reached for my arm.

I flung his hand away. "No. Get off!"

"Jess, we need to go. Now."

I weaved through the running people. "Dad! Dad, where are you?"

Bobby caught up with me. "Major Martinez ordered me to get you to safety. Come on, Jess. Please?" His eyes pulsed with fear.

"No. David won't hurt me." I backed away.

"I really doubt your friend is at the controls of that thing."

The wind whipped up, blowing my hair over my face. Above, the ship rose slightly, and began to tilt.

"Come on," Bobby yelled, grasping my jacket. I struggled against him, but he dragged me back toward the road, and a jeep waiting with its lights on.

Thomp.

Early dawn turned to day. Bobby stopped pulling, but continued to hold my wrist in a death grip. Above, sparkling amber light illuminated the runways.

"We're leaving, now!" Bobby yanked my wrist.

My hand tingled. Pins and needles numbed my fingers as I fought him. Twisting madly, I released the zipper on my jacket and wrenched away. My arm jostled free as the fleece slid off. I ran toward the center of the ship and the growing tube of light beneath.

"David. David stop!" The hum drowned out my desperate pleas. The ground shook beneath my sneakers. "David!"

The asphalt cracked. Dry, brown earth billowed from beneath, raising the tarmac, blocking me from the light.

"David!"

I tripped over the shaking gravel and slid down the newly formed slant of earth. Before me, the ebony ship lowered. Flickering amber sparkled, widened, and changed to deep, angry orange.

"No," I whispered, through gritted teeth. "No!" I shouted with all my might, but the shaking earth and increasing wind sucked the word from the air. I screamed, frustrated, but my voice was lost—even to my own ears.

"David!" My lips moved, but the roar overcame. The orange glow expanded.

I raised my hands into the air, and stepped into the light.

The roaring stopped. Orange swirls surrounded me, dancing and swaying in a non-existent breeze. My eyelids lowered, heavy, demanding.

Tired. So tired.

I forced them open, struggling against the intense need to sleep.

The lights above darkened, and I fought to hold my breath. My body shook as my skin heated.

No. This wasn't happening.

I clamped my jaw shut. Pressure invaded my nostrils.

Tendrils searched me—clawing, gnawing with invisible fingers.

Exhausted and suffocating, I exhaled. My hands reached for my throat as I gasped for a live-giving breath that didn't come. The tarmac scraped my knees as I collapsed.

Gazing up into the light, I used the last air in my lungs. "I trust you David. You would never hurt me."

My shoulder hit the pavement, and I rolled onto my back. The blinding light above singed my eyes. The world disappeared into an orange glow, pounding, throbbing, slowing with the pulse beating in my temples.

"David?" I whispered.

The world succumbed to darkness.

***

Bright dark spots swayed before me.

Breathe.

Ringing accosted my ears.

Breathe.

The muscles in my chest burned. Ached. Needed.

Breathe.

I coughed, sucking in sweet, cool air. Orange orbs marred my vision. Eyes opened or closed, the strange lights taunted— blinding and searing. A push of my arm propelled me onto my stomach, and I inched up to my knees. I blinked three times as my eyesight struggled to return.

Blurry, broken asphalt surrounded me. The earth, quiet below my feet, cooled to the touch of my fingers. Above, the glossy ebony orb swirled.

Quiet. Waiting.

I lifted up to my feet. Soldiers ran across the desolated airfield, shouting into the sky—shouting without voices. Their boots pounded noiselessly on the pavement. A frightening blanket of silence surrounded me, until the sound of my heartbeat reached my ears.

A dull drone pressed my senses from above. Bobby came into focus across the airfield. His lips formed my name. He gestured for me to come to him.

The hum deepened, the world quiet—but loud at the same time. The drone morphed, swirling into a buzz. The high-pitched squeal agitating, poking.

"Jess, get away from there!" Bobby's distant voice nudged through the piercing ringing in my head.

A dismal thump sounded from the ship.

The activity around the craft stopped. Soldiers froze in place, staring into the molded ebony above. The sound of my own heavy breathing reached my ears, and I wrapped my arms around my shoulders, unable to do anything but study the gelatinous mass threatening us.

The ringing abated, replaced by a tingling hum from the air as the vessel's shiny hull spun, glistening in the early sunrise. The ship lowered, floating lazily until it hung not more than a meter above my head.

Bobby's voice nudged me from a distant place as a swirl of calm settled within me, easing away my darkest fears.

I smiled as the molten ebony coating the sky dappled and pinched, tucked and swirled.

A small waterfall formed, inching slowly toward my face. The dark mass shimmered, forming a four fingered hand. Long digits reached out and rubbed my chin.

I took a deep breath and closed my eyes. The cool fingertips gently stroked my cheek. The thumb brushed over my lips, the touch more tender than any I'd ever experienced. I relished the gentle gesture as the fingers drew tender lines down my neck and across my collarbone.

"David," I whispered.

The hand began to melt back into the molten darkness. A lump formed in my throat as its animation slackened. I reached up and grabbed what was left of the fingers before they disappeared. "David, don't go!"

The hand reanimated, tightening around my wrist, drawing me upwards. I winced as the ebony digits melted into the hull of the ship, sucking my hand in with them. Frigid cold stung my skin. My wrist scorched, the pressure constricting and cutting. Something hot touched my palm, and a heated grip forced my fingers closed around it.

The warm embrace released me, and the cold liquid propelled my fist downward. My hand slid free of the ship, leaving naught but a ripple in the shimmering ebony that quickly abated.

My skin, cold and ghostly, prickled as it met the morning air. I opened my fingers, and the chain of my mother's necklace tumbled out, catching on my pinky. The etching on the golden oval caught the rays of the rising sun, glinting happy sparkles of light onto the ship above.

"Everything's going to be all right," I whispered. "There's nothing to be afraid of anymore."

I reached up and dragged my fingers through the cool liquid metal. Short lines followed my hands, only to be swallowed up into glossy black perfection once again.

A gentle breeze caressed me as the swirling fluid of the ship lowered and gently brushed its cool surface against my forehead. Bliss seeped into my skin, wrapping every inch of my frame in a blanket of pure, simple delight. My body trembled, soaking in the ecstasy of unadulterated joy.

"I love you too, David."

The ship rose suddenly, sending debris scattering across the demolished airfield. Transfixed, I watched as the craft became a distant spec in the early daylight and finally disappeared.

The weight of a blanket covered my back, and a gentle tug guided me forward. "It's all right, Jess," my father's voice said. "I've got you."

A chair slipped under me. A light shone in my eyes.

"The ships are leaving, sir," an unfamiliar voice said. "All locations are reporting withdrawal."

Peace. Love. Contentment. Simply existing had become such an amazing gift. Joy swirled inside my very being, infusing itself and becoming part of me.

"Her pupils are dilating."

Blurry movement drew my attention to the trees as a rack of antlers faded into the forest.

"Jess, can you hear me?"

I blinked hard, and Dad's face came into focus. The creases

in his forehead had deepened, matching the worry in his eyes. Inching out of my inner swaddling of paradise, I conjured a reassuring smile.

"Thank God," he cried, pulling me closer. "I was so scared, Jess. I was so scared."

I leaned my head on his shoulder, taking in his warmth.

A flash blinded me, then another. I lifted my head in time to see a photographer back up a step and click off another round of shots. He had perfect placement: father holding daughter with the sun rising behind them. It was not quite how I wanted to get into National Geographic, but it would do for now.

I settled my head back on Dad's shoulder as the last traces of David's euphoria ebbed away, replaced by the security of my father's embrace. I reveled in his touch, finding love, comfort, joy, and safety despite the insanity still erupting around us.

In the space of a few days, my life—everyone's lives, had changed forever. I cuddled deeper into Dad's arms and relaxed in his warmth. Sometimes change was good.

I pressed the heated metal of my mother's pendant into my palm. Its strength renewed me, coursing through the delicate gold and settling into my heart.

"It's going to be okay, Jess," Dad said between tears. "Everything is going to be fine."

The leaves rustled in the forest, dancing in the dawn's most beautiful sunrise.

"Yes," I whispered. "I know."

AUTHOR'S NOTE

Thank you so much for reading FIRE IN THE WOODS. I hope you had as much fun reading Jess and David's adventure as I had writing their story.

As a special bonus, the first chapter of book two: ASHES IN THE SKY is included at the back of this book. Strap yourself in, because it's not over yet.

Enjoy!

Jennifer M. Eaton

ACKNOWLEDGEMENTS

Everyone thinks of writing as a solitary endeavor. Believe me, it is far from solitary. Jess and David did not just fly out of my fingers one day. They developed over time. (One year and ten months, to be exact)

I'd like to thank the Sisterhood of the Travelling Pens for helping me keep my head on straight through this whole process: Julie Reece, J. Keller Ford, Jocelyn Adams, Terri Rochenski, Joyce Mangola, Emaginette/Anna Simpson, Sheryl Winters, Claire Gillian, and Rebecca Hart

Thank you, Georgia McBride, for "getting it" and loving Jess's quirky voice as much as I did, and for your wonderful suggestions on making this story shine.

Trial and error were definitely key to developing this story, as well as simple nudges (or sometimes slaps) in the right direction from my wonderful pool of beta readers and critique partners, some who read only small parts, others who labored over several complete drafts. I could not have done this without you.

If I have forgotten to thank anyone, please attribute it to brain deterioration, and not to lack of appreciation.

My partners in saving the human race:

Julie Reece, Claire Gillian, Ciarla Rubertone (for checking Jess's voice), Caitlin Stern, Ravena Guron, Kevin Stanley, Dawn Burne, Victoria Lees, Joy Eaton (for your insight into living on an Air Force base), Ron Grainger, Krista Magrowski, Danielle Ackley-McPhail, Mike McPhail (for your advice on artillery), Celia Lucente, Michael Kellogg, Georgina Morales, Dani-Lyn Alexander, Susan A., and Kevin Hanrahan of khanrahan.com (for your insight on police dogs).

And special thanks to J. Keller Ford, who read a poorly-written first draft and said, "This might be *it* for you." Thank you for being Jess and David's first fan.

JENNIFER M. EATON

Jennifer M. Eaton is a contemporary blender of science fiction, dystopian, and romance. (Because you can never get enough of a good thing) While not off visiting other worlds, Jennifer calls the East Coast of the USA home, where she lives with her wonderfully supportive husband, three energetic boys, and a pepped up poodle who tortures the family's goldfish and frogs. Jennifer's perfect day includes long hikes in the woods, bicycling, swimming, snorkeling, and snuggling up by the fire with a great book; but her greatest joy is using her over-active imagination constructively: creating new worlds for everyone to enjoy.

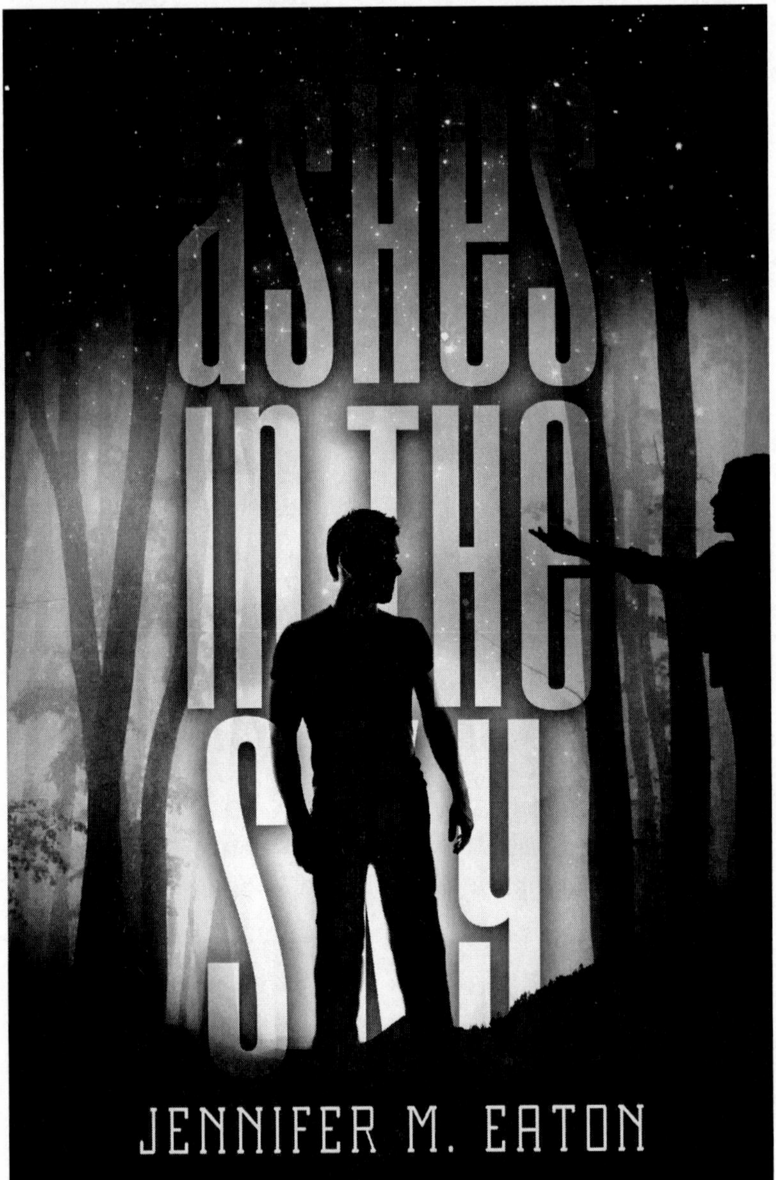
ASHES IN THE SKY
JENNIFER M. EATON

ASHES IN THE SKY PREVIEW

1

"You don't have to do this, Jess. We can turn around now and go home." Dad's hand shook on the limousine's armrest, making it look like we were moving despite having just parked.

Outside, police officers and several uniformed security guards held advancing reporters and camera crews on the sidewalks.

"Relax, Major," Elaine said, pulling out a compact and touching up her lipstick. "Two months after singlehandedly saving the world from an alien invasion, Earth's teenage savior returns to finish high school." She snapped the case shut. "This is the public interest story of the year."

Dad's nose flared. "Yes, she's supposed to be going to school, but you've made it a media circus. Why'd you have to schedule a press conference in the school?"

She slipped her lipstick back into her designer purse. "They would have been here anyway. The best way to calm a stalking fox is to invite him in for tea."

"Tea? I'll give you tea."

I held up my hand. "Dad…" I didn't have to finish. I never

did. Their arguments were always the same.

Elaine wasn't too bad, as far as publicists went. Not that I'd known any other publicists, but she'd been by my side since the very first press conference, and the hundred or so more over the past two months. She could be pushy, but she understood the power of a pint of *Death By Chocolate* ice cream at the end of a long day, which totally earned her brownie points in my book.

Dad's gaze returned to me. The deep lines around his eyes added to the weight of my own exhaustion. "We just got back. Do you really need to do another press conference?"

I shifted in my seat, my hands clammy against the leather interior. "If we go home, they'll be here again, tomorrow. Let's just get this over with, and maybe then we can get back to a normal life." I grabbed his hand. "I can do this."

Dad pressed his lips together. Of course he *knew* I could do this. Knowing, and *wanting* me to do this were two different things, and I loved him for it.

Elaine fluffed my hair and adjusted the collar on my shirt. "Show time." She tapped twice on the window, and the secret service agent outside opened the door for her. She slipped through the crowd with a practiced grace.

Camera-palooza erupted outside. Dang, there weren't this many photographers when I met the president.

Dad stepped out before me, an imposing figure in his combat uniform. Having an over-protective father did have its advantages. No one was getting by this bodyguard. No one.

I closed my eyes and took a deep breath. You would think I'd be used to the feeding frenzy by now. This was the longest fifteen minutes of fame ever.

Steadying myself on the limo door, I stood.

"Jess, look over here." Flash.

"Miss Martinez, how does it feel to be back at school?" Flash.

"Jessica, to your right." Flash. Flash.

The Secret Service closed in around us as Dad placed his hand on my back, guiding me to the front entrance. With a well-rehearsed smile, I made my way forward, hoping to avoid a repeat of tabloid-gate when the worst of the worst photos of me turned up on the cover of the National Daily.

I slipped my fingers into Dad's hand and squeezed. One more press conference. Just one more. I could do this.

We made our way through a throng of reporters, students, parents, and teachers to the auditorium. Hundreds of voices jumbled into one chaotic roar rebounding off the lockers.

A microphone appeared in front of my face. "Ms. Martinez how did you—"

Dad pulled me to his chest as two secret service agents pounced on the guy. The reporter sunk back into the crowd, disappearing like a stone thrown into water.

"There will be question and answer time after the presentation," Elaine called as we passed through the auditorium's stage door.

I exhaled, rubbing my arms. That had to be the worst crowd ever.

Dad circled the area behind the curtains and checked the cracks and crevices backstage. The Secret Service fanned out, covering the exits. I used to joke about their paranoia, until one of them actually found a bomb. Those guys in ugly suits quickly became my best friends.

"Did you practice your speech?" Elaine asked.

I raised an eyebrow. "No." You'd think she'd stop asking me that. I hadn't memorized one yet. Why would I start now?

I pulled aside the curtain and scoped out the auditorium. A sea of smiling, wide-eyed faces filled the room. Camera crews and reporters intermingled with the student body.

Going back to high school was supposed to help me get my life back.

This *was not* getting my life back. But maybe if I answered everyone's questions now, they wouldn't keep asking later.

Hey, a girl could dream.

Elaine tapped my shoulder before heading out past the curtains. Her heels clopped across the wooden stage as she passed a huge poster of National Geographic's "The Night the World Stood Still: Special Edition."

Steven Callup's cover photo was one of those shots every aspiring photographer dreamed of catching: perfect lighting, engaging subject, active backdrop, and undeniable emotional tone. I wasn't drooling over this masterpiece though, because the photograph was of me.

The flames over my shoulder were in crisp focus and flawlessly mirrored in my dark hair. The mottled hues of a fresh sunrise blended perfectly with the devastation in the background. And, Dad. My God, the expression on Dad's face as we embraced—the love in his eyes. That night would haunt me forever.

Something incredible had happened, and it had nothing to

do with an alien invasion. That cover immortalized the moment for all the world to see—a year after my mother's death, my father finally opened up and started to *feel* again.

I released the curtain, ready to face my peers knowing that no one gave a rat's ass about me *or* my dad.

They only wanted to know more about David.

I mean, I totally got it—an alien boy crash lands on Earth and has to escape before his people wipe the human race right off the planet. But David changed their minds, because of me. I was the heroine in the story of the millennia, whether I liked it or not.

I cringed, thinking of how many people had contacted me for the movie rights. *Ashes in the Sky*, they wanted to call it. *Ridiculous*. The world almost ended right in front of me. I didn't need to see it again on a big screen.

As Elaine announced my name, and the audience applauded, I wondered if anything would ever be as it was.

I took my place behind the microphone and squinted into the harsh auditorium lighting. I'd been in that audience dozens of times, but never on stage. The faces looking back at me were familiar, but distant, awestruck.

This was my school. My safe haven. Having the media here was wrong.

I grit my teeth and gripped the sides of the podium. This would be the absolute last time I talked about what happened to me in public. Ever.

Maggie's perky curls caught my attention from the third row. She beamed as she gave me a thumbs up. A little part of me relaxed, knowing I had a friend near.

Maggs was the only other person who'd known about David before the Army started chasing us. She even risked her own rear-end helping us escape. I sure hoped she didn't get in trouble for it.

Taking one last breath to steady myself, I leaned close to the mic. "You'd have to be dead not to know what happened two months ago. So I'm just going to open it up to questions."

Hundreds of hands shot into the air.

One of the moderators handed a bubbly girl with a blond ponytail a microphone. "Is it true that the alien looked just like Jared Linden?"

And it starts.

"Yes. David mimicked an advertisement, and looked just like Jared Linden's character in that movie *Fire in the Woods.*"

Okay, so that was only half of it. The truth was far too embarrassing. David pulled Jared Linden's features from my mind. He didn't really look exactly like Jared—just the hotter parts. The rest was an amalgamation of other cute guys he yanked out of my brain. There was no way I would admit to that, though.

A tall kid in a black band tee stood. "So what really happened out there? They were going to annihilate us. How'd you get them to change their minds?"

I cleared my throat. A flash of David's smile and the warmth of his touch sent a shiver down my spine. "It was luck, really. If David's plane hadn't crashed, we never would have met. It didn't take long until he realized that the human race was worth saving."

A teacher handed a microphone to a girl wearing glasses.

"How long will it take them to terraform Mars?"

Ugh. I tried to think of David's new home like Seattle or Los Angeles, but it wasn't. It was Mars. As in *not Earth*. Talk about your long distance romance.

"I really have no idea how long it will take them to make Mars, you know, livable. I do know that they are running short on supplies, so I'm hoping it will happen pretty quickly."

A girl in a cheerleader uniform flagged down the lady with the microphone. "Everyone says you and the alien were *doing it*. Inquiring minds want to know. Was he any good?"

Camera flashes singed my eyes as a teacher tried to pull the mic away from the girl.

"No," a reporter shouted. "Let's hear the answer."

The audience murmured, shifting like hyenas waiting to pounce on an unsuspecting foal. Beside the stage, Dad's face became an unnatural shade of crimson.

Crap.

"Well?" the cheerleader asked.

I wiped the sweat from my palms, remembering the shockwave that throttled through me when David's lips covered mine. The tabloids had reduced our relationship to supermarket trash, and Rah-Rah Girl probably wouldn't know a real emotional connection if it bit her.

David and I shared something so deeply intimate that it transcended *everything*. No one could possibly understand. I wasn't even sure I understood. All I knew was that I was in love, and I'd probably never see him again.

I blinked, realizing the room had gone quiet, awaiting my answer about *doing it*.

My hands fisted, but I forced a smile and rustled up the rote response Elaine had prepared for me. "I heard that rumor, too, but David and I were only friends." A tear formed in my heart. The thought of living the rest of my life with him on another planet was akin to living in the desert without water.

Was he out there somewhere, longing for me as much as I yearned for him?

My stomach fluttered. I hated how people's stupid questions dredged up feelings I'd worked hard to suppress. I had to get off that podium.

A kid in the back stood. "How does it feel to know that six million people died while you were out there hugging dear old dad?" He pointed over my shoulder to the huge magazine cover behind me. "How does it feel to know the death count is still rising?"

It was? "Umm—"

"When did you know they were hostile?" Someone else shouted.

My heart thumped against my ribcage. "I, uh—"

A teacher grabbed the microphone. "Do you really believe they won't come back and finish us off?"

The assembly grew louder. Cameras flashed as dozens of voices drowned one another out. So much for school being my safe haven.

Elaine gripped my shoulder and pulled me from the dais. "Thank you," she said. "That's all the questions we have time for today."

She scooted me past the curtains, Dad following close behind. The volume in the auditorium escalated.

"I'm sorry," she said. "We should've been ready for that. Next time—"

"There's not going to be a next time." I thrust my chin in the air. "That was my last public appearance. I'm already behind in school, and I need to graduate this year. I just want to get back to my classes and put this all behind me."

She smiled in that syrupy way adults do when they are about to get all condescending. "We'll talk about this later, honey."

Dad's gaze seared through her before he offered me a nod of approval.

No, Elaine. We would definitely *not* be talking about this later.

OTHER MONTH9BOOKS TITLES
YOU MIGHT LIKE

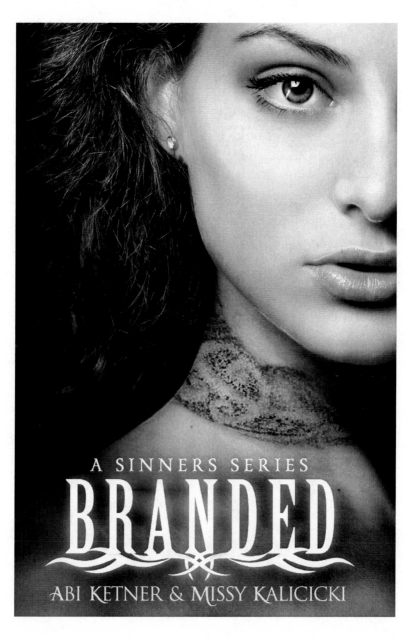

A SINNERS SERIES

BRANDED

ABI KETNER & MISSY KALICICKI

Forget everything you know.
Let the fire consume you.

INTO THE FIRE

BIRTH OF THE PHOENIX BOOK ONE

Kelly Hashway writing as

ASHELYN DRAKE

One slave girl will lead a rebellion.
One nameless boy will discover the truth.
When their paths collide, everything changes.

LIFER

BECK NICHOLAS

BOOK 1 IN THE PRAEFATIO SERIES

PRAEFATIO

A NOVEL

"This is teen fantasy at its most entertaining,
most heartbreaking, most compelling. Highly recommended." –Jonathan Maberry,
New York Times bestselling author of ROT & RUIN and FIRE & ASH

GEORGIA McBRIDE

Find more awesome Teen books at Month9Books.com

Connect with Month9Books online:
Facebook: www.Facebook.com/Month9Books
Twitter: @Month9Books
You Tube: www.youtube.com/user/Month9Books
Blog: www.month9booksblog.com
Request review copies via publicity@month9books.com